DO HU
THEIR

The spread of an alien culture across wide wastes of space, with its almost inevitable, remorseless destruction of human life, has chilling implications even for the liberal-minded. When mirrored in the bright, adventurous prism of modern sci-fi, it offers unparalleled opportunities to a writer of Lester del Rey's stature.

We're sure you agree that he scored a triumph in this brilliantly imaginative, highly entertaining yarn…

FOR A COMPLETE SECOND NOVEL, TURN TO PAGE 65

CAST OF CHARACTERS

DR. WILLIAM NORDEN
He survived an attack from The Aliens and now was saddled with protecting the whole human race from decimation. But could he trust his own shaky memory?

DR. HARDWICK
Killed in the same Alien attack, his notes and journals were the key to hiding Man's life force from the Alien invaders that sought to destroy the people of Earth.

GENERAL MILES
Head of the Moon Base. It fell upon him to make a risky and difficult decision. But would that decision help save the Earth—or hasten its destruction?

PAT MILES
Assigned to assist Dr. Norden, she was also the daughter of General Miles. She held her faith in Dr. Norden even when others began to doubt.

GENERAL ARMSWORTH
He was a hero for saving Dr. Norden. But sometimes heroes aren't always who they seem to be.

THE LIFE WATCH

By
LESTER DEL REY

ARMCHAIR FICTION
PO Box 4369, Medford, Oregon   97501-0168

*For more information about Armchair Books and products, visit our
website at...*

www.armchairfiction.com

Or email us at...

armchairfiction@yahoo.com

CHAPTER ONE

NORDEN COULD FEEL dread knot his mind as he watched the tiny blue speck against the black sky. It was a senseless, unnatural emotion, and he knew it. The searing blue point of flame could only mean that the approaching ship was powered by atomic rockets—and the Aliens drove their ships in some mysterious manner, without any kind of reaction motor. The object coming down toward the tiny asteroid could only be of terrestrial origin, powered by a human device.

Yet his fear grew worse. He shook his head, wondering again how close to insanity he had drifted. His eyes darted sideways, scanning the wreckage that had been his laboratory, then back to the descending ship. Mercifully, he couldn't remember most of what had happened. He only knew that it had been sufficiently bad to drive any human close to the brink of madness. It would have been torturing enough to be left alone for days in a wrecked and airless dome while the oxygen tanks were used up, one by one. But to have seen Hardwick's face when the Aliens caught him...

He tried to stop thinking about it. The Aliens were only vague shadows in his mind now—the picture of what must have happened as remote and unreal as his memories of struggling free from the wreckage.

Somehow, he'd survived against incredible odds, undetected by the Aliens. He'd dug out the emergency transmitter and tried signaling for help. Now apparently, before the last tank of oxygen on his back had been used up completely, rescue had come. He should have been ecstatic with relief.

The fear remained; some twisted reaction left over from the days of terror and hopelessness. He lifted his hands and studied them. They were steady enough; the fear was having no outward effect.

Already the ship was close enough for Norden to see glints of weak sunlight reflecting from its metal hull. The pilot must have been one of the best, for there was no wavering, or side-jetting to correct the course. It was coming, straight down, slowing to a drift. As Norden stared the exhaust hit the jagged surface of the asteroid and splashed out. Abruptly it cut off, and the ship dropped slowly the few remaining feet, to come to rest less than half a mile away.

Norden knew he should start running toward it, and stood up. But he couldn't give the order to his legs. He stared toward the ship, then back at the ruins. Maybe there was something he should take with him. He had air enough for another hour. Surely there was no need to rush things. Men would be coming here for him. And it wouldn't do any harm to put off meeting them a little longer. He didn't want to be subjected to their questions yet.

He started hesitantly toward the ship, trying to force himself to move. Men began to emerge and head toward him. He dropped onto a mess that had been a superspeed tape instrument recorder and waited.

His mind was running a rat race inside his head, and there was a gnawing tension. He cleared his throat and reached for the switch on his suit radio. The men were almost up to him. He got to his feet again, fumbling frantically with the little switch.

Then the harsh beam of a flashlight picked him out, and a gruff voice sounded in his headphones. "Dr. William Norden?"

He nodded, and rehearsed words stumbled to his lips. "Thank God, you got here! I was afraid the transmitter wouldn't work!"

There was a hint of something like kindness in the voice. "Take it easy, Dr. Norden! It did work, and we're here. What happened to Hardwick? Where is he?"

"Dead, I hope," Norden answered. "The Aliens got him!" He shuddered, glancing at the spot where it had happened.

The man wearing a general's insignia nodded, while sickness spread over his face. He motioned to one of the others. "Get pics of the wreck, and collect any records you can. The rest of you give Dr. Norden a hand. And hurry! They may have spotted us already!"

The man with the camera went resolutely to work, flashing his shots with a strobe light that blinked twenty-four times a second. Two others began unrolling a stretcher.

Norden shook his head in feeble protest. "I can walk. And I've already collected Hardwick's notebooks."

They set a pace closer to a run than a walk, bouncing ludicrously in the slight gravity of the asteroid. Norden kept up with them easily enough, trying to make sense of his reactions. Most of the fear and tension had left him, as if he'd passed over some hurdles, and was experiencing a resurge of confidence. The military efficiency of his rescuers had also a bracing effect. Maybe he hadn't believed in his rescue until now. But he did feel better, though his eyes went on studying the others cautiously, as if looking for any reaction that might inadvertently betray them.

They reached the ship, and began pulling themselves through its flexible hatch. The leader jerked off his helmet and suit, exposing iron-grey hair that contrasted rather startlingly with an almost youthful face. It was the face of a man who hadn't let himself grow soft during the years before the Aliens came. He swung toward Norden.

"How much gravity can you take, Dr. Norden?" he asked. "Six g's?"

"In a hammock, for a few minutes," Norden answered.

They were already heading up the ladder toward the nose of the ship. The general ripped a sling out of its case when they reached the control cabin. He snapped it to its lugs, motioned Norden onto it, and bound him in place in less time than he could have ordered the job done. Then he dropped to his own control seat. "Six g's for five minutes, then hold her at four until I order. Up ship!"

Norden didn't black out during the first five minutes, though the pressure was enough to drive the sling to its bottom mark and make its cables groan in protest. As they switched from six to four gravities, the pressure eased a little.

An hour crept by, and another. When the general finally ordered the drive cut, Norden estimated that they had been under acceleration for nearly five hours and were doing about two million miles an hour. Either the general was crazy, or the ship must have been stocked to the last bin with fuel. They were making more than five times the normal emergency speed.

Then the leader came back and began releasing Norden. "Sorry to give you such a beating after what you've been through, Dr. Norden," he said. "But we'll still be lucky if we have enough speed to slip past their detectors before they can trace our orbit and overhaul us. They've been getting worse lately."

He sighed, and his lips thinned. Then he shrugged. "We'll talk about that later. Right now you need food." He managed a smile, "I don't have to tell you that the doctor and psychiatrist will be biting their nails to give you the works. Oh, I'm Armsworth."

Norden felt the chill touch his mind again. He'd expected a doctor, and had been bracing himself for one. But the *psychiatrist*... He forced calmness into his voice. "I could eat a horse!"

"You probably will," Armsworth told him with quick, automatic humor. "This is the Space Service!"

The little cabin to which Armsworth took him was crowded alarmingly. There were the two men waiting for him, with their specialized equipment. In addition, there was the forbidding bulk of a large recording machine ready to take down every word he uttered. He acknowledged the introductions, and downed a glass of some over-sweetened fruit juice, which the doctor held out.

"It will get you ready for some real food," the physician told him. "Would you like to clean up while I look you over, before the main course comes?"

Norden seized on the chance. It would give him something to do besides tormenting himself, and it was obvious he needed grooming. His dark hair was matted, his face marked with dirt that had sunk into every wrinkle and line, and there was a thick growth of stubble on his skin. It was a thin, fairly good-looking face, as unfamiliar as if he'd just seen it for the first time in a photograph. He seemed to have forgotten *himself*, even.

While he washed and shaved, the doctor was busy. But the examination was less detailed than he had expected it would be, and finally the man stood back, nodding.

"For someone nearing forty, you're in excellent shape, Dr. Norden," he said. "You had a rough time of it, but I was sure you'd be all right physically when I heard you hadn't blacked out under high acceleration. Okay, go ahead and eat."

He moved toward the door, but showed no sign of leaving until his curiosity could be satisfied.

Norden had to force himself to eat, for he had no apparent appetite. The psychiatrist leaned forward casually, watching him. "Would you like to tell us about it, Dr. Norden?" he asked. "Precisely what happened to Hardwick?"

Norden shook his head, while the tension mounted again. The man would be on the alert for hidden meanings in his words, and he wasn't quite ready for that. Yet he was afraid to risk putting it off, "I'm not sure I can tell much. I—well, everything's pretty foggy. A lot of it I can't remember at all."

"Partial amnesia is fairly common," the psychiatrist said reassuringly. "In fact, everyone has touches of it. Try going back a bit—say to your childhood—to give you a running start. We've got plenty of time."

Norden had little interest in his childhood, and he skimmed over it with a few words. He'd done nothing unusual until he'd drifted into the new investigation of radiation outside the electromagnetic spectrum in his postgraduate college work. Then he'd suddenly developed, caught fire, and become something of a genius.

He was the first man ever to prove there was more than theory involved. He'd been called to Mars for the Widmark Interplanetary Award for his brilliant demonstration of protogravity after he'd floated two ounces of lead with a hundred thousand dollars worth of equipment that used twenty kilowatts of power.

In fifteen years at Mars Institute, he'd discovered four new types of extra-spectral radiation, become a full professor, and had *almost* discovered how to harness nuclear binding energy.

Then the Aliens had come. They had appeared abruptly near Pluto, apparently coming at a speed greater than that of light, in strange globular ships that defied radar detection.

Without provocation or mercy, they had sought out and destroyed every settlement between Pluto and Saturn, and had begun moving inward, systematically destroying all life in their path.

Nobody had ever seen an Alien—they invariably exploded to dust before they could be captured—but the horror of their senseless brutality was revealed in the hideous human corpses they left behind them.

Norden had been drafted while there was still optimism. Men could build a hundred ships to the Aliens' one, equally radar-proof, free from danger of magnetic or electronic detection, and nearly invisible in space. In anything like an even battle, men were certain to win. But they soon discovered it wasn't an even battle.

The Aliens had some means of detecting human ships accurately at distances of millions of miles, and blasting them with self-guided torpedoes, while remaining undetected themselves. And behind the torpedoes would come the dark globular ships to spray the wreckage with some force that left every cell utterly lifeless.

Hardwick had been a quasi-scientist, mixed up with certain weird cults, who maintained a private laboratory on an asteroid near Jupiter's orbit. And in the desperation that followed the first foolish optimism, his theory that the Aliens could detect life itself, or the presence of the questionable mitogenetic rays that were supposed to radiate from nerve endings, was actually taken seriously.

Surprisingly, the tests indicated that remote-controlled ships, which had been completely sterilized, went undetected, while ships carrying rats or other life were blasted. Norden, as the expert on all strange radiation, had been sent to work with Hardwick in attempting to devise a screen for the hypothetical life radiation.

He never learned whether Hardwick was a wild genius, or an even wilder lunatic. While he was wearing Hardwick's improvised shield during one of the attempts to test it, the Aliens had landed and broken in.

"What did they look like?" the psychologist asked casually—too casually, Norden felt.

"Well, they—" He frowned, trying to remember, but a clamp came down over his mind. "I—I can't remember. And they did—something—to Hardwick. I—I…"

Armsworth brushed the other question aside. "Never mind. You were wearing Hardwick's shield. Didn't they notice you?"

Norden shook his head doubtfully, "No, I don't think they did. It's all horribly blurred. I think I jumped for the spacesuit locker when they breeched the airlock on the dome. I must have gotten into a suit, and been hidden by the locker door. And I must have run out after they took Hardwick away."

At least he hadn't been hurt when the Alien bomb ruined the dome. He'd dug out the transmitter, sent the message, and then had spent the agony of waiting in trying to decipher the cryptic code in Hardwick's notebooks.

They went over his account several times, but he could tell then little more. Then there were tests, some of which he could understand and answer without trouble, while others left him taut with uncertainty and etched worried lines into the face of the psychiatrist. But at last the man nodded doubtfully.

"I think he'll do," he reported hesitantly to Armsworth. "A traumatic experience always leaves scars, but…"

"But or no he'd better do," Armsworth said gruffly. "No wonder they ordered us out to pick him up! He was within fifty feet of the Aliens, and they didn't locate him! Dr.

Norden, if that shield works and you can duplicate it, you'll be the most valuable man alive!"

"And the tiredest and sleepiest," Norden suggested. His eyes narrowed, and his mind darted about, seeking some sign of the wrong reaction. Then he relaxed as the doctor and psychiatrist picked up their equipment and went out with advice he hardly heard. Armsworth lingered, and Norden searched about in his mind for what seemed to be a safe question.

"How long until we reach Mars, general?" he asked.

"We don't!" Armsworth's voice was suddenly thick and bitter, "We've abandoned Mars. The Aliens have moved inward. We—ah, hell, we'll reach our new laboratory on the Moon base in about four days! And you'd better start praying that shield works, or my value to you won't be worth salvaging."

He shrugged abruptly and left, closing the cabin door quietly behind him. Norden slumped down on the bed, not bothering to remove his clothes.

Automatically, he lifted his arms until both his hands were pressing against the nape of his neck, settled into a comfortable position against the automatic straps, and began reviewing all the events of his rescue carefully. And bit by bit, the worry in his head quieted. He'd gotten away with it. What "it" was, he didn't know or even remotely suspect, but the horrible tension was gone.

CHAPTER TWO

It was a short-lived respite, for no sooner had Norden reached the base on the Moon where the frenzied activity of the new laboratories went on than the tension returned.

The taped interviews had been signaled ahead, together with Hardwick's notebooks and Norden's suggested list of equipment. Apparently, the information on him hadn't been satisfactory. He was rushed to a small, rectangular room where three men mumbled and complained unhappily as he was given tests that served no purpose that he could see.

And finally, he was forced to wait in the corridor outside for nearly an hour while the three conferred, before he was given an envelope of papers and led to the office of General Miles, head of the entire Moon base.

Miles skimmed through the reports and reached for the hushed phone. He was a man of indeterminate age, with a young voice and old eyes. There was a curious grace to his gaunt body, and a friendly smile on his rough-hewn face, despite telltale marks of exhaustion.

Norden watched him tensely, but his reactions were not revealing until he turned back abruptly, and extended his hand.

"You're in, Dr. Norden," he said. "What you urgently need is rest. You've had a devil of a time of it, and you show it. But we can't afford to let you go," He nodded grimly. "You're no more psychotic than I am, since you're able to work. And we need your work. The last settlement on Mars was just wiped out before we could evacuate it. Hardwick's notes are pure gobbledygook, so we *have* to depend on your help. Come on."

He stood up and led Norden through a narrow door, and into a tunnel that connected GHQ with a large Quonset-type building to the south.

"We've secured everything we could for you," he explained. "We even got you an assistant, and the exclusive use of our largest computer." He threw open the door to the laboratory, and gestured. "It's *all yours*. I'll be around from time to time, but if you need anything extra-special don't hesitate to ask for it. All of our work is important but you have top priority here."

Norden closed the door firmly as the general left, studying the equipment—more than he'd dreamed they could provide. To them, he was probably off balance. But at the moment, he was convinced they would have given top priority to a man who could do the Indian rope trick. It seemed like a careless way of running things, particularly since they hadn't put a guard over him, or hinted at a penalty for failure.

He moved slowly back through the laboratory, carefully studying the equipment. Once again, there was the disturbing sense that his experience had blanked out whole sections of his memory, until he had to puzzle out apparatus he must have used over a thousand times. But it was still obvious that the laboratory had everything he could possibly want—and more.

He wandered back and around the big computer, and almost collided with a small, brown-haired girl in a lab smock who looked up at him with eager interest, her slender hands busy with the keyboard.

"Dr. Norden? I'm Pat Miles, your assistant. I hope you won't let the fact that the general is my father disturb you. I had three years of extraspectral math and paraphysics at Chitec, and I'm a registered computer operator in my own right, grade one," She smiled at him.

He knew at once that she was the guard placed over him—an extremely attractive guard who would keep the general informed as to his progress. But a known factor was always better than an unknown one. He offered her his hand, and she took it quickly.

"Glad to have you, Pat," he said. "But until I can decode Hardwick's notes from what little I've learned of them, there won't be much to do."

He'd decided that it was a reasonable job, and one that would take up enough time for him to orient himself. After that…his mind skidded off the subject.

She pointed to the worktable by the machine where the notes lay spread out. "I've been systematizing it already. If you can supply half a dozen keys, the computer should be able to translate the rest."

It rocked him for a few seconds. He hadn't thought of the possibility, and it meant an end to stalling, long before he could be ready. But there was nothing he could do about it. He gathered up all of the notes, and began pointing out the handful of phrases he had learned, together with the only clear memory he seemed to possess of his time with Hardwick.

"The last page covers the final test," he told her. "Hardwick had some cockroaches and mosquitoes left over from an experiment with various vermin, and he put them in a glass case. I stood at one side with the screen he'd made on me, and he stood on the other. Apparently he figured the things could somehow sense the human aura, and the roaches should move toward my absence of one, the mosquitoes toward him for food. But there was no statistical evidence of its success."

She began feeding information to the machine, and reeling out the results, checking with him. At first, he begrudged the work, but then he found his interest quickening in the puzzle and its untangling. She was good at the work, though she found it hard to believe that the cult-inspired nonsense could be a correct translation.

He began trying to anticipate the problems of her programming, and to scan the results, cross-checking to reduce errors from his own confusion.

Finally she nodded. "That's it, Bill. The computer can crosscheck the rest itself. All I've got to do is cut the notes on a tape, and feed them in. Why don't you go to lunch while I'm doing it? Dad has you scheduled for his table, down in the GHQ basement cafeteria."

"What about you?" he asked.

She shook her head. "I want to finish this. Go on, don't keep Dad waiting."

Norden found most of the seats filled, but Miles saw him and waved him over. There was a round of introductions to names that were famous in their fields—famous enough for even Norden to recognize, though he'd stuck pretty closely to his own specialty.

"How's it shaping up?" Miles wanted to know.

"We should have the notes decoded tonight," Norden told him. "After that, it's a matter of how useful they'll be."

Miles grunted unhappily. "They'd better offer a more promising lead than the others we've had. And soon! At this rate, in two more weeks at most, the Aliens will be taking over the Moon—and if that happens, we may as well stay here waiting for them."

He turned to the head psychologist, while Norden was still hunting for the meaning of the implied threat he thought he could read into the words. "Jim, what about Enfield?"

"No dice," the psychologist answered. "He's obsessed with xenophobia—he hates the Aliens for breakfast, lunch and between meals. I can't treat him here. Of course, after what happened to his wife…"

Miles put his fork down and faced the group, but his eyes were on Norden. His words had the ring of an often-delivered but still vital lecture. "Damn it, we can't afford hatred. Maybe the mobs need it to keep them going. But we have serious things to do that take sound judgment. Why not hate disease germs or any other natural enemy?"

His voice hardened. "They don't kill for the pure love of evil. They're intelligent beings, doing what they believe *has* to be done. I think they're wrong, and I can't understand them—though I wish I could. I consider poisoning bedbugs a wise move, though no intelligent bedbug would agree with me. This expedition of theirs would be a major job for any race, and they're going at it just as we would—if we had to exterminate the boll weevil.

"Emotions haven't a thing to do with it. We're in a battle for raw survival, and we haven't the time to indulge our animal emotions. It's a scientific problem that has to be solved for our lives—like a plague."

Norden added another intangible to the puzzle—either Miles was setting a trap for him, or it was hard to understand how he'd gotten the five stars on his insignia. An enemy was an enemy! He decided on silence as the best course, and was glad when the others began to leave. He watched them moving out, shocked again at the pretense that was going on. Did they really think war to the death was a game?

He started to follow, then hesitated, swayed by a sudden impulse. Surely it could do no harm. He located one of the waiters and asked for a package of food to take to Pat. To his relief, the man showed no surprise, and he soon had a bag in his hand.

Pat was still sitting at the machine. She took the food with a pleased smile that told him he'd done the right thing. "Why so glum?" she asked.

"Frankly, I'm puzzled," he told her. On a sudden impulse, he mentioned the lecture and how it had disturbed him.

"Dad!" She smiled, then laughed outright, "He always talks like that to a new man. Bill, did you ever see a little boy fighting a bigger one, wading in, crying, whimpering, but so mad he couldn't stop—couldn't even see where he was hitting? That's hate-fighting. And it's senseless, because the other side may be just as right. Professional fighters don't really hate—they simply do everything they can to win, coldly and scientifically."

She touched his arm, "Bill, be sensible. You act as if we *couldn't* win."

"What makes you think we can?"

"The computer thinks so. I tried it. We'll win because we know how to be efficient. We'll experiment a bit, because we don't have a set pattern—because we've kept individuality. The Aliens act like a preset machine. Like a crew killing pests.

"Start at the outside of a circle and exterminate inwards! Nonsense! They should have hit Earth at once, even if they had to retrace their steps a few times. But they aren't trying to find out whether we act like the enemy they planned on. No—what's the proper way is the proper way. A lot of our nations attempted that once—and look where they are now."

He shook his head, not believing her, but it left him uncertain and disturbed. The fact was that the enemy was closing the net—closing it so fast he'd be a dead man in two weeks, if he couldn't find the solution. As to hatred...

He shook his head, and went into his office. There were copies of his own published works there, as well as magazines he hadn't yet seen. He dropped down to fill in the flaws his memory had developed.

Paraphysics was tricky stuff. For a long time men had known no other spectrum but the electromagnetic, running from heat up through cosmic rays. When atomic particles moved from one energy level to another, they produced quanta of energy in that spectrum, which was limited to the speed of light.

The kinetogravitic spectrum began with gravity and moved up through nuclear binding force toward some unknown band. Apparently it was the product of the behavior of some sub-particle finer than any known, and its speed of propagation was practically infinite. Other spectra were being considered, but no order or logic had fitted yet.

He found an article by a Japanese scientist that suggested there might be a spectrum related to the behavior of atoms in the molecule—with crystals in some cases acting on one level due to the electron drift, and on another due to atomic strains within the molecule. Colloids, polymers and even the encephalograph waves were dragged in, but the mathematics seemed sound enough.

Norden caught his breath, and began digging into the equation. The third manipulation suggested that magnetism might somehow be involved, and that would mean…

He couldn't dig the idea out. Just when it seemed about to open before him, his mind shied away and drifted off to other things. He was still working on it when Pat came in, and dropped a sheaf of papers on the table. Strips of tape had been pasted together to form a crude book.

"The whole thing," she reported. "But most of its nonsense. There's a page or two about some secret asteroid where the survivors of the fifth planet are waiting for men to mature before bringing the Great Millennium—or pages where Hardwick worked on the numerology of your name before he discovered your middle name had no H in it—or little notes to himself about buying a gross of Martian sand lizards. I had the machine go through it, strike out all meaningless matter, and come up with this."

It was a clip of five sheets. Norden skimmed through them, and groaned. The shield he had tested for Hardwick had been made of genuine mummy cloth, ground mandrake and a glue filled with bat blood.

"Yet you *did* live," Pat pointed out. "And he was right about their being able to detect life. We sent out sterile neoprene balloons loaded with live rabbits, and others with dead rabbits. Every balloon with the live rabbits was blasted—and none with the dead animals. We could use the same test to find out whether anyone of those things worked—or any combination of them."

"We'll have to," he decided. "And then it may have been the closet instead of the shield—or an accident to their detector that saved me. Pat, have they got some kind of library here?"

It was already quitting time, but she went with him while he persuaded the library attendant to let him in, before the next shift came on. Mummy cloth, it seemed, might become infused with a number of aromatic preservatives, products from the mummy, and such.

It was ridiculous—but hardly more ridiculous than using the byproducts of mold to cure disease must have seemed. Anything dealing with life was slightly implausible. And when he phoned in the order for the materials to Miles, there were no questions.

"Thanks, Pat," he told her after she'd shown him where his sleeping quarters were located.

She shrugged. "Why? If we *don't* find the answer, I'll be as dead as you in a few weeks."

He shuddered, and then put it out of his mind. Worrying about death wasn't decent, somehow. He found his bunk, stretched out with his hands behind his neck, and tried to review the serious events of the day, without the problem of hatred, over-efficiency, or Pat and her father. He saved those to worry about in his mind after he rolled over on his side, and gave up all ideas of sleeping.

Then abruptly there was a yell from down the hall, and lights snapped on, Norden sprang out with the others, to see the outer lock click shut. In the glare of the overhead lights, he could see a figure running desperately for the edge of a further Quonset—running in the airlessness of the exposed surface without a spacesuit!

More lights snapped on, and a guard in a suit suddenly came around the corner, throwing up a rifle. There was a tiny spurt of flame from the weapon, and the running man pitched forward. The guard started toward him just as a few men began to dart out of the huts in hastily-donned space suits.

A greenish-yellow effulgence bloomed shockingly where the runner had fallen, and the floor shook under Norden. The guard was thrown backwards, and the others stumbled. When the explosion was over there was no sign of the man who had run.

"Alien!" somebody muttered. "A damned Alien! They always blow up like that before you can get near them! I've seen it out in space!"

And Norden remembered the bomb that had wrecked the dome on the asteroid—a bomb that had flared up with the same greenish-yellow color.

Guards came up to drive the men back to their huts, but Norden seemed to have high enough rating to stay for a while. He learned that one of the workers was missing, and that it had been his badge, which the Alien had worn to enter the sleeping sections. Either the Alien had killed and destroyed the worker for his clothing or else he had been the worker!

And he had been discovered forcing the lock on the sub-section of the hut where Norden had been sleeping!

CHAPTER THREE

The invasion of the base by the Alien had shocked them all, and few people had slept during the night. On his way to breakfast, Norden could feel the attention that was riveted on him. To the others, he was probably one of the most likely targets for whatever attack had been intended. He'd wondered about it himself, sick with a feeling of close disaster; but he could find no logical basis for the fear.

Miles waited until they had finished with their food, his own face a study in grim anxiety. Then he stood up, and faced them, "No work this morning," he announced. "There's going to be a fluoroscopic test of every person on the base!"

Norden felt a wrench at his mind that left his thoughts spinning. He caught himself, just as he heard a gasp from Armsworth, a few places down. But Miles went on as if nothing had happened.

"The guards have already been checked. They'll lead us all down to the explosive test chamber. We'll go in, one at a time, and stand on a marked square. The fluoroscope results will show on a television screen visible to all of us. If you pass, you'll go across the chamber to the cleared rooms beyond.

"Any man resisting or proven non-human will be shot at once. The Alien last night *looked* human, but he didn't breathe oxygen, so his internal structure must be different.

However, if anyone wants to declare that he's an Alien, he'll be treated as a prisoner of war instead of a spy."

Nobody made such a declaration, and Miles nodded to the guards who had filed in, while fear-ridden faces were still staring at their neighbors. Norden wondered how long a confessed Alien would last before the men tore him to bits. Discounting hate was fine at long range—but not when the danger was at your elbow.

Miles and Pat went into the chamber first, with the expected result—human skeletons and shadowy organs showing up on the screen, Norden stared in fascination, while fear built up tensions inside him.

Armsworth passed in and found his position, with a face that was somehow both taut and frozen. The guards took a look at the screen and waved him on. He half staggered to the exit, his features distorted with an emotion that was unreadable.

Norden tried to fight down his own panic. Surely it would be madness to doubt the outcome. But a doubt began to throb in his mind. He could remember so little. He'd thought the Aliens had never found him. But if they had actually captured him, tampered with his mind, and turned him back again, would he know it? Suppose he was an Alien—one given a spurious, hypnotic belief he was Norden until the right signal to become himself again…

It was ridiculous, absurd! But the speculations ran on in his tormented mind. He didn't belong here. Men apparently took it for granted that a confessed spy could keep his life— and Norden took it equally for granted that death was the only answer. He didn't think like the rest of them. There had been that week on the asteroid. His memories were spotty…

"Dr. William Norden!" the speaker announced.

He shuddered convulsively. Then he caught himself, and forced his reluctant legs to move. The door shut behind him, and ahead lay the white square on which he was to stand. He approached the spot automatically, bracing himself to face straight ahead toward the fluoroscopic screen.

Now! It was almost a physical voice in his head. And his mind seemed to shift, to shout something down. *Not yet! Look!*

"Okay, Dr. Norden," the speaker said. His eyes flicked to the screen where a human skeleton showed dimly.

Crazy, he told himself. Hagridden with fears no sane human mind could have endured and retained its sanity. No wonder the psychologists had been uncertain about him. Unbalanced—but human!

Pat smiled weakly at him as he entered the room beyond, to join the ranks of the elect. Then they watched as their group passed successfully, to give place to a number of rocket men from the freight gang.

The sixth rocket man came through the door boldly enough—and suddenly leaped toward the side of the chamber where another door was. His hands were jolting at the locked barrier when the rifles sounded. A violent blast of greenish-yellow explosion rocked the chamber and shook the floors beyond. When it cleared, the Alien was dust and vapor, with nothing that could be studied for evidence.

Two workers who had been standing in line in a building beyond broke through the seal together, without waiting their turn, and headed with desperate haste for the shelter of a nearby barracks. A rifle bullet tore into one, and both exploded instantly.

By the time the rest had been proved safe in a testing ordeal as grim as death, it was the hour for lunch—a shocked, silent interlude at first. Then one of the men caught sight of a neighbor busily shaking his fork, and glancing sideways to emphasize some point. A tiny gadget appeared, and was concealed quickly under the steak on the man's plate. Ten seconds later, when the man cut into the meat, there was a cow-like bellow and the meat leaped six inches up, and two feet sideways. There was a shout of laughter that grew into a roar, and everything was suddenly normal again.

Norden shook his head. The incident appeared grotesque to him. Fluoroscope or not, something was wrong with him. He couldn't have been so different from other men before the ordeal on Hardwick's asteroid. That ruined steak had cost a small fortune to transport from Earth, and the man would lose valuable time while waiting for another to be cooked. And yet, Norden could see that somehow it had been effective therapy, had relieved an almost intolerable tension.

They spent the afternoon sending out the test "balloon" rockets with the various elements of Hardwick's screen. On the way back to the barracks, Norden noticed there were now six guards stationed about the laboratory, two of who instantly fell into step behind him. He had been shifted to the dormitory over the Headquarters building, where he would be in the least danger—and also have the least freedom from observation!

But he forgot it the next day as the results of the tests came in. The shields had been completely ineffective. Dead rabbits still were unmolested, but live ones had been picked off in everything they had sent out.

Miles accepted the result with a despairing shrug, but Pat was hit hard by it. None of the other research teams seemed to be getting anywhere. There was no way to detect Aliens, and no way to screen humans.

On the fourth day, when the last possible variation of Hardwick's formula had proved useless, and the Aliens had moved their lines up to fifty million miles from Earth's orbit. Pat was down early, re-checking the translation the computer had made, Norden came in, saw the results, and swore.

For three hours, he pored over the Japanese scientist's mathematics—and as before, he found his mind reaching for something, only to begin some useless side speculation that threw him off. It was as if he had a censor in his mind telling him he could go no further. He considered the grim prospect of ten days or more of life for himself, and the men here, until the noonday signal sounded.

Somebody had put a new plastic glue on the handle of his knife and fork, and it was fifteen minutes before he could locate a solvent that removed it. Pat laughed at his plight along with the others. He checked his anger, swallowed it— and suddenly realized that in a strange way, the practical jest played on him was a mark of acceptance.

He went back to the laboratory trying to think of something ingenious enough to enable him to live up to their queer code. An idea that had nagged him tantalizingly, just below consciousness, nibbled again at his mind, but he let it go. If he could fit a protogravity generator under a plate...

And abruptly, he was digging for the complete set of Hardwick's notes, and scanning the nonsense that the computer had declared meaningless. He picked up the telephone and called the library. "Give me what you've got on Martian sand lizards!"

Most of it was useless. They were typical low-grade Martian life, tiny things covered with fur, but vaguely lizard-like. Then the significant part came, "The females demonstrate a remarkable ability to locate the rare males at extreme distances. Janiekowski found that a female with all sense organs removed could locate a male at a distance of five kilometers, even when the male was enclosed in an airtight box of laminated copper and soundboard. No satisfactory explanation is known."

It *had* to be some form of telepathy or sensitivity to the life forces of the male lizards! He went over the work done with the creatures a dozen times and could find no other explanation. And suddenly his mind was milling about, trying to slide away from it again.

"Taboo!" he muttered, "*Damn* the taboo!" It was too late for a taboo to interfere now, whatever the reasons behind it. And fortified by his growing certainty that something had been done to him, it only served to confirm the fact that he was on the right track at last.

Pat listened to his summary of what he'd found, and nodded hopeful agreement. "A quick test! It's what we need, all right. We still may not find the insulator for the shield, but we can run tests fast enough to have a chance. Metals first, then the other broad classifications, until something vital turns up. Bill, I guess this makes me, and the computer look pretty silly. And after all the yelling I've done about flexibility being needed, too. I hope some zoo or laboratory on Earth has a collection of the little beasts."

It turned out that Harvard was well stocked as a result of a research plan to rework Janiekowski's experiments. In less than five hours, twelve females and two rare males were lying in front of Norden. They looked like small lizards covered with chinchilla hair, and possessing eight legs apiece. The females, with scant modesty, were trying busily to break down the wall that kept them from the males.

Pat had already installed three television pickups and cages at various distant points, doing the work herself to insure secrecy, and picking places most difficult to break into. Now she came back to move the females to their new homes, where they immediately began trying to crawl toward the torpid males, as shown by the television screens. The walls of their cages were equipped with pressure, measuring devices to test the strength of their efforts.

The mummy cloth drew a complete blank, as did the bat's blood. But the ground mandrake set the males to pawing at their cake with their triple tongues out, trying to reach it, while the distant females went berserk.

Pat took the stuff away, snorting at them. "They'll die of frustration in another minute. To them an active male seems to be a combination billionaire, video star, and accomplished Cassanova in the art of love. I guess I know how they feel."

He was getting better at reading her glances, and he frowned as her eyes rested upon him. He liked Pat, but sometimes she—

She laughed. "Forget it, Bill. I was only ribbing you. You have about as much romantic appeal to me as my grandfather."

It was ten minutes later before he realized what a typical masculine *human* reaction to such a remark would have been. He frowned, while his mind chilled at the implications. How could he doubt any longer that the Aliens had caught him and done something to him—something drastic? He wasn't quite human, despite what the bones of his body had seemed to confirm.

And that could only mean that Hardwick's shield had never worked. He stopped short, and then reconsidered. The difficulty he had forcing his mind to think about tests for the lizards still spelled a taboo in his mind—and that indicated there might be a shield. It left him exactly where he was, except for the problem of what the Aliens wanted. If he could solve that, and defeat it...

Nothing they tried gave any positive result, though Pat thought that the variation in the female activity had been slightly more than normal when they'd tried the potassium salt solution around the males. They gave up late, and Norden went back to his bunk, and to the familiar pattern of lulling himself into a semi-conscious condition by the ritual of reviewing the day with his hands locked behind his head.

Then he swore. It was a pointless habit. He returned his arms to his side and held them rigid, while his head squirmed unpleasantly. Habits could be broken—and any compulsion he had as a result of whatever had happened to him was a luxury he couldn't permit himself.

There would be no recovery until he had overcome the taboos and filled all the gaps in his mind with useful things. Perhaps the Aliens had already succeeded. They might have decided somehow that he was the only man who *could* solve the problem, and had tampered just enough to make sure he'd fail, while keeping him competent enough to insure that no other man would replace him.

He yanked his arms down again, and started to turn over. Fifteen minutes later, he came out of a complete blackout with his hands at the back of his neck again and a queer feeling that his mind had remained active, with only his memory of its activities missing. His glance darted to the door, but it was still locked, and his clothes lay on the floor where he'd kicked them.

Apparently he hadn't moved from the bed while he'd been short-circuited from his memory, at least.

He thrust himself up from the bed in disgust, pulled on his clothes, and headed down the hall, back towards the laboratory. He passed the cubicle where General Miles should have been sleeping and noticed a trace of light shining under the door. For a second, he remembered the man's words—a spy who confessed would be treated as an honorable prisoner of war.

Only damn it, he wasn't a spy, whatever else he might be. And there was no time left to find someone else to solve the problem that had been dumped into his lap. He couldn't turn himself in while that problem remained a race with death.

Inside his mind was a slowly growing hatred of the Aliens, and he clung to it tenaciously. They'd denied him his right to be a normal human being—and while their imposed attitudes made it impossible for him to understand the absurd conduct of men, he was beginning to realize that the fault lay with him, and not with the rest of humanity. It was not a pleasant thought.

Fresh guards had replaced the original pair. They swung in behind him, and then stopped at the entrance of the laboratory. He'd insisted that they stay outside, since he wanted no one to watch his experiments with the lizards. Complete ignorance of events was the only sure protection against spies.

He headed around the computer by letting his feet guide him, and reached for the switch. It clicked, just as a voice sounded in front of him.

"Norden, you damned fool! Leave those lights off!"

But they were already on, showing the tall, unmoving figure of Armsworth standing before the cage of the lizards with a knife in his hand.

CHAPTER FOUR

Norden felt a wave of hate boil up in him, and made no attempt to check it. As he returned Armsworth's stare his mind reacted to the situation before he could realize more than a few of the implications.

Obviously, Armsworth was a spy who knew of the work here, and had come to wreck it. With his rank, it would be easy enough for him to get in. Also, the man stood there with none of the fear he should have shown on being discovered, and Norden felt the sick confirmation of his being a pawn for the Aliens.

But the fact itself gave him some chance. He lifted his arm to the switch, and then dropped it. "The guards would suspect something if I cut it off now," he admitted candidly. "Any suggestions?"

"I could kill the lizards, let you discover me, and chase me out to explode," Armsworth said thoughtfully, without any emotional color to the suggestion. He shook his head. "I don't know. It's funny they can't trust you to stall off the Miles girl and have to send me here. With replacements scarce, I'd hate to blow up unless it's absolutely necessary."

Then his eyes narrowed in incredulous alarm, "Wait a minute. You weren't supposed to know my identity."

Norden's hand swept up, hit the light switch. His other arm jerked out for the big tongs he had noticed. He heard the spy leap, and recoiled just in time to avoid the rush. His arm came down with the instrument, and there was a solid thud. When he turned the lights on again, Armsworth lay on the floor with a gash across his head an inch deep.

For a moment Norden was only aware of his own harsh breathing. Then, slowly and horribly, the corpse sat up and began hitching along the floor toward the cage of lizards.

Norden bent, picked up the little cage and swung towards the door. He took one step forward, stopped abruptly, and bent again. His hand gripped the collar of the thing on the floor and, straightening, he heaved it up against the light gravity of the Moon.

The thing sailed across the laboratory, heading toward the rear of the heavy protogravity generator. Norden cushioned the cage of lizards against his chest and dropped to the floor in the shelter of the computer.

There was a blast that nearly ruptured his eardrums and the accompanying glare of greenish-yellow light burned through his eyelids into his brain. The floor heaved and shook, while sections of the curved roof began falling. The air gushed upwards, and the floor jarred again as the automatic airseal dropped, cutting off other sections.

Norden jumped toward a plainly market closet, and threw it open. He yanked down one of the spacesuits stored there for emergency purposes, thrust the lizard cage inside, closed it, and turned on the oxygen.

Adapted to the thin air of Mars, it seemed likely the animals would remain alive. He groped about until he located another suit that would fit, cursed as he found it zippered closed, and finally worked it open. Once in, he sealed it, and headed toward the personnel lock on the big emergency airseal.

He got through just as the guards were about to enter in their own spacesuits, dragging rescue equipment. Miles was with them, waiting impatiently while Norden slipped his helmet off. "Who was it?" he demanded.

"Armsworth," Norden told him. "After he passed the fluoroscope test!"

Miles sighed, but there was no surprise. "Damn! I should have had him checked when he came back from inspecting the other side. They must have had a spy all ready to make the switch as soon as they got him. Or maybe the test doesn't mean anything."

The guards had come back. One of them began to report on what they had seen. Most of the damage had been confined to the roof of the building, and to the big protogravity generator, which apparently had shielded the rest of the equipment.

Norden and Pat, who had finally been called, went inside in their suits to supervise clearing away the debris. Outside, a crew was already erecting a new roof on the laboratory, using prefab sheets. Aside from the generator they had never used, nothing irreplaceable had been hurt. And the two little male lizards were doing well enough. Inside of two hours the laboratory was back in full operation.

By common consent, Pat and Norden abandoned all idea of sleeping. Norden started to draw up a list of new tests, and then went back to the potassium shield. It seemed to produce a very slight quantitative difference in the reaction of the females. He consulted the vague speculations in his own works on possible other spectra, and came back.

The trouble was that he wasn't working with any natural phenomenon, but with life. He grimaced at the twist of his logic, but the sense remained. Something came into the back of his mind from a phrase in Hardwick's notes. It teased him, until his mind almost had it, and then another taboo clamped down on his thoughts.

He fought it out, standing still while Pat stared at him doubtfully. Twice he could feel himself almost black out, but he tracked the taboo down in his mind, pursued it into its lair, and strangled it. It died hard, but left his answer available.

"K-40," he said. His voice was steady, and Pat relaxed, unable to see the complete fatigue inside him. Disciplining himself seemed to be the hardest possible task. "Radioactive potassium isotope. It's supposed to be mixed up somehow with the life processes. Some scientists claim it's essential to life."

She reached for the phone, and spoke into it briefly. Then there was a wait, before she handed it over, and a voice came on. "This is General Dawes at Oak Ridge. Who's calling?"

"William Norden, Project A-sub-zero, Moon Base. I want five pounds of K-40 up here in four hours. Use my top priority and mark the shipment for delivery to me only."

There was the usual few seconds of waiting while the message traveled to Earth, and back. "Five *pounds?*" the voice asked, incredulously.

"Five pounds! And I may want more as fast as it can be gathered."

Pat was on another phone. Before Earth could answer again, there was a click, and General Miles' voice broke in sharply. "This is Miles, Dawes. *Give Norden what he wants.*"

A sputter of protest began, but it ended abruptly as Miles' voice reached Earth. The silence was broken by a sigh, "Okay, Norden, we'll get it to you in four hours somehow."

It arrived in less time, and Norden and Pat began the tricky job of getting the highly active elements into a container, which was both, chemically and radioactively safe. They clamped it over the cage at last, and watched the pressure on the female cages.

The results weren't spectacular, but they were unquestionable. And later, when they had reduced the amount of K-40 to a thin coating, it still worked. The quantity of potassium made very little difference beyond a certain minimum.

The effects still weren't good enough. They tried painting various substances with the chloride of the potassium, with equally good results and much greater ease of handling. The nitrate was even better to work with.

But it took them until late that night before they learned that coating the nitrate over cleaned iron was a major step forward. Until then it had been all hit and miss, except for vague directional hunches.

Norden looked at Pat, who seemed ready to drop, "Better go back for some rest," he suggested. She shook her head, but did agree to lie down while he began rechecking their results to date. Their best efforts had quieted the excitement of the females by no more than ten percent.

He reduced everything he could to a consistent basis, and added other formulae, which might apply from the incomplete relationship tables that strove to, reconcile the two recognized spectra. Those might also indicate something about any third spectrum. Either his memory was coming back or his reading of the books and articles was beginning to take effect, he was pleased to notice.

Pat worked the computer, which had fortunately suffered only minor damages, and had been repaired. From the computations, they made the indicated experiments, and fed the results into the machine. This time, it gave only seven suggested answers, with a rough weighing of them. The second one called for one of several organic substances soaked in potassium ferrocyanide and grounded.

While they waited for the chemistry shed to handle that with due precautions on the radioactive isotope, they tried the others. One gave a better than fifty percent reduction, which meant that the females were only mildly crazy.

"Don't they ever relax?" Pat wondered, unwrapping one of the sandwiches Miles had ordered sent in to them.

The female sand lizard's libido mattered less than nothing to Norden at the moment. He was staring at the work he had done in relating hints and fragments of information with pure hunches to get new facts, and realizing that he could never have done that, even before the Aliens had tampered with him. Either he was mysteriously more capable, now that he'd managed to overcome a few of the taboos in his mind, or else the loss of so much of his memory had left his thoughts freer to operate.

"We'll call this the Hardwick spectrum," he decided aloud. "The man was a crackpot cultist, but he was a genius, all the same. And with this, we'll pay those damned Aliens back for what they did to him."

"We wouldn't be able to if you hadn't had time to get the males and yourself into oxygen suits before Armsworth exploded," Pat told him. "They're the only males left alive, now that Mars has been scoured by the Aliens."

He swung around in surprise, "I never..."

The phone saved him from finishing. He hadn't had time to get into a space suit immediately. After the blast he had fumbled around searching for one And he'd arrived outside the lock without ever having felt discomfort from living in a vacuum for *five full minutes!*

His self-satisfaction vanished, and revulsion took its place. He stared at his body in horror. No human body could have endured such punishment. But he had taken it without noticing it!

Pat came back at a run. "Come on, Bill. A messenger just arrived from Earth with five hundred pounds of K-40!"

"Five hundred?" Norden could almost hear again the amazed voice of General Dawes when he asked for a mere five pounds—a quantity nearly impossible to secure.

Pat's face confirmed his suspicions. Earth couldn't have made five hundred pounds so rapidly.

They found the guards already waiting to take them to where Miles was, and followed them down to the entrance of the explosion-testing chamber. Miles was smiling and chatting with a man who appeared to be a perfectly normal rocket pilot, and who seemed bored until he saw Norden. He consulted a picture on some kind of tape recording and stepped forward.

"I have orders to deliver the K-40 to you, Dr. Norden," the pilot said. "But it's pretty bulky in its containers. If you'll come out to the ship and okay it…"

Miles cut in blandly, "I've been explaining the new regulations, Dr. Norden." He winked slightly, with a faint motion toward the chamber.

"Go ahead and clear through," Norden told the pilot. "I'll wait, and then we can look at your cargo. It's a damned nuisance having to hold things up while everyone is X-rayed. But we've new regulations now." He caught Miles' look of approval, and he knew he'd reacted correctly.

The pilot shrugged. "Why not? Let me know if you find any dangerous diseases." He chuckled, and stepped through the entrance, and out toward the fluoroscope set-up.

The picture on the screen was satisfactory and the guards started to relax beside the slits where their guns projected into the chamber. Miles glanced at them, and his voice was urgent, commanding. "*Shoot to miss. And keep getting closer.*"

Another screen showed the pilot turning to leave, just as the first bullet splintered the floor a yard from his boots. He jumped back with a terrified gesture. Another bullet came closer, and a third barely missed him. Shock hit his face, and vanished as he turned into a bright splash of greenish-yellow light.

"They over-estimated our production and under-estimated our ability to bluff," Miles said. "Good shooting, men. I'm glad he decided he'd failed the test before you had to shave it closer."

Norden stood staring at the blasted area and back toward the screen that had shown the image of a normal human standing before a fluoroscope. Breathing vacuum for five minutes hadn't hit him as hard. Subconsciously, he'd counted on the fluoroscopic evidence—and it had proved to be a lie.

"He couldn't have been an Alien with that kind of a skeleton!" he whispered.

Miles shook his head. "He wasn't. As near as our cyberneticists could gather, he was some kind of a robot, designed to mix with us. We left automatic televisors on Mars to catch a few telephotos of the Aliens, and they look a little like octopi on stubby legs. Nothing could make them look human."

"But a robot with a human skeleton?" Pat asked.

"It's possible, with enough advanced development. Hide the metal works in the so-called bones and skull, and shape everything else to the right form and transparency. Probably the first ones we caught were meant to mislead us. Hughes swears that any race capable of developing such an advanced cybernetic brain could handle the rest—down to letting him get his energy out of our food."

Miles' face was more fatigued than ever, but he found enough strength for a smile, "Thanks for playing along with me, Bill. Now get back to work, if you can stand it. The chem lab delivered your stuff while you were coming here."

The stuff from the chemists looked like wool, impregnated with the K-40 salt, Pat slashed off a yard or so of the coarse cloth and draped it around the cage, after a quick check with the Geiger-Mueller counter. She formed a rope of it and then connected the cage-cover to the nearest pipe.

And the images of the females in the screens were suddenly still, as if all of them had gone to sleep at once. Pat yanked the cover off and instantly the females were dashing at the gates of their cages again.

Pat let out a yell and reached for the phone, Norden tried to echo her enthusiasm, but there was no resiliency left in him. He stared at the answer to their problems, while part of his mind estimated that the pilots could stand the radioactivity from suits of such cloth long enough to accomplish their purpose, if an undersuit of lead-cloth could be worn also.

But the rest of his mind was in his own private hell. *Robot*, it shouted at him—*robot and spy!* It was plain enough now that his periods of "relaxation" and review of the day's events had been a mechanism for leaking important information to the Aliens. His unexpected and rebellious attempt to end it had been the signal to send Armsworth against the male lizards. Hands-behind-the-head-Norden, he thought—the robot too dumb to recognize the working of an automatic transmitter switch.

He fondled the cloth cover slowly, tasting the anticipation of revenge. The Aliens had taken a man named William Jon Norden from a lonely asteroid, and had drained him of his life history and knowledge. They'd built a poor dupe of a robot, and had sent it out to spy for them, and to believe for a while that it was human and alive. Now let them feel the defeat they'd earned when they built their robot too close to the original.

Then he considered the thin thread on which his hopes rested. He had something that stopped some form of energy from being detected by the lizards—an unknown band-width of an unknown spectrum, which might not even be the right one.

He swung around to check Pat's call, but it was too late. The word had already spread, judging by the whoops or rejoicing coming from beyond the laboratory.

CHAPTER FIVE

Norden broke away from the men who refused to listen to his warnings as quickly as possible. Pat had already gone to her bunk, worn out completely by the brief burst of hope, and he headed for his own cubicle. There was no physical fatigue—how could there be in a robot? But his mind was dulled with too many shocks. He dropped to the bunk, and his arms came up automatically.

He forced them down, and this time he was ready when his brain tried to black out on him. The compulsions that acted on him to make him pass on his information to the Aliens were partly under his control.

He managed to sidetrack his thoughts before blacking out, and to keep his arms down. He lay there, cursing himself and the things, which had created him, fighting his battle silently, until he knew he had won.

His legs were unsteady when he finally stood up. The effort of will had shocked even his motor control impulses, but the damage was not permanent, and by the time he passed Miles' darkened doorway, he was moving smoothly enough again. He saw surprised looks exchanged by his guards as they followed him back to the laboratory.

"You might as well come in," he told them. "I'll be here all night, and there's nothing secret about my work now. I think there's a deck of cards in the desk over there."

One of them looked and came back, holding the deck and grinning. "Thanks, Doc," he said. "You're all right."

For a second, Norden experienced a warming glow as he turned into his office. He could find some acceptance among men now. Then he grimaced bitterly, as he realized what they'd think of him if they knew the truth about him. It was one thing to ape humanity, quite another to belong.

The article on speculative spectra by the Japanese scientist was still on his desk, and he began poring over it. Almost at once, his mind swerved away on a flight of curiosity about the card game the men had been playing. He pulled it back, and his imagination started in on hatred of the Aliens.

He fought against that too, tempting as it was. He'd licked the compulsion to communicate with them in two hours. There was hope that he could lick the taboo against investigating into a forbidden field. The fact that it was forbidden made it doubly worth studying.

Bit by bit he traced down the mathematics, but in the end the taboo threw him. It required all the effort he could bring to the problem to follow the tricky formula, and it couldn't be done while fighting the treachery of his own mind. He gave up in disgust, and turned to the computer.

He'd seen Pat use it often enough, and apparently his robot mind was good at memorizing. He searched through the available tapes of information until he came to one that covered the more vital aspects of Einstein's unified field theory.

He fed it in, and began adding the spectra relation data from the books, carefully storing them in the memory circuits of the machine. The mathematics of the article went in next. He made sure the material they had used to locate the screen was still active, and brought it up to date.

Finally he set the machine to deriving all possible extensions of the mathematics he couldn't handle himself.

When that was finished, there was no longer any need to worry about the taboo. The computer had done what he had failed to do, and more. He stared at the sheaf of papers. The assembled material would save years of work on extraspectral radiation. And his suspicion that magnetism was the vital link seemed to be confirmed. It appeared to be something of a universal transformer, when properly handled.

But the machine couldn't tell him what section of the Hardwick spectrum involved life. The field used by the lizards to locate each other lay well up in it, in a band relationship somewhat analogous to the X-rays of the normal spectrum. But if that failed, there was no clue to what might work.

In any new field, one fresh fact could open up tremendous stores of knowledge—but there would always be even greater ones awaiting discovery.

He put in a call to the library for more material on Janiekowski's work with the lizards, and was told that they'd have to secure a tape from Earth. Earth promised a ship with the tape, and other material he'd requested within three hours. There was no questioning of the priorities this time.

Then he glanced at the clock, and was shocked to find it already past noon. He got up impatiently, heading toward the lunchroom. It was strange that Pat had failed to join him.

He found her and Miles searching for him the cafeteria, and one look was enough. Miles motioned Norden to follow him, and led the way to his office. Once there, he closed the door, and threw the decoded dispatches down for Norden to see.

"The Aliens have narrowed the invasion area to ten million miles from Earth," he said wearily. We've been holding out by a clever tactical subterfuge. Send out a hundred ships near each other, and the Aliens can't handle them all at once. If we're lucky, and spot the first torpedoes, we can trace them back and a few ships may survive long enough to send visual, pattern-seeking atomic torpedoes toward the Alien ship.

"But we can't get closer than a few hundred thousand miles with any life aboard a ship, because the radiation—or whatever it is they use—is fatal so long as they can detect us. You can see why Command rushed through all the screen suits they could, and struck this morning. They had to."

Norden picked up the dispatches, and scanned them grimly. Seven hundred pilots out of twice that many thousand had been screened. A third of the total number had returned—but none of the spared ships had been theoretically protected.

The Aliens had apparently not only spotted all of the protected ships, but had concentrated their torpedo fire on them. The experiment was complete failure!

There was no use in reminding Miles that he's tried to warn him. Earth hadn't been able to heed such warnings. He handed the papers back, his mind tormented by a picture of seven hundred men—men probably like the guards who'd called him all right—who had lost their marginal chance to live because a robot had failed. It was nonsense, his mind told him. Soldiers were meant to die. But the picture remained.

"So what happens to me now?" he asked.

You'll try again, of course," Miles answered, apparently surprised at the question. "At least the fact that they worked that hard to eliminate the ships with the screen indicates you're on the right track."

Norden stared at him despairfully. "It's like tracing a single drop of water in the ocean—or looking for trace of life that can be detected for millions of miles when you're in the middle of hordes of living creatures. I've been working on that already. And the only reason we *could* detect and screen the lizard signals was because they were unique.

Hardwick was right about that, too. You have to look for life forces where they're scarce. I need isolation from people, animals—even from germs and viruses, probably."

Pat gestured to a map on the wall. "There are the mine installations on the other side of the Moon. Would they do?"

He had no idea, but it was the best he could hope for. He nodded slowly, and she towards the door.

"Then what are we waiting for?" she asked. "we've got too little time now."

"You're not going, Pat," he told her. "Nobody is. I need isolation from life, remember! Besides, if there's any means of communication between here and there, I'll need you here to work the communicator."

There was television link that was still useful, as a quick check showed. And there were ships to carry as much equipment as he needed, including two rabbits, and a male and female sand lizard in little airtight cages where oxygen could be supplied from tanks. He had no idea of what he might need, and had to take everything he could imagine as being useful.

CHAPTER SIX

Three hours later, he stood alone in the building that had served as a barracks for a mine crew. He watched the rockets leave, and began opening the airlocks to space. Any bacteria left by the former men would quickly perish, he felt sure. But he had to be thorough.

He had no hope of success yet. He might be keeping a deathwatch over the human race as the Aliens moved in—or a life watch, since he was seeking life while they were intent on ending it. But he, at least, was no living thing, and the life detectors of the Aliens should miss him. Somehow, he'd learn enough to seek vengeance among them.

They'd made a mistake in creating him with all the ability of the original William Norden, and the thinking speed of a robot. They'd made a bigger mistake in assuming that a robot was only a robot, and that orders in the form of compulsions would be followed without question.

For their mistakes, they'd pay. He had twenty-four hours out of each day for work, and, until they caught him, to learn their further weaknesses.

He flooded the front entrance, where the television link to Moon base stood, with air to make speech possible, and rigged up a flexible seal to the rest of the building.

Janiekowski had dissected countless sand lizards, and the pictures were included in the reel of tape from Earth. He studied them, digging into what the calculator had supplied about radiation, and its behavior in the third spectrum. He found, as he had expected, that a tiny bit of radioactive material lay at the base of the microscopic receptor in the female, and that a similar mechanism was to be found in the organ which the male used to generate the force.

There was a tiny helix of superfine, wirelike construction around the radioactive material, but he had no idea of what the conductor was composed, or how the animals generated the faint currents of electricity they'd need. He was only sure the helix was a tiny electromagnet.

He built a model as best he could, and tried to find some indication that it picked up a signal form the male. Finally he was forced to anesthetize the female and remove her receptor for examination under the portable electron microscope.

It took eleven tries before he was able to detect anything of importance. Then the result surprised him. The faint, almost invisible glow from the radioactive disintegration in his device abruptly faded. He had been expecting it to increase, but whatever force the male broadcast seemingly acted to decrease the "unchangeable" rate of decay of a bit of K-40.

He called Pat, asking for information. Her face was haggard with worry, and her anxiety to remain constantly vigilant and alert. She wrote down his questions, and cut off without wasting time. Half an hour later, she called back.

"You're right. Uranium-bearing ores from far out in space contain much less uranium in proportion to lead than similar ores on Earth. Geologists say it's because those space-borne rocks are older, and cosmic radiation acts on them more continuously."

They're wrong," he said flatly, "It's because radioactivity is inhibited by the life processes. I don't know how. But I do know I need that data fed into the computer."

It meant they'd have to revise all of their figures about the age of the Earth upwards. Since the beginning of life on Earth and Mars, no radioactive half-life had been natural. Probably the rate of decay had varied slightly with each century, as the amount of life changed.

He fed her a list of calculations, and waited while the machine ground out its answers. Pat came back to the screen while it worked on automatically.

"They're bombing the base now," she reported dully. "We've been able to miss being hit by keeping a cover of volunteers up to attract the seeking units before they reach us. And the Aliens are within three million miles. We can't hold out much longer."

"Don't forget your optimism," he said. He'd meant it for reassurance, but she stared back as if he'd slapped her. "I mean your computer calculations on victory for Earth. How come they moved in so quickly?"

"It's been three days," she told him, "Don't you know how long you've been out there?"

He hadn't kept track. The cluck of the computer ending its work interrupted them, and she held the results up to the screen for him to copy with the camera at his end.

He studied the formulae for long, wasted minutes before he could accept them. Then he went on to other work.

There was no shield possible for any object bigger than about twice the size of the cage they had used. There could never be any way to protect a man from the Aliens.

It was to be a deathwatch he kept, apparently. And Pat must have known it when she saw the formulae, since she had picked up sufficient basic knowledge to read it.

He stood staring up at the space above him, letting the hate harden inside him, while he pictured the base in the hands of the invaders! Humans were beyond saving,

50

according to the figures he had now. But it was still not too late for vengeance.

This time he deliberately sought for a taboo in his mind to discourage thought along hindering lines. The forbidden topic was the question of why the Aliens had to exterminate life as they advanced. He wrestled with it briefly, rejoicing in the knowledge that he seemed to be gaining ease in overcoming the compulsory behavior which had been imposed on him.

Life must be poison to the Aliens! Probably it was for that reason that they had been able to detect it in the first place. And they could never rest until it was wiped out to the last living cell. He glanced at his formulae again, and nodded. If their existence were somehow based on the breakdown of radioactive isotopes, and if protoplasmic life slowed up that process, then they *had* to exterminate it.

How? He asked it automatically, remembering the force they used to sterilize space before them. And that had an answer, too. Even protoplasmic life apparently needed a tiny, incredibly small amount of radioactivity to function. Blast enough of the raw life force against it, and all nuclear breakdown would stop—and with the stopping of that, there would be no life.

It was logical that the weapon of the Aliens should be the one thing that they themselves feared most.

Tiny—incredibly weak—as the energy of those life forces were, they could do more in their inhibiting of the great force of nuclear readjustment than ten million atomic bombs!

He drew up his plans this time with sureness. He was no longer amazed at the progress he'd made in understanding extraspectral phenomena. It might very well represent the work of generations of scientists, but he was a robot designed to understand human science, even from the few smatterings the Aliens had been able to learn before he had been created.

He finished the designs, wrote down the proper formulae, and stacked the paper in front of the television pick-up, pressing the call button. Without waiting for an answer, he went back into the workshop, and began assembling the tiny, radioactive strontium batteries and tubes of protein plastic, wound with layers of iron wire. He had enough for what he needed.

The device was set to work both as a detector and a generator of the radiation involved. He tuned one, setting it to receive. It took a few minutes to replace the antenna of the small radar set with the new device, and he forced himself to work faster by the sheer drive of his will.

Then he stepped aside, letting mechanism revolve on the antenna mount. He began increasing the current that controlled the degree of electromagnetism in the wire, which served to tune the device.

A pip appeared on the screen, pointing toward the cage where the male and crippled female lay peacefully together. Norden raised the frequency until another pip appeared, this time pointing to the rabbits. He adjusted it for maximum brightness. In the section, which should cover the direction of Moon base below him, a brilliant glow sprang up, indicating radiation that cut straight through all the layers of the Moon. He adjusted the instrument again.

He found the exact frequency, and the whole screen suddenly blazed, blanked out by overloading of the amplifier. Apparently all life of terrestrial origin radiated at the same frequency. He cranked up the control, expecting nothing more. Then he bent sharply forward as other pips appeared, indicating objects far out in space!

The Aliens also radiated in the same spectrum—but at such an incredibly high frequency that no atomic nucleus was small enough to be affected by the radiation.

As Norden watched, the central pip suddenly began to grow brighter, holding its position in a way that indicated a straight descent toward his detector! Terror struck at his nerves.

Obviously the Aliens had detectors for every frequency, and his detector was just crude enough to radiate a faint trace of its own. He'd been located, and the exterminating force was on the way.

CHAPTER SEVEN

Norden cursed his own stupidity, and estimated the time it would take. If they decided to come in, and spray the area with their own force, or to capture it, he had several minutes. If they sent one of their superspeed torpedoes, he was on borrowed time. His mind raced furiously.

With a few minutes to spare, he could tune the tube he'd designed as a weapon, and spray them with that. Its straight-line efficiency would insure that no dangerous amount of its radiation would reach the men two thousand miles away. Vengeance was his for the taking.

He reached for the other tube, hesitated, and picked up a piece of paper and a pencil. The men at the base had the working plans of his device by now. They had to be warned how dangerous it would be not to make absolutely sure that their radiation generators and detectors couldn't spill dangerous radiation at random. Also that the Aliens could detect an inefficient search ray.

Norden headed for the flexible seal at a full run, while his steady hands pencilled the final information on the radiation frequencies needed. He broke through into the air of the entrance, yanked the diagrams off the pickup rack, and snapped in the new instructions. He turned with a single motion, and headed for the workroom again. And stopped!

Beyond the entrance, the gleaming fins of a rocket were visible. And the red light on the airlock indicated someone was coming through. As his eyes focussed, he saw the inner lock open, and Miles and Pat emerged in the red glare.

They started to shout something, but he cut them off. "For God's sake, stay here. There's no air beyond, Alien ship!"

He jumped through the seal. His hands swept up the tube that was to be a weapon, and his eyes darted to the screen. The pip was bigger now, and at maximum brightness. The Alien ship must be only tens of thousands of miles above, braking down to attack with deadly precision.

Less than a hundred feet away, the two humans waited, at the mercy of any energy that might spill from his weapon! He would have to score with a perfect piece of marksmanship, with all the radiation directed in a straight line.

The formulae of its propagation seemed like an endless belt in his mind. He tightened the helix of wire about the radioactive lode, trying to be sure they were even. With time, there were a number of things he might have done, but he had no time to spare. He might harm Miles and Pat—but the Alien beam would leave nothing to chance.

The thought of Miles and Pat jolted through his mind in a delayed reaction. They'd seen him come into this airless space without a helmet. They knew now he wasn't human! Discovered! *Explode the...*

"No!" he shouted silently into the airless room. He had to get the Alien first!

He had no idea how much time he had left as he snapped a flashlight battery into place, and tried to line the weapon into resonance with the detector settings. He lifted his eyes, to stare up through the open roof of the building. He knew there should be a faint black dot in the sky, but he couldn't see it against the blackness of space.

He lifted the weapon, pointed it toward where the Aliens should be, and depressed the little trigger, moving the rheostat back and forth to be sure he had the lethal frequency well covered.

He felt a tremor on the floor beside him, and his eyes caught a glimpse of Pat at his side before he could force his gaze toward space again. She was shouting something inside her helmet.

Then he caught the first visible sign of the Alien ship, already within miles of the building, and big enough to show in the sidelight of the sun. It came rushing down in an unchecked plunge, apparently heading straight for him! He strained his eyes, tracing its path. Then he relaxed. It was moving sideways and would land a mile away. *The weapon had worked.* No ship would have risked such speed so near the surface if the pilot had been alive.

He gripped Pat by the shoulder, and dragged her to the floor, away from the threat of falling debris. There was no sound, but a tremendous jolt rocked the floor of the building, and for a terror-fraught moment the ground seemed to dance madly. A shaft of greenish-yellow radiance merged with a glaring red that lit up the sky for miles. The ship had struck at a terrific speed—fast enough to reduce everything inside it to a pulp. The instant everything was quiet, Norden sprang to his feet.

Now! There is no time to be lost!

He caught the thought in time. He couldn't let himself explode in the workroom. He had to get outside, away from the two humans. The compulsion squeezed and writhed in his mind, and he could not throw it off. It was tenfold as strong as the previous commands—and the need to overcome it a hundred times as great.

He stumbled toward the seal as Pat stood by. His body slipped through the seal, and he almost bumped into Miles, who was apparently waiting for him. Norden had no spare effort for speech or thought. He headed dumbly for the airlock, determined to get outside as quickly as possible.

"Norden!" The general had grabbed his arm, and was following him. "Norden, if you go out there, I'm going with you. Whatever happens will happen to me, too. *You've got to listen!*"

He tried to force his way ahead, shaking his arm to free it. The other arm was also carrying a dead weight, and he could see Pat's face close to his own.

She was screaming at him, "Bill! Bill, you must listen! We knew it all along! We *knew* you were a robot! It doesn't matter. If you explode, you'll take us with you!"

He hit the lock in savage desperation and the words froze meaninglessly in his ears as he held back the driving urge until he could escape from them.

Miles clung grimly. "It's the Aliens, Bill! They want you to explode. The damned Aliens who want to kill you! Do you love them so much you'll kill us all? Or do you hate them?"

Slowly it penetrated the red haze of torment in his mind. The Aliens wanted to kill him. They'd played with him, had turned him into a monster to do their malicious bidding. They'd given him nothing in return. And now they wanted everything. His own life, worthless though it might be—and the life of his friends.

The hate washed through him—the cold, hard hate that had a greater strength for its very lack of endocrine instability.

"I'm all right," he said slowly. "You're safe. You can go back to the base."

Miles stared at him with a warm and friendly understanding. "We really did know about you, Bill," he said. "That business about your being the only undetected human on the asteroid looked suspicious, and the psychologists weren't fooled. We were gambling on a chance to get some information on the Aliens' detector out of you before you could do anything dangerous.

"Hardwick was the only man who could have known enough to have any chance. With him dead, we had to hope they'd give you information enough to act in his place, Pat volunteered to watch you. And we had ultra-violet cameras in every room where you ever were, watching you every second."

He paused, but Norden could think of nothing to say. He looked at Pat for confirmation, and she nodded. "We set the whole thing up for you, Bill. But we found we were wrong. The Aliens had done too good a job on you for their own good. They made you too human—so human that you had to begin thinking *our* way. After that business with Armsworth, we stopped worrying."

"But you came out here…" he began.

"Not to spy on you, Bill," Miles told him, "Earth's evacuating the Moon, now that you found us weapons to handle the Aliens. We're needed to supervise things back at the factories, Pat and I just came to pick you up, when you wouldn't answer your calls. We're taking you home."

He stared at them silently, and there was a complex of feelings in his mind that made thinking almost impossible. Bitterness was heavier than anything else.

"That's fine for someone who won't hate an enemy— though you're quick enough to employ hate when it's useful." He looked at Miles steadily. "What about the rest of the world? Will they welcome a bomb-carrying robot monster as a friend?" Bill Norden wanted to know.

Miles put his hands on Norden's shoulders, while Pat went back into the workroom. "Sit down on the desk, Bill," he urged. The only people who know are the two of us, and Jim—the psychologist who predicted exactly how you'd react from the beginning. He also gave you a test that first day that involved our top-grade X-ray machine—not one of those fluoroscopic toys. It's a good thing you've got your brains all through you, because when I get done, you'll be literally empty-headed."

Pat came back with a collection of equipment. Norden stared, trying to sit up. "You must be insane. Do you want to be killed if I blow? Are all humans crazy?"

Miles tightened his grip on Norden's shoulder. "Hold still. It shouldn't hurt. We're going to leave the communication gadget where it is, as it may be useful, later. But that bomb must come out." He smiled abruptly. "As to humans—well, you should know."

CHAPTER EIGHT

Three days later Bill Norden took his hands from the back of his neck, and sat up abruptly. He joined General Miles and Pat at the screen of the big life-force "radar." Far out in space, a large group of shiny, swiftly moving objects were drawing together, according to the pips that traced their course. They formed into clusters and began heading outwards.

The pips grew dimmer almost instantly, though they should have lost only half their brightness after a billion miles of traveling.

"Obviously faster than the speed of light, and on a heading straight toward Sirius," General Miles said slowly. "The poor devils! Until some damned, misguided fool from Earth travels there some day in an effort to formalize a peace agreement with them, they're going to live every single hour of their lives with the knowledge of the horrible certainty that we can wipe them out whenever we choose—and that the best their race could do was a total failure. They'll probably have sunk back to being scared, unhappy savages before we reach them."

Norden then thought of the charts that had been shown to him while he lay in the communicating position. Earth certainly had enough life-force projectors to sweep the skies with lethal radiation already, and she had just begun to tool up.

The Aliens had guessed wrongly about every step—they had tried to follow a logical pattern against a race that defied logic.

And somehow, his hatred of them was gone. "You'll have the superlight drive next year, probably," he guessed. "There are enough of their ships out there now with Aliens who died before they could set off their bombs for you to figure that out. Earth will be sending a ship there before they can revert to complete savagery."

"And I suppose you want to be on it?" Pat asked. She looked at her father, smiling thoughtfully as he grinned in answer to her lifted eyebrow, "I imagine the three of us could swing permission, at that."

Norden gave a quick nod. He'd planned it all out. He'd have to go back to university work, pretending to explore the new trails of science that had opened with the discovery of Hardwick's spectrum. The formulae he'd developed had been destroyed, but he could always remember enough to keep up with the eager young men who would go plunging into the field.

Maybe, that way, by the time the probable levels of telepathy and other psi-phenomenon had been discovered, the world would be ready for them. He had no intention of acting as a super-brain, however well equipped he might be. With the emergency over, the human race could discover enough by itself.

Miles and his daughter would be busy with the long and difficult job of trying to re-settle the numerous planets that the Aliens had despoiled. But all three of them would be ready when the first ship capable of reaching the stars had been built.

Norden drew himself up.

"Yes," he said. "Yes, I guess I want to be on it. I helped teach the Aliens enough about human beings as enemies. Now I'd like to teach them about us as friends."

THE END

If you've enjoyed this book, you will not want to miss these terrific titles…

ARMCHAIR SCI-FI & HORROR DOUBLE NOVELS, $12.95 each

D-11   **PERIL OF THE STARMEN** by Kris Neville
           THE STRANGE INVASION by Murray Leinster

D-12   **THE STAR LORD** by Boyd Ellanby
           CAPTIVES OF THE FLAME by Samuel R. Delaney

D-13   **MEN OF THE MORNING STAR** by Edmund Hamilton
           PLANET FOR PLUNDER by Hal Clement and Sam Merwin, Jr.

D-14   **ICE CITY OF THE GORGON** by Chester S. Geier and Richard S. Shaver
           WHEN THE WORLD TOTTERED by Lester Del Rey

D-15   **WORLDS WITHOUT END** by Clifford D. Simak
           THE LAVENDER VINE OF DEATH by Don Wilcox

D-16   **SHADOW ON THE MOON** by Joe Gibson
           ARMAGEDDON EARTH by Geoff St. Reynard

D-17   **THE GIRL WHO LOVED DEATH** by Paul W. Fairman
           SLAVE PLANET by Laurence M. Janifer

D-18   **SECOND CHANCE** by J. F. Bone
           MISSION TO A DISTANT STAR by Frank Belknap Long

D-19   **THE SYNDIC** by C. M. Kornbluth
           FLIGHT TO FOREVER by Poul Anderson

D-20   **SOMEWHERE I'LL FIND YOU** by Milton Lesser
           THE TIME ARMADA by Fox B. Holden

ARMCHAIR SCIENCE FICTION CLASSICS, $12.95 each

C-3   **INTO PLUTONIAN DEPTHS**
          by Stanton A. Coblentz

C-4   **CORPUS EARTHLING**
          by Louis Charbonneau

C-5   **THE TIME DISSOLVER**
          by Jerry Sohl

C-6   **WEST OF THE SUN**
          by Edgar Pangborn

ARMCHAIR SCIENCE FICTION & HORROR GEMS SERIES, $12.95 each

G-1   **SCIENCE FICTION GEMS, Vol. One**
          Isaac Asimov and others

G-2   **HORROR GEMS, Vol. One**
          Carl Jacobi and others

If you've enjoyed this book, you will not want to miss these terrific titles…

ARMCHAIR SCI-FI, FANTASY, & HORROR DOUBLE NOVELS, $12.95 each

D-21 **EMPIRE OF EVIL** by Robert Arnette
         THE SIGN OF THE TIGER by Alan E. Nourse & J. A. Meyer

D-22 **OPERATION SQUARE PEG** by Frank Belknap Long
         ENCHANTRESS OF VENUS by Leigh Brackett

D-23 **THE LIFE WATCH** by Lester Del Rey
         CREATURES OF THE ABYSS by Murray Leinster

D-24 **LEGION OF LAZARUS** by Edmond Hamilton
         STAR HUNTER by Andre Norton

D-25 **EMPIRE OF WOMEN** by John Fletcher
         ONE OF OUR CITIES IS MISSING by Irving Cox

D-26 **THE WRONG SIDE OF PARADISE** by Raymond F. Jones
         THE INVOLUNTARY IMMORTALS by Rog Phillips

D-27 **EARTH QUARTER** by Damon Knight
         ENVOY TO NEW WORLDS by Keith Laumer

D-28 **SLAVES TO THE METAL HORDE** by Milton Lesser
         HUNTERS OUT OF TIME by Joseph E. Kelleam

D-29 **RX JUPITER SAVE US** by Ward Moore
         BEWARE THE USURPERS by Geoff St. Reynard

D-30 **SECRET OF THE SERPENT** by Don Wilcox
         CRUSADE ACROSS THE VOID by Dwight V. Swain

ARMCHAIR SCIENCE FICTION CLASSICS, $12.95 each

C-7 **THE SHAVER MYSTERY, pt. 1**
        by Richard S. Shaver

C-8 **THE SHAVER MYSTERY, pt. 2**
        by Richard S. Shaver

C-9 **MURDER IN SPACE** by David V. Reed
        by David V. Reed

ARMCHAIR MASTERS OF SCIENCE FICTION SERIES, $16.95 each

M-3 **MASTERS OF SCIENCE FICTION, Vol. Three**
Robert   Sheckley

M-4 **MASTERS OF SCIENCE FICTION, Vol. Four**
        Mack Reynolds, part one

THE LISTENERS...

"Orejas de ellos," the things who listen, whispered the superstitious fishermen when the strange occurrences began off the Philippine coast. How else explain the sudden disappearance of a vessel beneath a mysterious curtain of foam? The writhings of thousands of maddened fish trapped in a coffin-like area of ocean? What monsters gorged at the bottom of Luzon Deep and what were their plans?

Radar expert Terry Holt and the crew of the Esperance had to devise a weapon against the horrifying creatures which threatened mankind with extinction.

Here are terror, excitement, and the clutch of cold death as combined by a master hand in the field of science-fiction, Murray Leinster.

CAST OF CHARACTERS

TERRY HOLT
He was offered a ton of money to design a new undersea device and go on a long cruise. He just wasn't allowed to ask why…

DEIRDRE DAVIS
It took deep sea monsters, aliens from space, and a long sea voyage to get this brainy woman into the swing of things.

CAPTAIN DAVIS
He knew there were aliens landing in the Earth's oceans. But what was their purpose, and most of all…could he prove it?

DR. MORTON
In charge of the China Sea tracking station for satellites, he had an interesting theory concerning strange meteorite activity...

POLICE CAPTAIN FELICIO HORTA
Just an average cop from the Philippines—not a scientist. What then was his interest in a famed scientist from the U.S?

THE CREW-CUTS
Nick Alden, an M.I.T. graduate, Tony Drake, from Harvard. Jug Bell, a Princeton graduate, and Doug Holmes, from Yale. These four brawny young men rounded out the crew of The Esperance.

CREATURES OF THE ABYSS

By
MURRAY LEINSTER

ARMCHAIR FICTION
PO Box 4369, Medford, Oregon   97501-0168

*For more information about Armchair Books and products, visit our
website at…*

www.armchairfiction.com

Or email us at…

armchairfiction@yahoo.com

CHAPTER ONE

The moment arrived when Terry Holt realized that he was simply holding the bag for Jimenez y Cía.—Jimenez and Company—in the city of Manila. He wasn't getting anywhere, himself. So, painfully, he prepared to wind up the company's affairs and his own, and start over. It seemed appropriate to take inventory, consult the police—they'd been both amiable and cooperative—and then make new plans. But first it would be a good idea to go somewhere else for a while, until the problem presented by *La Rubia* and radar and fish and *orejas de ellos* had been settled. He was at work on the inventory when the door opened, the warning-bell tinkled, and the girl came into the shop.

He looked up with a wary eye, glancing over the partition separating the workshop area in which the merchandise sold by Jimenez y Cía. was assembled. There were certain people he felt should not come into the shop. The police agreed with him. He was prepared to throw out anybody who came either to demand that he build something or else, or to demand that he not build it or else. In such forcible ejection's he would be backed by the authorities of the city and the Philippine Republic.

But this customer was a girl. She was a pretty girl. She was pleasantly tanned. Her make-up, if she wore any, looked natural, and she carried a sizable parcel under her arm. She turned to close the door behind her. She was definitely from the United States. So Terry said in English, "Good afternoon. Can I do something for you?"

She looked relieved.

"Ah! We can talk English," she said gratefully. "I was afraid I'd have trouble. I do have trouble with Spanish."

Terry came out from behind the partition marking off the workshop. The shop was seventeen feet wide and its larger expanse of plate glass said, *"Jimenez y Cía."* in large letters.

Terry's now-vanished partner Jimenez had liked to see his name in large print. Under the name was the line *"Especialidades Electrónicas y Físicas."* This was Terry's angle. He assembled specialties in the line of electronics and modem physics. Jimenez had sold them, not wisely but too well. At the bottom corner of the window there was a modest statement: *"Orejas de Ellos,"* which meant nothing to anybody but certain commercial fishermen, all of whom would deny it.

The girl looked dubiously about her. The front of the shop displayed two glaringly white electric washing machines, four electric refrigerators, and two deep-freeze cabinets.

"But I'm not sure this is the right shop," she said. "I'm not looking for iceboxes."

"They're window-dressing," said Terry. "My former business associate tried to run an appliance shop. But the people who buy such things in Manila only want the latest models. He got stuck with these from last year. So we do—I did do—*especialidades electrónicas y físicas*. But I'm shutting up shop. What are you looking for?"

The shop was in an appropriate place for its former products. Outside on the Calle Enero there were places where one could buy sea food in quantity, mother-of-pearl, pitch, coir rope, bêche-de-mer, copra, fuel oil, Diesel repair-parts and edible birds' nests. *Especialidades* fitted in. But though it was certainly respectable enough, this neighborhood wasn't exactly where one would have expected to find a girl like this shopping for what a girl like this would shop for.

"I'm looking," she explained, "for somebody to make up a special device, probably electronic, for my father's boat."

"Ah!" said Terry regretfully. "That's my line exactly, as is evidenced in Spanish on the window and in Tagalog, Malay and Chinese on cards you can read through the glass. But I'm suspending operations for a while. What kind of special device? Radar— No. I doubt you'd want *orejas de ellos...*"

"What are they?"

"Submarine ears," said Terry. "For fishing boats. The name is no clue at all. They pick up underwater sounds, enabling one to hear surf a long way off. Which may be useful. And some fish make noises and the fishermen use these ears to eavesdrop on them and catch them. You wouldn't be interested in anything of that sort!"

The girl brightened visibly.

"But I am! Something very much like it, at any rate. Take a look at this and see what my father wants to have made."

She put her parcel on a deep-freeze unit and pulled off its paper covering. The object inside was a sort of curved paddle with a handle at one end. It was about three feet long, made of a light-colored fibrous wood, and on the convex part of its curvature it was deeply carved in peculiar transverse ridges.

"A fish-driving paddle," she explained. "From Alua." He looked it over. He knew vaguely that Alua was an island somewhere near Bohol.

"Naturally a fish-driving paddle is used to drive fish," she said. "To—herd them, you might say. People go out in shallow water and form a line. Then they whack paddles like these on the surface of the water. Fish try to get away from the sound and the people herd them where they want them—into fish-traps, usually. I've tried this, while wearing a bathing suit. It makes your skin tingle—smart, rather. It's a sort of pins-and-needles sensation. Fish would swim away from an underwater noise like that!"

Terry examined the carving.

"Well?"

"Of course we think there's something special about the noise these paddles make. Maybe a special wave-form?"

"Possibly," he admitted. "But—"

"We want something else to do the same trick on a bigger scale. Directional, if possible. Not a paddle, of course. Better. Bigger. Stronger. Continuous. We want to drive fish and this paddle's limited in its effect."

"Why drive fish?" asked Terry.

"Why not?" asked the girl. She watched his face.

He frowned a little, considering the problem the girl posed.

"Oh, *ellos* might object," he said absently.

"Who?"

"*Ellos*," he repeated. "It's a superstition. The word means 'they' or 'them.' Things under the ocean who listen to the fish and the fishermen."

"You're not serious." It was a statement.

"No," he admitted, still eyeing the paddle. "But the modern, businesslike fishermen who buy submarine ears for sound business reasons call them *orejas de ellos* and everybody knows what they mean, even in the modernized fishing fleet."

"Which," said the girl, "Jimenez y Cía. has had a big hand in modernizing. That's why I came to you. Your name is Terry Holt, I think. An American Navy Captain said you could make what my father wants."

Terry nodded suddenly to himself.

"What you want," he said abruptly, "might be done with a tape-recorder, a submarine ear, and an underwater horn. You'd make a tape-recording of what these whacking's sound like under water, edit the tape to make the whacking's practically continuous, and then play the tape through an underwater horn to reproduce the sounds at will. That should do the trick."

"Good! How soon can you do it?" she asked.

"I'm afraid not at all," said Terry. "I find I've been a little too efficient in updating the fishing fleet. I'm leaving the city for the city's good."

She looked at him inquiringly.

"No," he assured her. "The police haven't asked me to leave. They're glad I'm going, but they're cordial enough and it's agreed that I'll come back when somebody else finds out how *La Rubia* catches her fish."

"*La Rubia?*"

"*The Redhead*," he told her. "It's the name of a fishing boat. She's found some place where fish practically fight to get into her nets. For months, now, she's come back from every trip loaded down gunwale-deep. And she makes her trips fast! Naturally the other fishermen want to get in on the party."

"So?"

"The bonanza voyages," Terry explained, "started immediately after *La Rubia* had submarine ears installed. Immediately all the other boats installed them. My former partner sold them faster than I could assemble them. And nobody regrets them. They do increase the catches. But they don't match *La Rubia*. She's making a mint of money! She's found some place or she has some trick that loads her down deep every time she puts out to sea."

The girl made an interrogative sound.

"The other fishermen think it's a place," Terry added, "so they ganged up on her. Two months back, when she sailed, the entire fishing fleet trailed her. They stuck to her closer than brothers. So she sailed around for a solid week and never put a net overboard. Then she came back to Manila—empty. They were furious. The price of fish had gone sky-high in their absence. They went to sea to make some money regardless. When they got back they found *La Rubia* had sailed after they left, got back before they returned—and she was just loaded with fish, and the market was back to normal. There was bad feeling. There were fights. Some fishermen landed in the hospital and some in jail."

A motor truck rolled by on the street outside the shop of the now moribund Jimenez y Cía. The girl automatically turned her eyes to the source of the noise. Then she looked back at Terry.

"And then my erstwhile associate Jimenez had a brainstorm," said Terry ruefully. "He sold the skipper of *La Rubia* on the idea of short-range radar. I built a set for him. It was good for possibly twenty miles. So *La Rubia* sailed in the dark of the moon with fifty fishing boats swearing violent oaths that they'd follow her to hell-and-gone. When night fell *La Rubia* put out her lights, used her radar to locate the other boats who couldn't see her, and sneaked out from their midst. She came back loaded down with fish. There were more fights and more men in the hospital and in jail. Some of *La Rubia*'s men boasted that they'd used radar to dodge their rivals. And that's how the police got interested in me."

The girl had listened interestedly.

"Why?"

"Oh, Jimenez began to take orders for radar from other fishing boat owners. If *La Rubia* could dodge them by radar, they could trail her by radar even in the dark. So the skipper and crew of *La Rubia* promised blood-curdling things as Jimenez's fate if he delivered a radar set to anybody else. Then the skippers and crews of other boats made even more blood-curdling threats if he didn't deliver radar to them. So Jimenez ran away, leaving me to hold the bag."

The girl nodded.

"And therefore," said Terry, "I'm shutting up shop.

I'll turn the inventory over to the police and go off somewhere until someone learns where *La Rubia* gets her fish. When things calm down again, I'll come back and start up business once more—without Jimenez. I'll probably stick to electric-eye doors, burglar alarms, closed-circuit television systems and things like that. Then I might make this underwater broadcasting device, if your father still wants it. I'd better not now."

"We heard about your problem," said the girl. "Almost exactly the way you just explained it."

Terry stared. Then he said politely, "Oh. You did?"

"Yes, I thought—"

"Then you knew," said Terry more politely still, "that I was leaving town and couldn't make the gadget you want? You knew it before you came here?"

"Why," said the girl, "your plans seemed to fit in very nicely with ours. We've got a sixty-five-foot schooner and we're sailing around. My father wants something like—what you described. So since you want to—well—travel around for a time, why not come on board our boat and make the thing we want there? We'll land you anywhere you like when it's finished."

"Thanks," said Terry with very great politeness indeed. "I think I made a fool of myself, explaining. You knew it all beforehand. I'm afraid I bored you horribly. You probably even know that Jimenez took all the funds when he ran away."

She hesitated, and then said, "Y-yes. We thought—"

"That I should have trouble raising steamer-fare to any place at all," he said without cordiality. "And I will. You had that information too, didn't you?"

"Please!" she said with distress. "You make it sound—"

"Did you have any idea what I'd charge to assemble the device you want?"

"If you'll name a price."

Terry named one. He was angry. The sum was far from a small one. It was, in fact, exorbitant. But he felt that he'd made a fool of himself, responding to her encouragement by telling her things she already knew.

She opened her purse and peeled off bills. She put them down.

"I'll leave the paddle with you," she said crisply.

"Our boat is the *Esperance*. You'll find it…" She named the anchorage, which was that of Manila's most expensive yacht club. "There's a launch which will bring you out whenever you're ready to sail. It would be nice if you could sail tomorrow—and nicer if you could come aboard today."

She nodded in friendly fashion, opened the door—the bell jangled—and went out.

Terry blinked. Then he swore and snatched up the pile of bills. Two fluttered to the floor and he lost time picking them up. He went out after her, the money in his hand.

He saw a taxicab door close behind her, three or four doors down the street. Instantly the cab was in mad career away. The taxicabs of Manila are driven by a special breed of chauffeurs. It is said that they are all escaped lunatics with homicidal tendencies. The cab went roaring down the Calle Enero's cluttered length and turned the corner.

Terry went back to the shop. He swore again. He looked at the money in his hand. It totaled exactly the excessive amount he'd named as the price of an electronic fish-driving unit, including an underwater horn.

"The devil!" he said angrily.

He felt the special indignation some men feel when they are in difficulties, which their pride requires them to surmount by themselves, and somebody tries to help. The indignation is the greater as they see less chance of success on their own.

Terry's situation was offensive to him because he shouldn't be in this kind of situation at all, or rather; his troubles were not foreseeable by the most competent of graduate electronic engineers. He'd trained for the work he'd undertaken. He'd prepared himself for competence. At graduation he'd encountered the representatives of at least three large corporations who were snapping up engineers as soon as they left the cloistered halls of learning. Terry'd asked how many men were employed in the category he'd fit in. When one representative boasted that ten thousand such engineers were on his company's payroll, Terry declined at once. He wanted to accomplish something himself, not as part of a team of some thousands of members. The smaller the organization, the better one's chance for personal satisfaction. He wouldn't make as much money, but—

It was a matter of simple logic. If he was better off with a really small company, he'd be best off on his own. And he'd nearly managed it. He'd worked only with Jimenez. Jimenez was the sales organization. Terry was the production staff. In Manila there was certainly room for special electronic equipment—*especialidades electrónicas y físicas*. He should have had an excellent chance to build up a good business. Starting small, even without capital, he'd confidently expected to be going strong within months. There were taxi fleets to be equipped with short-wave radio. There were burglar alarms to be designed and installed, and all sorts of setups to be engineered. And these things were still in demand. His expectations had a solid foundation. Nobody could have anticipated the disaster caused by *La Rubia*'s phenomenal success in commercial fishery. It was even irrational for it to be a disaster to Terry. But it was.

More immediately, though, he was indignant because this girl had known all about him when she came into the shop. She'd probably even known about his gimmicking a standard-design submarine listening device so it was really good and really directional. But she'd let him talk; asking seemingly interested questions, when she knew the whole business beforehand. And at the end she'd done a most infuriating thing by paying him in advance for something he'd refused to do, thereby forcing him into the obligation to do it.

He fretted. He needed the money. But he objected to being tricked. He went back to the probably senseless business of taking an inventory. Time passed. Nothing happened. Nobody came to the shop. The police had been firm about *La Rubia* crewmen calling on Terry to make threats. They'd been equally firm about other people calling to make counter-threats. No casual customers entered. Two hours went by.

At four o'clock the door opened—with the sound of its tinkling bell—and Police Captain Felicio Horta came in.

"*Buenas tardes*," he said cordially.

Terry grunted at him.

"I hear," said Horta, "that you leave Manila."

Terry asked evenly, "Is that a way of asking me to hurry up and do it?"

"*Pero no! Por supuesto no!*" protested Horta. "But it is said that you have new and definite plans."

"What do you know about them?" demanded Terry.

Police Captain Horta said pleasantly, "Officially, nothing. Privately, that you will aid some *ricos americanos* to do experiments in—*oceanografía?* Some study of oceanic things. That you regret having agreed to do so. That you consider changing your mind. That you are angry."

The girl, of course, could have inferred all this from his angry charge out of the shop with the money in his hand, too late to stop her taxicab. But Terry snapped, "Now, who the devil told you that?"

Police Captain Horta shrugged.

"One hears. I hope it is not true."

"That what's not true? That I leave? Or that I don't?"

"I hope," said Horta benignly, "that you do as you please. I am not on duty at the moment. I have my car. I offer myself to chauffeur you if there is any place you wish to go—to a steamer or anywhere else. If you do not wish to go anywhere, I will take my leave. With no pre...prejudice," he finished. "We have been friendly. I hope we remain so."

Terry stared at him estimatingly. Police Captain Horta was a reasonable and honest man. He knew that Terry had contributed to matters giving the police some trouble, but he knew it was accidental on Terry's part. He would hold no grudge.

"Just why," asked Terry measuredly, "did you come here to offer to drive me somewhere? Is there any special reason to want me to get out of town?"

"That is not it," said Horta. "It could be wished that you would—take a certain course of action. Yes. But not because you would be absent from here. It is because you would be present at a special other place. The matter connects with *La Rubia*, but in a manner you could not possibly guess. Yet you are wholly a free agent. You will do as you please. I would like to make it—convenient. That is all."

He paused. Terry stared at him, frowning. Horta tried again.

"Let us say that I have much interest in *oceanografía*. I would like to see certain research carried on."

"Being, I'm sure, especially interested in fish-driving," said Terry skeptically. "You sound as if you were acting unofficially to get something done that officially you can't talk about."

Horta smiled warmly at him.

"That," he pronounced, "is a logical conclusion."

"What's the object of the—research, if that's what it is? And why pick me?"

Horta shrugged and did not answer.

"Why not tell me?"

"Amigo," said Horta, "I would like nothing better than to tell you. I would be interested to see your reception of the idea. But it would be fatal. You would think me cr-azy. And also more important persons. But especially me."

It was Terry's turn to shrug his shoulders. He hesitated for a long moment. If Horta had tried to apply pressure, he'd have turned obstinate on the instant. But there was no pressure. First the girl and now Horta tried to lure him with mystery and assurance of interest in high places.

"And *La Rubia*'s involved in the secret?" demanded Terry.

"Innocently," said Horta promptly. "As you are."

"Thank you for faith in my innocence," said Terry with irony. "All right. If I'm involved, I'm involved. I'll try to devolve out of being involved by playing along."

He turned to the workshop space at the back of the store. He found boxes to pack his working tools and the considerable stock of small parts needed to make such things as burglar alarms, submarine ears and the assorted electronic devices modern business finds increasingly necessary. He began to pack them. Surprisingly, Horta helped. Any man of Spanish blood is apt to be sensitive about manual labor. If he has an official position his sensitiveness is apt to be extreme. But Horta not only helped pack the boxes with Terry's stock of parts; he helped carry them to his car outside. He helped to load them.

Terry turned the key in the door and handed it to him, with the nearly complete inventory of the shop's contents.

"Jimenez having run away, I leave the shop in your hands," he observed.

Horta put the key and document away. He started the motor of his car and drove along the Calle Enero. He drove with surprising moderation for a police officer authorized to ignore traffic rules on occasion. Presently the dock-area of Manila was left behind, and then the rest of the commercial district, and then for a time the car tooled along wide streets past the impressive residences of the wealthy. Some of the architecture was remarkable. A little further, and the harbor—the bay— appeared again. The car entered the grounds of Manila's swankiest yacht club. The design of the clubhouse was astounding. The car stopped by the small-boat pier. There were two men waiting there. Without being given any orders, they accepted the parcels Horta handed out. Also without orders, they carried them out to the float. They loaded them into the brass-trimmed motor tender, which waited there.

"They knew we were coming," said Terry shortly. "Would I have been brought anyhow?"

"Pero no," said Horta. "But there are telephones. When we left the shop, one was used."

The men who'd carried out the parcels vanished. Terry and Horta stepped aboard. The tender cast off and headed out into the harbor. There was a Philippine gunboat and a minelayer and an American flattop in plain view. There were tankers and tramp steamers and a vast array of smaller craft at anchor. A seemingly top-heavy steamer ploughed across oily water two miles distant. The tender headed for a trim sixty-five-foot schooner anchored a mile from shore. It grew larger and seemed more trim as the tender approached it.

The smaller boat passed under the larger one's stern, and the name *Esperance* showed plainly. On the starboard side a boat boom projected. The tender ran deftly up and a man in a sweat shirt and duck trousers snubbed the line. He said cheerfully, "How do you do, Mr. Holt?" Then he nodded to Horta. "Good to see you, Captain." He offered his hand as Terry straightened up on deck. "My name's Davis. We'll have your stuff aboard right away."

Two young men in dungarees and with crew cuts appeared and took over the motley lot of cartons that Terry and Horta had made ready.

"Have you everything you need?" asked Davis anxiously. "Would some extra stuff be useful?"

"I could do with a few items," said Terry, stiffly.

He had quickly developed an acute dislike for the patent attempt to induce him to join the *Esperance*. He had no reason for his objection, save that he had not been informed about the task he was urged to undertake.

"Also," he added abruptly, "Captain Horta didn't think to stop at my hotel so I could get my baggage."

"Write a list of what you want," suggested Davis. "I'm sure something can be done about your baggage. Make the list complete. If something's left over, it won't matter. There's a desk in the cabin for you to write at." He turned to Horta. "Captain, what's the news about *La Rubia*?"

"She sailed again yesterday," said Horta ruefully. "She was followed by many other boats. And now there is a moon. It rises late, but it rises. Many sailors will be watching her from mastheads. It is said that all the night glasses in Manila have been bought by fishermen…"

His voice died away as Terry went down the companion ladder. Belowdecks was attractive. There was no ostentation, but the decor was obviously expensive. There were armchairs, electric lamps, a desk, and shelves filled with books—two or three on electronics and a highly controversial one on marine monsters and sea serpents. There were some on anthropology. On skin diving. On astronomy. Two thick volumes on abyssal fish. There was a shelf of fiction and other shelves of reference books for navigation, radio and Diesel maintenance and repair. There were obvious reasons for these last, but no reason that could be imagined for two books on the solar planets.

Terry sat at the desk and compiled a list of electronic parts that he was sure wouldn't be available in Manila. He was annoyed as he realized afresh the smoothness of the operation that had brought him to the *Esperance*. He found satisfaction in asking for some multi-element vacuum tubes that simply couldn't be had except on special order from the manufacturers back in the United States. But it took time to think of them.

When he went abovedecks, half an hour later, he had listed just six electronic components. The tender was gone, and Horta with it. Davis greeted Terry as cordially as before.

"The tender's left," said Terry with restraint. "Here's my list."

Davis did not even glance at it, but beckoned to one of the crew-cut young men who'd unloaded the tender.

"This is Nick Alden," he said to Terry. "He's one of the gang. See about this list, Nick."

The crew-cut young man put out his hand and Terry shook it. It seemed expected. He went forward with the list and vanished down the forecastle ladder. Davis looked at his watch.

"Five-thirty," he observed. "A drink might not be a bad thing."

He went below, and Terry surveyed the *Esperance*. She had the look of a pleasure craft, but was built along the lines of something more reliable. There was an unusual power winch amidships, with an extraordinarily large reel. Next to it there was a heavy spar by which to swing something outboard. There were two boats, well stowed against heavy weather, and a number of often-omitted bits of equipment, so that the schooner was not convincing as the hobby of a mere yachtsman.

Then Terry saw the brass-trimmed tender heading out from the yacht-club float again. Foam spread out from its bow. A figure in it waved. Terry recognized the girl who'd come into the shop of Jimenez y Cía. She was smiling, and as the launch came nearer it seemed to Terry that there was triumph in her smile. He bristled. Then he saw some parcels in the bow of the tender. Next to the parcels—and he unbelievingly suspected what they were—he suddenly recognized something else: his suitcases and steamer trunk. In order to sail with the *Esperance* he need not go ashore to get his belongings. They were brought to him. He became totally convinced that these people had assumed he'd do what they wanted him to, without consulting him. He rebelled. Immediately. Any time other people took for granted that they could make plans for him, he would become obstinate. When he was in a fix and now he was practically stranded in Manila with a need to go elsewhere for a time and no money with which to do it—he was especially touchy. He found himself scowling and angry, and the more angry because what was required of him would have been very convenient if there'd been no attempt to inveigle him into it.

The launch came around the *Esperance's* stern. Davis came from below with two glasses. The girl said cheerfully, "Howdo! We've got your extra items. All of them. And your baggage."

Terry said curtly, "How did my list get ashore?"

"Nick phoned it," said Davis. "By short-wave."

"And where the devil did you find the stuff I named?"

"That," said Davis, "is part of the mystery you don't like."

"Right!" said Terry grimly. "I don't like it. I don't think I'll play. I'll go ashore in the tender."

"Hold it!" said Davis. But he was speaking to the operator of the tender. The crew-cut Nick was in the act of handing up the first piece of baggage. Davis waved it back. "I'm sorry," he said to Terry. "We'll stay at anchor here. If you change your mind, the tender will bring you out any time."

Terry brought out the sheaf of bills the girl had left in the shop of the vanished Jimenez. He held them out to the girl. She put her hands behind her back and shook her head.

"We put you to trouble," she said pleasantly, "and we haven't been frank with you. That's to make up for it."

"I won't accept it," said Terry stiffly. "I insist."

"We won't have it back," said Davis. "And we insist!"

Terry felt idiotic. There was enough of a breeze to make it impractical simply to put the batch of bank notes down. They'd blow away. The girl looked at him regretfully.

"I'm truly sorry," she said. "I planned the way we went after you. You are exactly the person we're sure to need. We decided to try to get you to join us. We couldn't explain. So we asked what you were like. And you're not the sort of person who can be hired to do what he's told and no questions asked. Captain Horta said you were a gentleman. So since we couldn't ask you to volunteer blindly—though I think you would volunteer if you knew what we're about to do—we tried to make you come for the adventure of it. It didn't work. I'm sorry."

Terry had the singular conviction that she told the exact truth. And she was a very pretty girl, but she wasn't using her looks to persuade him. She spoke as one person to another. He unwillingly found himself mollified.

"Look!" he said vexedly. "I was leaving Manila. I need to be away for a while. I am coming back. I can do any crazy thing I want for some weeks, or even a couple of months. But I don't like to be pushed around! I don't like—"

The girl smiled suddenly.

"All right, I'll keep the money."

The girl smiled more widely and said, "Mr. Holt, we are off on a cruise. We'll put in at various ports from time to time. We think you would fit into our party. We invite you to come on this cruise as our guest. You can be helpful or not, as you please. And we will *not* try to pay you for anything!"

Davis nodded. Terry frowned. Then he spoke painfully.

"I have a gift for making a fool of myself," he said ruefully. "When it's put that way, fine! I'll come along. But I reserve the right to make guesses."

"That's good!" said Davis warmly. "If you do find out what we won't tell you, you'll see why we didn't."

He waved to Nick and the tender operator. The parcels came onto the *Esperance's* deck. His baggage followed. He picked up one of the new cardboard parcels and examined its markings.

"This," he said more ruefully still, "has me stymied. I'd have sworn you couldn't get one of these special tubes nearer than Schenectady, New York. But you found one in Manila in minutes! How did you do it?"

The girl laughed.

"Terribly simple!" she said. "We'll tell you. But not until we're under way, or you might be so disgusted with the simplicity of it that you'd want to go ashore again."

CHAPTER TWO

The edge of the sun touched the horizon and sank below it, out of sight. There were magnificent tints in the sky, and the gently rippling harbor water reflected them in innumerable swirlings of color. The *Esperance* swayed very slightly and very gracefully on the low swells. In minutes two of the dungareed members of the ship's company got the anchor up with professional efficiency. One of them went below, and the *Esperance's* engine began to rumble. Davis casually took the wheel, and the small yacht began to move toward the open sea while Nick played a salt-water hose on the anchor before lashing it fast. The brief twilight of the tropics transformed itself swiftly into night. Lights winked and glittered ashore and on the water.

Terry felt more than a little absurd. The girl said pleasantly, at his side, "My name's Deirdre, in case you don't know."

"Mine's Terry, but you do know."

"Naturally!" she said briskly. "I should explain that I'm the ship's cook, and the boys forward aren't professional sailors, and my father isn't—"

"Isn't in this business for money," said Terry. "It's strictly for something else. And I don't think it's buried treasure or anything like that."

"Nothing so sensible," she agreed. "Now, if you want to join a watch, you'll do it. If you don't, you won't. The port cabin, the little one, is yours. You are our guest. If you want anything, ask for it. I'm going below to cook dinner."

She left him. He surveyed the deck again, and presently went back to where Davis sat nonchalantly by the *Esperance's* wheel. Davis nodded.

"Now that you've, well, joined up," he said meditatively, "I've been trying to think how to, well, justify all the mystery. Part of it was Deirdre's idea. She thought it would make our proposition more interesting, so you'd be more likely to take it up. But when I think about explaining, I bog down immediately."

Terry sat down. The *Esperance* drove on. Her bow lifted and dipped and lifted and dipped. The water was no longer nearly smooth. There was the beginning of a land breeze.

"There's *La Rubia*," said Davis uncomfortably. "You outfitted her with underwater ears and radar, at least. Was there anything else?"

"No," said Terry curtly. "Nothing else."

"She catches the devil of a lot of fish," said Davis.

He frowned. "Some of them you might call very queer fish. You haven't heard anything about that?"

"No," said Terry. "Nothing."

"I think, then," said Davis, "that I'd better not expose myself to scorn. I'd like to be able to read her skipper's mind, though. But it's possible he simply thinks he's lucky. And it's possible he's right."

Terry waited. Davis puffed on his pipe. Then he said abruptly, "Anyhow you're a good man at making gadgets. We'll let it go at that, for the time being."

The sea became less and less smooth. There were little slapping sounds of waves against the yacht's bow. The muted rumble of her engine was not intrusive. The breeze increased. Davis gave a definite impression of having said all he intended to say for the time being. Terry stirred.

"You want me to build a gadget," he said. "To drive fish. Would you want to give me some details?"

Davis considered. A few drops of spray came over the *Esperance's* side.

"N-o-o-o," said Davis. "Not just yet. There's a possibility it will fit in. I'd like you to make one, and maybe it will fit in somewhere. But *La Rubia's* the best angle we've got so far.

There is one gadget I'd give a lot to have! You know, a depth-finder. It sends a pulse of sound down to the bottom and times the echo coming back. Very much like radar, in away. Both send out a pulse and time its return."

Terry nodded. There was no mystery about depth-finders or radars.

"We've got a depth-finder on board," said Davis. "If I sail a straight course and keep the depth-finder running, I can make a profile of the sea bottom under me. If I had a row of ships doing the same thing, we could get profiles and have a relief map of the bottom."

"That's right," agreed Terry.

"What I'd give a lot for," said Davis, "would be a depth-finder that would send spot-pulses, like radar does. Aimed sound-pulses. And an arrangement made so it could scan the ocean bottom like radar scans the sky. One boat could make a graph of the bottom in depths and heights, mapping even hummocks and hills underwater. Could something like that be done?"

"Probably," Terry told him. "It might take a good deal of doing, though."

"I wish you'd think about it," said Davis. "I know a place where I'd like to use such a thing. It's in the Luzon Deep. I really would like to have a detailed picture of the bottom at a certain spot there!"

Terry said nothing. He'd been made angry, then mollified, and now he felt tempted to grow angry again. There was nothing definite in what was wanted of him, after elaborate machinations to get him aboard the *Esperance*. He was disappointed.

"Good breeze," said Davis in a different voice. "We might as well hoist sail and cut off the engine. Take the wheel?"

Terry took the wheel. Davis went forward. Four dungareed figures came up out of the forecastle. The sails went up and filled. The engine stopped. The motion of the boat changed.

More spray came aboard, but the movement was steadier. Davis came back and took the wheel once more.

"I think," he said, "that we're acting in a way to—hm—be annoying. I ought to lay my cards on the table. But I can't. For one thing, I haven't drawn a full hand yet. For another, there are some things you'll have to find out for yourself, in a situation like this."

"Such as—"

"Well," said Davis with a sudden dogged air, "take those *orejas de ellos*, for an example. *Ellos* are supposed to be some sort of beings at the bottom of the sea who listen to fish and fishermen. It's a superstition pure and simple. Suppose I said I was investigating the possibility that there were such-beings. You'd think I was crazy, wouldn't you?"

Terry shrugged.

"What I am interested in," said Davis, "has enough credit behind it for me to get some pretty rare electronic parts from the flattop in harbor back yonder. Nick called them by short-wave, they sent the parts ashore and gave them to Deirdre, and she brought them out to you."

Terry blinked. Then he realized. Of course, that was where just about any imaginable component for electronic devices would be found—in the electronics stores of a flattop! They needed to have such things at hand. They'd carry them in store. Davis said drily, "They wouldn't supply parts to a civilian who was investigating imaginary gods or devils. So what I'm bothered with isn't a superstition. Right?"

"Y-yes," agreed Terry.

It was true. The Navy would not stretch regulations for a crackpot civilian. It was not likely, either, that Horta would have implied so definitely that the Philippine Government wanted somebody with Terry's qualifications to go for a cruise on the *Esperance*.

Deirdre put her head up through the after-cabin hatch. "Dinner is served," she said cheerfully.

"The wheel," said Davis to Terry.

He went forward. All four of the non-professional seamen came with him when he returned.

"This is the rest of the gang," said Davis. "You met Nick. The others are Tony Drake, Jug Bell, and Doug Holmes." He made an embracing gesture as they shook hands in turn. "Harvard, Princeton, Yale—and Nick's M. I. T. It's your turn at the wheel, Tony."

One of the four took over. The others filed below after Davis and Terry. Terry was silent. Davis had wanted to show that he was being informative, and yet he'd said exactly nothing about the interests or the purpose of the *Esperance's* complement.

Dinner in the after-cabin was almost as confusing to Terry. Seen at close range across a table, the four dungareed young men could not possibly be anything but college undergraduates. They were respectful to Davis as an older man and they tended to be a little cagey about Terry, because he was slightly older than themselves but not an honorary contemporary. They plainly regarded Deirdre with the warmest possible approval.

Conversation began, at first cryptic but suddenly only preposterous. There was an argument about the supposed intelligence of porpoises, based on recent studies of their brain structure. Tony observed profoundly that without an opposable thumb intelligence could not lead to artifacts, and hence no culture and no great effective intelligence was possible. Jug denied the meaningfulness of brain structure as an indication of intellect. Intellect would be useless to a creature, which could neither make nor use a tool. Doug argued hotly that the point was absurd. He pointed to spastic children once rated as morons but actually having high I.Q.'s. They had intellects, though they had been useless because of their inability to communicate. But Nick asserted that without tools they'd have nothing to talk about but food, danger, and who went where with whom for what. All of which, he observed, needed no brains.

Davis listened amusedly. Deirdre threw in the suggestion that without hands or tools an intelligent creature could compose poetry, and Jug protested that that was nothing to use a brain for—and the talk turned into a violent argument about poetry. Doug insisted vehemently that the finest possible intellects were required for the composition and appreciation of true poetry. Then Davis said, "Tony's still at the wheel."

The argument died down and the crew-cuts devoted themselves to eating, so one of them could get through and relieve him.

Afterward, Davis settled down below to a delicate short-wave tuning process to get music from an improbable distance. Deirdre served Tony his meal and talked with him while he ate it. Terry went abovedecks and paced back and forth as the *Esperance* sailed on through the night.

He couldn't make out anything at all about the crew or the purpose behind the *Esperance's* chosen task and purpose. He felt dubious about the whole business. Like most technically-minded men, he could become absorbed in a problem, especially if it was a device difficult to design or a design that somehow didn't work. Such things fascinated him. But the *Esperance's* crew was not concerned with a problem like that. There was no pattern in their talk or behavior to match the way a technical mind would go about finding a solution. The problem was bafflingly vague, yet there *was* one.

La Rubia was an element in it. Possibly Davis' wistful mention of a partial map of the bottom of the Luzon Deep fitted in somewhere. Davis had spoken of *orejas de ellos* with some familiarity, but certainly no Navy ship would cooperate in the investigation of a fisherman's superstition in which even fishermen didn't believe any longer. The Philippine fishing fleet was modern and efficient. Fishermen used submarine ears without superstitious fears, and if they referred to imaginary *ellos* it was as an American would say "knock on wood," with no actual belief that it meant anything.

CREATURES OF THE ABYSS

Whatever the *Esperance's* purpose was, there was nothing mystical about it—not if a flattop parted with rare and expensive specialized vacuum tubes to try to help, and the police department of Manila urged Terry tactfully—through Horta—to join the yacht, and no less than a Navy Captain had named him as someone to be recruited.

Deirdre came abovedecks and replaced Tony at the wheel. The *Esperance* sailed on. A last-quarter moon was now shining low on the eastern horizon. It seemed larger and nearer to the earth than when seen from more temperate climes. The wake of the yacht glowed in the moonlight.

The wide expanse of canvas made stark contrast between its moonlit top and its shadow on the deck. The only illumination on the ship was the binnacle lights and the red and green running lights. Deirdre kept the *Esperance* on course.

Terry went up to where she sat, beside the wheel.

"I've been making guesses," he told her. "Your father...I believe that his curiosity has been aroused by something, and he's resolved to track it down. I strongly suspect that at some time or another he's gotten bored with making money and decided to have some fun."

Deirdre nodded.

"Very good! Almost completely true. But what he's interested in is a good deal more important than fun."

Terry nodded in his turn.

"I suspected that too. And it's rather likely that you've got a volunteer crew instead of a professional one because these young men consider it a fascinating adventure into the absurd, and because they'll keep their mouths shut if something turns out to be classified information."

"My father's doing this strictly on his own!" said Deirdre quickly. "There's nothing official about it. There isn't any classified information about it. This is a private affair from the beginning!"

"But in the end it may turn out to be something else," said Terry.

"Y-yes. We don't know, though. It's impossible to know! It's—ridiculous!"

"And my explanation for your being so mysterious with me is that you and your father insist that I find out everything for myself because I'd think it foolish if you told me."

Deirdre did not answer for a moment. There was a movement behind Terry, and Davis came on deck.

"That was good music!" he said pleasedly. "You missed some very interesting sounds, Deirdre! You too, Holt."

"He's decided," said Deirdre, "that we're a little bit ashamed of our enterprise and won't tell him about it for fear he'll simply laugh at us."

Terry protested, "Not at all! Nothing like that!"

"When some forty-odd people have been killed by something inexplicable at one time that we know of," said Davis, "—and we don't know how many others have been killed at other times, or may be killed by it in the future—I don't think that's a laughing matter."

He surveyed what should be the direction of the land.

A light showed there and vanished, then came on again and vanished. A minute later it showed and disappeared, then came on again twice. It was very far away. Davis said in a different tone, "We can change course now, Deirdre. You know the new one."

The *Esperance's* bowsprit forsook the star at which it had been aiming. It swung to another. Davis moved about, adjusting the sheets alone. On the new heading the yacht heeled over a little more and the water rushing past her hull had a different sound. The sky seemed larger and more remote than it ever appears from a city. The yacht's wake streamed behind her in a trail of bluish brightness. Even the moon was strange. It had the cold enormousness of something very near and menacing. It looked as close as when seen through a telescope of moderate power.

The *Esperance* seemed very lonely on the immense waste of waters.

Next morning, of course, the sense of loneliness was gone. There was neither land nor any ship in sight, but gulls fluttered and squawked overhead, and the waves seemed to leap and gambol in the sunshine. Just before the foremast a metal plate in the decking had been lifted up, and a new, stubby, extensible mast rose or almost as high as the crosstrees. A tiny basket-like object rotated monotonously at its upper end. It was a radar-bowl, and somehow it was not unusual, except in the manner in which it was mounted. Yet, such a collapsible radar mast was reasonable on a sailing yacht with many lines aloft that could be fouled. Anyhow, the radar was concerned with human affairs, and so it was company.

The housekeeping work on the boat was in progress. Doug and Jug scrubbed the deck. The other crew-cuts gave signs of industry from time to time, appearing and vanishing. Davis smoked tranquilly at the wheel. Terry felt useless, as well as puzzled.

"Can I do anything?" he asked awkwardly. "You're your own boss," said Davis.

"Then I might as well see what can be done about that submarine noisemaker."

"If you feel like it," said Davis, "fine!"

But he did not urge. Terry waited a moment. There was a sort of contagion of purposefulness in this eccentric small group on the *Esperance*. They had something they were trying to do, and it seemed important to them. But Terry was an outsider and would remain one until he became active in their joint effort.

He got out his equipment and materials and spread them out. There was no need to build a recorder, since there was one among the supplies. The rest wouldn't be unduly difficult. He established a working space and set systematically to work. The task he'd accepted was essentially simple. A submarine ear was to pick up underwater sounds. He had to modify a microphone and enclose it in a water-tight housing, with certain special features that would make it highly directional. The recorder would take the pick-up and register it on magnetic tape, while playing it for simultaneous listening. Then he had to assemble a machine for playing back the taped sounds under water. That required a unit for a submarine horn, to broadcast the amplified sound. It isn't difficult to make a sound under water. One can knock two stones together under the surface and a swimmer can hear it a mile or more away. But a horn to reproduce specific sounds is more difficult to build. It needs extra power. A sound-truck in a city, competing with all the traffic noises, will turn no more than fifteen watts of electricity into noise. But much more power would be needed to produce a similar volume under water.

Terry modified the mike into a submarine ear—an *orejas de ellos*. Then he began to assemble an audio amplifier to build up the volume of the sounds already taped for re-use under the sea. He had the parts. It was mostly just finicky labor. He sat cross-legged in the sunshine, not far from the *Esperance's* unusual winch.

Nick came up from below and went aft. He spoke to Davis. Terry couldn't hear what was said, but Davis gave orders.

The *Esperance* heeled over; away, away over. The four crew-cuts adjusted the sheets for maximum effect of the sails on the new direction of motion. The yacht seemed to tear through the water like a racing boat. Terry had to rescue some of his smaller parts, which started for the scuppers. He looked up. Deirdre said cheerfully, "Our radar picked up a boat that's probably *La Rubia* on the way back to Manila. We don't want her to see us."

Terry blinked. "Why?"

"We're going to take a look at the spot where we think she catches her fish," said Deirdre. "It's strange enough that she catches so many, but what's even stranger is the kind of fish she catches at times."

"How?"

Deirdre shrugged. Then she said irrelevantly, "*La Rubia's* skipper would like to have the only radar in the world, as you've reason to know, and he doesn't think of radars, except his own and possible competitors. But there are lots of others. We're probably a blip on somebody's radar-screen right now. In fact, we're supposed to be. So when my father got interested in *La Rubia* and her—catches, he was able to have somebody notice where she goes every time she slips away from the fishing fleet. And so he was told. It was all quite unofficial, of course."

Terry bent over his task again while the *Esperance* sped along over the offshore swells. There was no land in sight anywhere. An albatross glided overhead for a time, as if inspecting the *Esperance* as a possible source of food. When Terry looked for it later it was gone. Once there was a flurry in many wave-flanks, and a small school of flying fish darted out of the sea with hazy, beating fins, and dived back into the sea many yards from where they started.

But nothing of any consequence happened anywhere. Terry fitted and soldered and tested. By noon he had a rather powerful audio amplifying unit, set up to magnify any sound the tape-recorder fed into it. Deirdre prepared a meal. The galley of the *Esperance* was admirably supplied with all kinds of food. After the noon meal the yacht changed course again to a line which would intersect her original morning course at some point.

Terry found himself fuming. He'd set to work to make something that Davis apparently wanted, but his most elementary questions still ran against a blank refusal to answer. Both Davis and Deirdre had spoken of oddities in the catches of *La Rubia*. There could not possibly be any reason for them to refuse to tell him what they were. Terry worked himself into irritability, recalling how he volunteered to come on the *Esperance* but not thinking that he would be treated as someone who wasn't allowed to know what everybody else aboard most certainly did.

In the afternoon there was guitar music down in the forecastle, and Doug came out and settled himself on the bowsprit with a book of poetry. Presently Nick sat down close by Terry and watched interestedly as he put mysterious-looking electronic elements together into incomprehensible groups. When he had finished, Terry did not admire his handiwork. The noisemaking unit came last. The electrical part had to be enclosed, watertight, with a diaphragm exposed to the water on one side and its working parts protected from all moisture on the other. The device looked cobbled, but it worked, and made monstrous sounds in the air.

Now he plugged the submarine ear into the recorder. He dropped it overside and taped the random noises of the sea: the washings of sea water against the *Esperance's* hull, frequent splashings, and very faint, chirping noises from who-knew-what.

"Watch the volume, will you?" Terry pointed out the indication that should not be exceeded. Nick nodded. "I'm going to whack the paddle overside and see what we get in the way of noise."

Nick hesitated. Then he said uneasily, "Wait a minute." He went aft to Davis, apparently somnolent at the wheel. Deirdre joined the two of them in a seemingly very serious discussion. Then she walked over to Terry.

"I hate to say it," she told him with evident concern, "but my father thinks it would be wiser to try out the paddle in shallow water. Do you mind?"

"Yes," snapped Terry. "I do mind, since I'm not allowed to know the reason for that or anything else."

He put away his tools and the unused parts. He pointed to the machines he had already built.

"This is what your father wanted, I think. After it's tested I'll ask you to put me ashore."

He went below, where he fretted to himself. But no one came, either to inform him of Davis' reasons, or to tell him to do as he pleased. He felt like a child who isn't allowed to play with other children; who is arbitrarily excluded from the purpose and the excitement of his fellows. Thinking in such terms did not make him feel any better. His irritation increased. The *Esperance* was engaged in an enterprise that these people considered very much worth doing. He'd joined them to accomplish it, and they wouldn't tell him what it was. He hadn't the temperament to be content with just following blindly. And somehow the fact that Deirdre was aboard and a participant in the secret made his exclusion an insult.

He felt about Deirdre that urgent concern that a man may feel about one or two, or at most three girls during his whole lifetime. It wasn't a romantic interest, at this stage, but he wanted to look well in her eyes, and he was enormously interested in anything she said and did. H he left the *Esperance* and ceased to know her, he knew he'd be nagged at by the feeling that he'd made a very bad mistake. He didn't want to stop knowing her. But he refused to be patronized.

He saw an open book on the after-cabin table and glanced restlessly at it. There were three or four photographs and a newspaper clipping stuck into its pages. The book itself dealt with physics at post-graduate levels—which meant that it included a good deal about electronics.

Still fuming, Terry glanced at the pictures. The first was of a spherical object made of transparent plastic and probably of small size. It had a number of metallic elements clearly visible through the transparent case. It looked as if it might be an electronic device itself, but there was no sign of lead-in contacts, and the parts inside made no sense at all. The second and third photographs were of a similar yet slightly different object. The fourth photograph was a picture of what looked like ocean water, taken from a plane. The horizon showed in one corner. The center of the picture was an irregularly shaped mass of white. On close examination it appeared to be foam. But it looked as if it were piled up in masses above the surface. If the water around it was ocean—and it was—and the visible crest-lines were of waves—and they were—that heap of foam must have been hundreds of yards in diameter and piled many feet high on the surface. Foam does not form in such masses in the open sea. It would not last if it did.

On the margin of this picture a date had been inked—three days before—and a position in degrees of latitude and longitude.

Terry turned to the chart rack. He pulled out a chart and looked up the position. Someone had made a pencil-dot there. It was close to Thrawn Island, on the very brink of the Luzon Deep, that incredible submarine chasm in which the entire Himalayan chain could be sunk without showing a single pinnacle above the surface.

He went back to the clipping. It was dated Manila, two years earlier. It was an obviously skeptical article on a report made by the crewmen of a sailing ship that stopped by Manila. Sailing ships are rare enough in modern times. This ship reported that she had sighted another of her own kind at sea. The two ships altered course to speak to each other. And the one which came into Manila declared that when the other vessel was no more than two miles away, white foam suddenly appeared on the sea just in front of her. A geyser of unsubstantial white stuff spouted up and spread, shooting up about thirty feet on the water. The bow of the other sailing ship entered the foam patch. And suddenly her bow tilted downward, her masts swayed forward, and the entire ship vanished into the white stuff, exactly as if she had sailed over a precipice. She did not sink. She dropped. She "fell" under water—under the foam—her sails still spread. One instant she sailed proudly. The next instant she was gone.

The position of such an incredible happening was roughly given. It was almost exactly the same as the position written on the photograph of foam taken from the air. At the margin of the Luzon Deep.

Terry found that his indignation had evaporated. The reason for it still remained, but now he wanted to know more about this happening and about the spheres of plastic with those deftly designed but enigmatic inclusions. The plastic objects had a purpose. He wanted to know what. And the news clipping...

Having announced crossly that he would ask to be set ashore as soon as the fish-driving unit was tested, he was ashamed to take it back. He stayed below, now angry with himself again. Nobody came below. Deirdre did not descend to cook. Night fell. Well after nightfall he heard movements on deck, and presently a voice which sounded oddly distant. The *Esperance's* course changed abruptly. The quality of her motion altered once more.

He went abovedecks. Twilight was long over, but the moon was not yet up. Here and there a wave-tip frothed, and blue luminescence appeared. Here and there a streak of dim blue light could be seen under water, where some fish darted. But those dartings were rare. Despite the yacht's shining wake and the curling wave-tips, the sea was darker than usual.

Nick's voice came from aloft, faint and eerie and seeming to come from the stars.

"…farther to port…Two points…"

Terry could see the masthead weaving and swaying against the stars, with a small dark silhouette clinging to it: Nick. The yacht began to swing. On one bearing she pounded heavily. The seas could hit her squarely, and they did. Figures moved swiftly about the deck, loosening sheets or tightening them. Nick's voice again, from overhead.

"Stea-a-a-dy!"

The *Esperance* ceased to turn. Rushing, pounding water sprayed in the air. The waves splashed upon the hull of the yacht, which was sweeping along on a quartering wind.

For a while no one talked. Tony stood at the wheel, with Davis nearby, by the binnacle light. Terry could see Davis glancing into the binnacle, then gazing at the horizon ahead, and then aloft, where Nick seemed to swing among low-hanging stars.

"Ri-i-i-ght!" he called from high overhead. "Steady as she goes."

The *Esperance* sailed on, over the surging seas. Waves came out of nowhere, leaped beside the yacht and then went by—to nowhere. It was hard to believe that the yacht actually moved forward. She seemed to stay perpetually in the one spot. But there was a winding, sinuous wake, and there was froth under her forefoot.

Then a vague brightness appeared on the sea, at the limit of vision. It spread out more widely as the *Esperance* approached. Presently it was clearly visible.

Dead ahead, the beam of the headlight suddenly revealed an incredible spectacle. Until then there had been just a few flashes in the water, where some fish darted away from the yacht's bulk. But here the entire surface of the water shone with thousands and thousands of fish. They were packed in a sharply delimited circle about a mile wide. When the *Esperance* got close enough, she hauled up into the wind to look.

From a spot fifty yards ahead, the sea was alive with a million frantic dartings of swimming things. They were crowded, packed almost fin-to-fin. And it was not a surface phenomenon only. From the yacht's deck the streaks of light were visible deep down, as far as the clear water would let them be seen. They formed a column of glittering chaos. The vast circle, to an indefinite depth, was packed solid with agitated fish. At that edge of brightness the thronging creatures were splashing in a mad frenzy. Solid shining shapes leaped crazily from the water. Some leaped again and again, until they reached the spot where the flashes were thickest, and got lost in the multitude of their fellows. A few escaped to the darker surrounding sea. They seemed to run away in stark terror. But those were only a few. The greatest mass of fish milled crazily inside the circle. There were even porpoises, darting about as if frightened beyond all normal behaviors, not even trying to feed on the equally fear-maddened creatures all about them.

CHAPTER THREE

Terry stared incredulously. Someone moved beside him. It was Davis. He spoke in a dry voice. "I would think," he said detachedly, "that *La Rubia* could catch a boatload of fish in that water with a single haul of her nets. Certainly with two."

Terry turned his head.

"But what is it? What makes these fish gather like this?"

"An interesting question," said Davis. "We'll try to find out how it happens. Even more interesting, I'd like to know why."

He moved away along the deck. Terry went close to the side rail. A few minutes later the startling glare of one of the side searchlights smote upon the water away from the incredible scene. It moved slowly back and forth. Where the light struck, the sea seemed totally commonplace. No fish could be seen. Then the white beam swept here and there in jerky leapings. There was nothing unusual on the surface, nothing beyond the limit of brightness, where the sea turned dark.

Deirdre said at Terry's side. "We didn't really expect this! I'm going to get a sample of the water, Terry. Want to help?"

She ignored his haughty withdrawal of the afternoon, and he could not stand on his dignity in the presence of such an incredible phenomenon. She got a water bucket from the nearby rack. A wave sprung up as she tried to fill the bucket overside. It touched her hand and she cried out. Terry jerked her back by the shoulder. The bucket bumped against the *Esperance's* side, hanging on the line attached to the rail.

"What's the matter?"

"It stung! The water stung! Like a nettle!" Shaking a little, Deirdre rubbed her wet hand with the other. "It doesn't hurt now, but it was like a stinging nettle—or an electric shock!"

Terry hauled in the bucket and set it down. He leaned far over the rail. He plunged his hand into a lifting pinnacle of the sea. Instantly, his skin felt as if pricked by ten thousand needles. But his muscles did not contract as they would in an electric shock. The sensation was on the surface of his skin alone.

He shook his head impatiently. He put his finger in the bucket he'd lifted to the deck. There was no unusual sensation. He dipped overside again. Again acute and startling hurt, from the mere contact with the water.

Deirdre still rubbed her hand. She said in a queer, surprised voice.

"Like pins and needles. It's like—like the fish-driving paddle! But worse! Much worse!"

Terry looked again at the sea glittering with the swarms of fish in hopeless, panicked agitation, confined in a specific narrow compass by something unguessable. The searchlight continued to flick here and there. The *Esperance* drifted away from the edge of brightness. Terry put his hand overside once more, and once more he felt the stinging, nettle-like sensation. He got a fresh bucket of water from overside. On deck, there was no strange sensation when he dipped his hand in it.

The searchlight went out abruptly and only a faint and quickly dimming reddish glow came from it. That too died.

Davis' voice gave orders. Terry said sharply, "Wait a minute!" He began to explain about the stinging of the water. But then he said, "Deirdre, you tell him! I'm going to put a submarine ear overboard. At the least we'll get fish noises on a new scale. But I've got an idea...don't sail into the bright circle yet."

He got out the submarine ear and the recorder he'd made ready that afternoon. He started the recorder. Then he trailed the microphone overside. The sounds would be heard live through the speaker and they would be taped at the same time. At first, a blaring, confused sound came through. Terry turned down the volume.

He heard gruntings and chirpings and rustlings. Fish made those noises—not all fish, but certain species. These shrill, squeaking noises were the protests of frightened porpoises. But under and through all other sounds, a steady, unvarying hum could be easily detected. Terry had never heard anything quite like it. Its pitch was the same as that of a sixty-cycle frequency, but its tone quality was somehow sardonic and snarling. The word that came into Terry's mind was "nasty." Yes, it was a nasty sound. One didn't like it. One would want to get away from it. In the air the same unpleasant sensation is produced by noises that make one's flesh crawl.

Terry straightened up from where the recorder played upon the wet deck. Davis and Deirdre had come to listen, in the strange darkness under the sails of the *Esperance.*

"I've got a sort of hunch," said Terry slowly. "Let's sail across the bright patch. I'll record the sea noises all the way. I've a feeling that that hum means something."

"It's not what you'd call an ordinary sound," said Davis.

He raised his voice. One of the crew-cuts was at the schooner's wheel. He spun it. The sails filled, and the rattling of flapping canvas died away. The *Esperance* gathered way and moved swiftly from the glittering circle, came about, and sailed again toward the shining area. She got closer and closer to the boundary.

The recorder continued to give out the confused and frightened noises of the sea creatures, but under and through their sounds there remained the nasty and sardonic hum. It grew louder and more unpleasant—much louder in proportion to the fish sounds. At the very boundary of the bright space it was loudest of all.

But as the yacht went on, the hum dimmed. At the very center of the circle where the glitterings were brightest, the humming sound was overwhelmed by the submarine tumult of senseless fish voices. Terry dipped his hand here. The tingling was almost tolerable, but not quite.

Davis hauled more buckets of water to the deck. In two of them he found some fish, so dense was the finny multitude. Then the yacht neared the farthest limit of the bright circle. The hum from the recording instrument grew progressively louder. Again, at the very edge of the shining water, it was loudest.

The *Esperance* sailed across the live boundary and into the dark sea. As the boat went on, the sound dimmed...

"Definitely loudest," said Terry absorbedly, "at the edge of the circle of fish. At the line the fish couldn't cross to escape. It is if there was an electric fence in the sea. It felt like that, too. But there isn't any fence."

Davis asked evenly, "Question: what holds them crowded?"

Terry said again, groping in his mind, "They act like fish in a closing net. I've seen something like this once, when a purse-seine was hauled. Those fish were frantic because they couldn't get away. Just like these."

"Why can't they get away?" asked Davis grimly. "We haven't seen anything holding them."

"But we heard something," pointed out Deirdre. "The hum. That may be what closes them in."

Her father made a grunting noise. "We'll see about that."

He moved away, back to the stern. In moments, the *Esperance* was beating upwind. Presently, she headed back toward her previous position, but outside the brightness. Terry could see dark silhouettes moving about near the yacht's wheel. Then he saw another brightness at the eastern horizon, but that was in the sky. Almost as soon as he noticed it, the moon peered over the edge of the world, and climbed slowly to full view, and then swam up among the lower-hanging stars.

Immediately, the look of the sea was different. The waves no longer seemed to race the darkness with only star glitters on their flanks. The figures at the *Esperance's* stern were now quite distinct in the moonlight.

"You said a very sensible thing, Deirdre," said Terry. "I thought of the fish-driving paddle and its effects, but I was ashamed to mention it. I thought it would sound foolish. But when you said it, it didn't."

"I have a talent," said Deirdre, "for making foolish things sound sensible. Or perhaps the reverse. I'm going to say a sensible thing now. We haven't had dinner. I'm going to fix something to eat."

"You won't get anybody to go belowdecks right now!" said Terry.

"I thought of that," she told him. "Sandwiches."

She went below. Terry continued to watch, while figures at the stern of the schooner went through an involved process of visual measurement. It was not simple to determine the dimensions of a patch of shimmering light flashes from a boat in motion. But presently, Davis came toward him.

"It's thirteen hundred yards across," he told Terry. "Plus or minus twenty."

"I didn't expect all this," Davis said, frowning. "I've been making guesses and hoping fervently that I was wrong. And I have been, but each time the proof that I was wrong has led to new guesses, and I'm afraid to think those guesses may be right."

"I can't begin to guess yet," said Terry.

"You will!" Davis assured him. "You will! You try to add up things... A half-mile-wide patch of foam that piles up thirty feet above the sea..."

"And into which," Terry interrupted, "a sailing ship does not sink but drops out of sight as if there were a hole in the sea."

Davis turned sharply toward him.

"There were some photographs and a newspaper clipping on the cabin table," explained Terry. "I suspected they might have been put there for me to see."

"Deirdre, perhaps," said Davis. "She's resolved to involve you in this. You've got scruples, so she suspects you of having brains. Yes. You'll add those things up. You'll include the remarkable success of a fishing boat named *La Rubia* and the fact that she sometimes brings in very strange fish... And then you'll add..."

His eyes flickered aloft. A shooting star streaked across one-third of the sky leaving a trail of light behind it. Then it went out.

"You'll even be tempted," said Davis, "to include something like that in your guesses! And then you'll try to come up with a total for the lot. Then you'll be as troubled as I am."

He paused a moment.

"You said you wanted to be put ashore as soon as the gadget you made today was tested. I hope you've changed your mind, or will. That tape-recording may mean something to somebody. We wouldn't have heard that very singular noise but for you."

"I withdraw the business of going ashore," said Terry uncomfortably. "I'm going to ask another question. What are those little spheres that I saw in the photographs on the cabin table? Were they found fastened to the fish?"

"So I'm told," said Davis. "They are made of plastic. One was on a fish caught by a chief petty officer of the United States Navy. Four have been found on fish brought into the market by *La Rubia*. They could conceivably be a joke, but it's very elaborate! Somebody tried to cut one open and it burst to hell-and-gone. Terrific pressure inside. The metal parts inside were iridium. The others haven't been cut open. They're—" Davis' tone was dry. "They're being studied."

A figure came out of the forecastle and walked aft. It was Nick. He stopped to say, "I called Manila and got a loran fix on us. We're right at the place *La Rubia* heads for every time she sneaks away from the rest of the fishing fleet. It seems that she hauls her nets yonder."

He nodded toward the circular area of luminosity on the sea. "It looks smaller than when I went below deck."

Davis stared. He seemed to stiffen.

"It does. We'll make sure."

He went aft. Deirdre came up with sandwiches. Terry took the tray from her and followed her toward the others.

"Cigars, cigarettes, candy, sandwiches?" she asked cheerfully.

Davis was back at the task of measuring the angle subtended by the patch of shining sea, and then closely estimating its distance from the *Esperance*. He said, "It is smaller. Eleven hundred yards, now."

"When *La Rubia* was here today," said Terry, "it might have been a couple of miles across. Even that would be a terrific concentration of fish! They're not all at the surface."

Davis said with impatience, seemingly directed against himself, "It's narrowed two hundred yards in the past half-hour. It must be tending toward something! There has to be a conclusion to it! Something must be about to happen!"

Deirdre said slowly, "If it's the equivalent of a seine being hauled, with a hum instead of a net, what's going to happen when it's time for the fish to be boated?"

Davis ignored her for a moment. Then he said irritably, "Everyone seems to have more brains than I do! Tony, break out those gun-cameras. Nick, get back and report if the bright spot's getting any smaller. I wish you weren't here, Deirdre!"

The two crew-cuts moved to obey. Terry, alone, had no specific duty assigned to him on the yacht, unless tending to the recorder was it. He bent over the instrument, which was playing in the air anything that a trailing microphone picked up under water. He raised the volume a trifle. He could still hear the singular noises of the agitated fish mixed in with the thin, strangely offensive humming sound. He heard small thumping's, and realized that they were the footfalls of his companions on the deck of the *Esperance*, transmitted to the water. He heard...

Tony came abovedecks with an armful of mysterious-looking objects, which could not be seen quite clearly, in the slanting moonlight. He put two of them down by the wheel and passed out the others. He silently left one for Terry and another for Deirdre, while Terry adjusted tone and volume on the recorder for maximum clarity.

"What are those?" asked Terry.

"Cameras," said Deirdre. "Mounted on rifle stocks, with flash bulbs in the reflectors. You aim, pull the trigger, and the shutter opens as the flash bulb goes off. So you get a picture of whatever you aim at, night or day."

"Why..."

"There was a time when my father thought they might be useful," said Deirdre. "Then it looked like they wouldn't. Now it looks like they may."

Terry was tempted to say, "Useful for what?" But Davis' vague talk of unpleasant wrong guesses, which led to even less pleasant ones, had already been an admission that no convincing answer could be given him. Davis came over to him.

"This has me worried," he said in a frustrated tone of indecision. "We must be near the end of some process that I didn't suspect, and the conclusion of which I can't guess. I don't know what it is, and I don't know what it's for. I only know what it's tied in with."

Terry said absorbedly, "Two or three times I've picked up some new kinds of sounds. You might call them mooing noises. They're very faint, as if they were far away, and there are long intervals between them. I don't think they come from the surface."

Davis made an irresolute gesture. He seemed to hesitate over something he was inclined to accept. Deirdre protested before he could speak. "I don't think what you're thinking is right!" she said firmly. "Not a bit of it! Whatever happens will be connected with the fish. *La Rubia* has been around this sort of thing over and over again! We haven't been running the engine and we haven't been making any specific noises in the water to arouse curiosity! If anything were going to happen to us, it would have happened to *La Rubia* before now! It would be ridiculous to run away just because I'm on board!"

Terry, bent intently over the recorder, suddenly felt a cold chill run up and down his spine. His mind told him it was ridiculous to associate distant mooing sounds, underwater, with a completely unprecedented, frantic gathering of fish into one small area, and come up with the thought that something monstrous and plaintive was coming blindly to feed upon fellow creatures of the sea. There was nothing to justify the thought. It was out of all reason. But his spine crawled, just the same.

"The circle's only eight hundred yards across, now," said Davis, uneasily. "The fish can't crowd together any closer! But Doug went overboard with diving goggles, and he says there's a column of brightness as far down as he can make out."

Terry looked up.

"He went overboard? Didn't he tingle?"

"He said it was like baby nettles all over," Davis protested, as if it were someone's fault. "But he didn't sting after he came out. It must be..."

A mooing sound came out of the recorder. It was fainter than the other sounds and very far away. It must have been of terrific volume where it originated. It lasted for many seconds, then stopped.

"I should have been recording," said Terry. "That sound comes up about every five minutes. I'll catch it next time."

Davis went away, as if he wanted to miss the noise and the decision it would force upon him. Yet Terry told himself obstinately that there was no reason to connect the mooing sound with the crazed fish herd half a mile away. But somehow he couldn't help thinking there might be a connection.

The ship's clock sounded seven bells. Deirdre said, "The brightness is really smaller now!" The patch of flashes was no more than half its original size. Terry pressed the recording button and straightened up to look more closely. Right then Deirdre said sharply, "Listen!"

Something new and quite unlike the mooing noise now came out of the recorder.

"Get your father," commanded Terry. "Something's coming from somewhere!"

Deirdre ran across the heaving deck. Terry shifted position so he could manipulate the microphone hanging over the yacht's side into the water. Davis arrived. His voice was suddenly strained and grim. "Something's coming?" he demanded. "Can you hear any engine noise?"

"Listen to it," said Terry. "I'm trying to get its bearing."

He turned the wire by which the submarine ear hung from the rail. The chirpings and squealings and squeakings changed volume as the microphone turned. But the new sound, of something rushing at high speed through the water—that did not change. Terry rotated the mike through a full circle. The fish noises dwindled to almost nothing, and then increased again. The volume of the steady hum changed with them. But the rushing sound remained steady. Rather, it grew in loudness, as if approaching. But the directional microphone didn't register any difference, whether it received sound from the north, east, south, or west.

It was a booming sound. It was a rushing sound. It was the sound of an object moving at terrific speed through the water. There was no engine noise, but something thrust furiously through the sea, and the sound grew louder and louder.

"It's not coming from any compass course," said Terry shortly. "How deep is the water here?"

"We're just over the edge of the Luzon Deep," said Davis. "Four thousand fathoms. Five. Maybe six."

"Then it can only be coming from one direction," said Terry. "It's coming from below. And it's coming up."

For three heartbeats Davis stood perfectly still. Then he said, with extreme grimness, "Since you mention it that would be where it's coming from."

He turned away and shouted a few orders. The crewmen scurried swiftly. The yacht's head fell away from the wind. Terry listened again to the rushing sound. There seemed to be regular throbbings in it, but still no engine noise. It was a steady drone.

"Bazooka shells ought to discourage anything," Davis said in an icy voice. "If it attacks, let go at it. But try to use the gun-cameras first."

The *Esperance* rolled and wallowed. Her bows lifted and fell. Her sails were black against the starry sky overhead. Two of the crew-cuts settled themselves at the starboard rail. They had long tubes in their hands, tubes whose details could not be seen. The wind hummed and shuttered in the rigging. Reef-points pattered. Near the port rail the recorder poured out the amplified sounds its microphone picked up from the sea.

The sound of the coming thing became louder than all the other noises combined. It was literally a booming noise. The water started to bubble furiously as it parted to let something rise to the surface from unthinkable depths.

Doug put two magazine-rifles beside Terry and Deirdre, then he moved away. Deirdre had a clumsy object in her hands. It had a rifle-stock and a trigger. What should have been the barrel was huge—six inches or more in diameter—but very short. That was the flashbulb reflector. The actual camera was small and on top, like a sight.

"We'll aim these at anything we see," said Deirdre composedly, "and pull the trigger. Then we'll pick up the real rifles and see if we must shoot. Is that all right?"

She faced the shining patch of ocean. Davis and the crew-cut at the wheel faced that way. Tony and Jug stood with the clumsy tubes of bazookas facing the same direction. Doug had taken a post forward, with a camera-gun and a magazine rifle. He had the camera in hand, to use first.

It seemed that hours passed, but it must have been just a few minutes. Nothing out of the ordinary seemed to be taking place anywhere. The moon now shone down from a sky in which a few thin wisps of cloud glowed among the stars. Sharp-peaked waves came from one horizon and sped busily toward the other. The yacht pitched and rolled its company strangely armed and expectant. The recorder gave out a droning, booming, rushing sound, which grew louder with ever-increasing rapidity. Now the sound reached a climax.

From the very center of the glinting circle of sea, there was a monstrous splashing sound. A phosphorescent column rose furiously from the waves. It leaped. Water fell back and…something soared into the air. Sharp, stabbing flashes of almost intolerably white light flared up. The gun-cameras fired their flash bulbs without a sound.

It was then that Terry saw it—in mid-air. He swung the gun-camera, and a flash from another gun showed him that he would miss. He jerked the gun to bear and pulled the trigger. The flash illuminated *it* vividly. Then night again.

It was torpedo-shaped and excessively slender but very long. It could have been a living thing, frozen by the instantaneous flash. It could have been something made of metal. It leaped a full fifty feet clear of the waves and then tumbled back into the ocean with a colossal splash. Then there was silence, except for the sounds of the sea. Terry had the magazine-rifle still in his hands. Tony and Jug waited with their bazookas ready. It occurred to Terry that yachts are not customarily armed with bazookas.

"That—wasn't a whale," said Deirdre unsteadily.

The recorder bellowed suddenly. It was the hum that had been heard before: the nasty, sixty-cycle hum that surrounded the captive fish. But it was ten, twenty, fifty times as loud as before.

The fish in the bright-sea area went mad. The entire surface whipped itself to spray, as fish leaped frenziedly to get out of the water, which stung and burned where it touched.

Then, very strangely, the splashing stopped. The brightness of the sea decreased. A while later the enormous snarling sound was noticeably less loud than it had been at that first horrible moment.

The wind blew. The waves raced. The *Esperance's* bow lifted and dipped. The noise from the loudspeaker system—the noises from the sea—decreased even more. One could hear the squeakings and chitterings of fish again. But they were very much fainter. Presently the humming was no louder than before the strange apparition. By that time the fish-sound had died away altogether. The nearer normal noises remained. The hum was receding. Downward.

Davis came to Terry, where he stood by the recording instrument.

"The fish have gone," he said in a flat voice, "they've gone away. They didn't scatter. We'd have seen it. Do you realize where they went?"

Terry nodded.

"Straight down. Do you want to hear an impossible explanation?"

"I've thought of several," said Davis.

Doug came and picked up the gun-cameras that Terry and Deirdre had used and went away with them.

"There's a kind of sound," said Terry, "that fish don't like. They won't go where it is. They try to get away from it."

Deirdre said quietly, "I would too, if I were swimming."

"Sound," said Terry, "in water as in air, can be reflected and directed, just as light can be. A megaphone turns out one's voice in a cone of noise, like a reflector on a light. It should be possible to project it. One can project a hollow cone of light. Why not a hollow cone of sound, in water?"

Davis said with an unconvincingly ironic and skeptical air, "Indeed, why not?"

"If such a thing were done," said Terry, "then when the cone of sound was turned on, the fish inside it would be captured as if by a conical net. They couldn't swim through the walls of sound. And then one can imagine the cone made smaller; the walls drawn closer together. The fish would be crowded together in what was increasingly like a vertical, conical net, but with walls of unbearable noise instead of cord. It would be as if the sea was electrified and the fish were shocked when they tried to pass a given spot."

"Preposterous, of course," said Davis. But his tone was not at all unbelieving.

"Then suppose something were sent up to the top of the cone, and it projected some kind of a cover of sound on the top of the cone and imprisoned the fish with a lid of sound they couldn't endure. And then suppose that thing sank into the water again. The fish couldn't swim through the walls of noise around them. They couldn't swim through the lid of sound above them. They'd have to swim downward, just as if a hood were closing on them from above."

"Very neat," said Davis. "But of course you don't believe anything of the sort."

"I can't imagine what would produce that sound in that way and send up a cork of sound to take the fish below. And I can't imagine why it would be done. So I can't say I believe it."

Davis said slowly, "I think we begin to understand each other. We'll stay as close to this place as we can until dawn, when we will find nothing to show that anything out of the ordinary happened here."

"Still less," said Terry, "to hint at its meaning. I've been doing sums in my head. That bright water was almost solid with fish. I'd say there was at least a pound of fish to every cubic foot of sea."

"An underestimate," said Davis judicially.

"When the bright patch was a thousand yards across—and it was even more—there'd have been four hundred tons of fish in the top three-foot layer."

Davis seemed to start. But it was true. Terry added, "The water was clear. We could see that the packing went on down a long way. Say fifty yards at least."

"Y-yes," agreed Davis. "All of that."

"So in the top fifty yards, at one time, there were at least twenty thousand tons of fish gathered together. Probably very much more. What *La Rubia* carried away couldn't be noticed. All those thousands of tons of fish were pushed straight down. Tell me," said Terry, "what would be the point in all those fish being dragged to the bottom? I can't ask who or what did it, or even why. I'm asking, what results from it?"

Davis grunted.

"My mind stalls on who or what and why. And I'd rather not mention my guesses. I…No!"

He moved abruptly away.

The *Esperance* remained under sail near the patch of sea that had glittered earlier and now looked exactly like any other square mile of ocean. The recorder verified the position by giving out, faintly, the same unpleasant humming noise, either louder or fainter. A soft warm wind blew across the waters. The land was somewhere below the horizon. The reel of recorder-tape ran out. It was notable that there were very few fish sounds to be heard, now. Very few. But the hum continued.

CREATURES OF THE ABYSS

Toward morning it stopped abruptly. Then there was nothing out of the ordinary to be observed anywhere.

The sun rose in magnificent colorings. The sky was clear of clouds. Again the waves looked like living, leaping, joyous things. Gulls were squawking.

Doug came up from belowdecks. He carried some photographic prints in his hand. He'd developed and printed what the gun-cameras had photographed when the mysterious object, or beast, leaped clear of the sea. There were seven different pictures. Four showed flashbulb-lighted sections of empty ocean. One showed a column of sea water rising at fantastic height from the sea. Another one showed the edge of something at the very edge of the film.

The seventh picture Terry recognized. It was what he'd seen when the flash bulb of his gun-camera went off. The focus was not sharp. But it was neither a whale nor a blackfish—not even a small one—nor was it a shark. It was not a squid. It was not even a giant manta. The picture was a blurry representation of something unreal made for an unimaginable purpose, under abnormal conditions.

Deirdre looked at it over his shoulder. It could be a living creature. It could be…anything.

"You said you didn't like mysteries," commented Deirdre. "Are you sorry you came?"

CHAPTER FOUR

The next morning the *Esperance* headed southeast over a sunlit sea. First, of course, the crew examined the sea's surface for miles around. As expected, there was nothing remarkable to be observed. Davis did point out that there were no fish jumping, which was an indication that there were not as many fish as usual in this part of the ocean. But it was hard to be sure. There is no normal number of times when fish will be seen to jump. They usually jump to escape larger fish that want to eat them. The number is pure chance. But there seemed to be almost no jumps at all this morning.

It was not discussed at length, however. All the ship's company was curiously reluctant to refer to the events of the previous night. In broad daylight, a detached review was simply impractical. With gulls squawking all about, with seas glinting in the sunshine, with decks to be washed and breakfast to be eaten, and commonplace, routine ship-keeping to be done, the adventure of the patch of shining sea seemed highly improbable. Terry felt that it couldn't really have happened. To discuss it seriously would be like a daylight ghost tale. One was unable to believe it in daylight. It was better ignored.

Terry, though, did get out his tools to make a minor modification in the underwater microphone. It had been designed to be directional, so that the sound of surf or fish could be located by turning the mike, but he hadn't been able to point it vertically downward, and last night that had been the key direction—right under the yacht's keel. So now he improvised gimbals for the microphone, and a mounting for it similar to that of a compass, so it could tilt in any desired direction, as well as turn.

Which, of course, was a tacit admission that something peculiar had happened. Presently, Deirdre came and watched him.

"What's that for?" she asked, when he fitted the gimbals in place.

He told her. She said hesitantly, "Yesterday, when I asked you not to try the paddle until we got to shallow water, you got angry and said you'd ask to be put ashore. We're headed for Barca now. Someone there is building something for my father, the same thing I had asked you to build—a fish-driving instrument. If you still want to go, you can get a bus from there to Manila. But I hope you have changed your mind."

"I have," said Terry dourly. "I told your father so. I was irritated because I couldn't get any answers to the questions I asked. Now I've got some questions your father wants answers to. And I'm going to try to find them out."

Deirdre sighed, perhaps in relief.

"I put some pictures and a clipping in a book on the cabin table," she said. "Did you see them?"

He nodded.

"What did you think?"

"That you put them for me to see," he said.

"It was to make you realize that we can't answer every question, which you know now."

"I still think you could answer a few more than you have," he observed. "But let it go. Is the Barca harbor shallow?"

"Ten, fifteen feet at low tide," she informed him. "We're having a sort of dredge made there. Something to go down into the sea, take pictures, get samples of the bottom, and then come up again. There's an oceanographic ship due in Manila shortly, by the way. It will have a bathyscaphe on board. Maybe that will help find out some answers." Then she said uncomfortably, "I have a feeling the bathyscaphe isn't...safe."

He glanced up.

"*Ellos?*" He grinned as she looked sharply at him. Then he said, "This dredge: isn't it pretty ambitious for a boat this size to try to dredge some thousands of fathoms down?"

"It's a free dredge," she said. "It will sink by itself and come up by itself. There's no cable. What are you doing now?"

He'd put away the submarine microphone he'd just altered and was now taking out the still untested underwater horn.

"I'm going to try to make this directional, too," he said. "In fact, I'm going to try to make it project sound in a beam shaped like a fan. A hollow cone may come later."

She was silent. The *Esperance* sailed on.

"Ever talk to the skipper of *La Rubia?*" he asked presently.

She shook her head.

"You should. He's a stupendous, self-confident liar," said Terry. "He lies automatically. Gratuitously. A completely amiable man, but he can't tell the truth without stopping to think."

"We found that out," said Deirdre. "I didn't. Someone else."

"Is this another censored subject, or can I ask what happened?"

"I'd better see about lunch," said Deirdre quickly.

She got up and left. Terry shrugged. The day before yesterday, or even yesterday, he'd have been indignant. But then he'd known these people had secrets in which he had no share. Today he was beginning to share those secrets, and he had fabulously nonsensical material on which to work on his own. He had strange ideas about the event of last night. He did not quite believe them, but he thought he had devised some ways to see how much of truth they contained, if any. Deirdre could keep her secrets, so long as he did not have to disclose his own wildly imaginative ideas.

The routine of the yacht went on. It was in a way a very casual routine. Davis gave orders when the need arose, but there was no formal discipline; there was cooperation. Terry heard one of the crew-cuts ask Deirdre a question using her first name. It would have been highly improbable in a paid crew, but it was reasonable enough in a volunteer expedition. He heard Deirdre say, "Why don't you ask him?"

The crew-cut, Tony, came to the part of the deck where Terry worked.

"We got into an argument," he said without preface. "We were talking about that...'whale' last night."

Terry nodded. The use of the term "whale" was a deliberate pretense that the previous night's events were natural and normal.

"How fast do you think it was traveling when it broached?" asked Tony. "I know a whale can jump clear of the water. I've seen it in the movies. But that one jumped awfully high!"

"I hadn't tried to estimate it," said Terry.

"You've got a tape of the noise," said Tony. "Could you time the interval between the sound when it left the water, and the splash when it fell back?"

"Mmm. Yes," said Terry. He looked up. "Of course."

"It would be interesting to do it," said Tony, semi-casually. Then he added hastily, "I've read somewhere that whales have been clocked at pretty high speeds. If we can find out how long its leap lasted, we could know how fast it was going."

Terry considered for a moment, and then got out the recorder. He played the tape for a moment, and skipped forward to later parts of the record until he came to the place where the unpleasant humming sound was loud, and finally reached the beginning of the rushing noise. That, in turn, had preceded the leap of the object photographed by the gun-cameras.

Terry glanced at his watch when the rushing started. He timed the period of ascent of the noise, while it grew louder and louder and became a booming sound, which was at its loudest the instant before it ceased. At that moment the mysterious object had leaped out of the sea. The splash of its re-entry came long seconds later.

Tony timed the leap. When the splash came he made his calculations absorbedly, while Terry switched off the recorder.

"It would take the same amount of time going up as it does coming down," said Tony, scribbling numbers. "Since we know how fast things fall, when we know how long they fall we can tell how fast they were traveling when they landed, and therefore when they leaped."

He multiplied and divided.

"Sixty miles an hour, roughly," he pronounced. "The whale was going sixty miles an hour straight up when it left the water! What can swim that fast?"

"That's your question," said Terry. "Here's one of mine. We heard it coming for five minutes ten seconds. How deep is the water where we were?"

"About forty-five hundred fathoms."

"If we assume that it came from the bottom, it must have been traveling at least sixty miles an hour when it broke surface," said Terry.

"But can a whale swim sixty miles an hour?"

"No," said Terry.

Tony hesitated, opened his mouth, closed it, and went away.

Terry returned to the changing of the submarine horn. Sound has its own tricks underwater. If you know something about them you can produce some remarkable results. A deliberately made underwater signal can be heard through an unbelievable number of thousands of miles of seawater. But, except through a yet untested fish-driving paddle, Terry had never heard of fish being herded by sound. Still, fish can be stunned or killed by concussions. They have been known to be made unconscious by the noise of a very near submarine bell. It wasn't unreasonable that a specific loud noise could make a barrier no fish would try to cross. But there were still some parts of last night's events that did not fit into any rational explanation.

Davis came over to Terry.

"I think," he said, "that we may have missed a lot of information by not having submarine ears before. There may have been all sorts of noises we could have heard."

"Possibly," agreed Terry.

"We're more or less in the position of savages faced with phenomena they don't understand," said Davis vexedly. "The simple problems of savages range from what produces thunder to what makes people die of disease. Savages come up with ideas of gods or devils doing such things for reasons of their own. We can't accept ideas of that sort, of course!"

"No," agreed Terry, "we can't."

"But what happened last night," said Davis, "is almost as mysterious to us as thunder to a savage. A savage would blame it on devils or whatnot."

"Or on *ellos*," said Terry.

"He'd imagine a personality behind it, yes," said Davis. "He does things because he wants to, so he thinks all natural phenomena occur because somebody wants them to. He has no idea of natural law, so he tries to imagine what kind of person— what kind of god or devil—does the things he notices. It's a natural way to think."

"Very likely," admitted Terry. "But the point?"

"Is that we mustn't fall into a savage's way of thinking about last night's affair."

Terry said, "I couldn't agree with you more. But just what are you driving at?"

"There's a dredge being made for me in Barca. I'm afraid you may suspect that I'm trying to—stir up something with it. To poke something we *know* is somewhere but can't identify. I didn't want you to try the fish-paddle in deep water, that's true. But…"

"You're explaining," said Terry, "that you didn't want me to whack a fish-driving paddle overside in deep water."

Davis hesitated, and then nodded.

"The phenomena you're interested in are under water?"

"Yes," said Davis. "They are in the Luzon Deep area."

"Then, to be cooperative, I'll test this contrivance in ten to fifteen feet of water in the Barca harbor. And I will not get temperamental about your suggestions that I should not mess up your deep-water inquiries."

"Thanks," said Davis.

He went forward to meet Nick, just coming abovedecks with a slip of paper in his hand. It occurred to Terry, suddenly, that somebody went below down the forecastle hatch just about every hour on the hour. They must be in short-wave communication with Manila. It had been mentioned last night—a loran fix on the *Esperance's* position. There were apparently frequent reports to somebody somewhere.

The afternoon went by. A tree-lined shore appeared to the eastward just when the gaudy colorings of a beautiful sunset filled all the western sky. The *Esperance* changed course and followed the coast line, some miles out. Night fell. The yacht sailed with a fine smooth motion over the ocean swells.

After dinner Davis was below, fiddling with the knobs to pick up short-wave music from San Francisco, and the muted sound of an argument came occasionally from the forecastle where the four crew-cuts resided. Terry and Deirdre went on deck.

"My father," said Deirdre "says you understand each other better, now. He doesn't think you're going to feel offended with us, and he's really pleased. He says your mind doesn't work like his, but you come to more or less the same conclusions, which makes it likely the conclusions are right."

Terry grimaced.

"My conclusion," he observed, "is that I haven't enough facts yet to come to any conclusion."

"Of course!" said Deirdre. "Just like my father!"

They sat in silence. It was not exactly a tranquil stillness. It was pleasant enough to be here on the slanting deck of a beautiful yacht, driving competently through dark seas under a canopy of stars. But now Terry realized he was constantly aware of Deirdre. He liked her. But he'd liked other people, male and female, without being continually conscious of their existence. Girls are usually more conscious of such things than men. At least ninety-nine per cent of the time, a man does not modify his behavior because of the age, sex, and marital status of the people he comes in contact with. It isn't relevant to most of what he says and does. But a girl frequently modifies her actions in just such circumstances. Deirdre was well aware of the slightly uneasy, extremely interested state of Terry's mind. There was silence for a long time. Then a shooting star went across the sky. It went out.

"Would you like to hear something really wild?" asked Deirdre, ruefully. "That shooting star, just then. It used to be true that more meteorites—shooting stars—had fallen and been recovered in Kansas than any other place in the world. But it would be ridiculous to think they aimed for Kansas, wouldn't it?"

Terry nodded, not following at all.

"At Thrawn Island," said Deirdre, "since the satellite tracking station has been built, space-radars have picked up more bolides—big meteors—coming in to fall in the Luzon Deep than ever in Kansas or anywhere else. I think my father frets over that, simply because he's so concerned about the Luzon Deep."

Terry heard himself saying irrelevantly, "I'd like to ask you a few strictly personal questions, Deirdre. What's your favorite food? What music do you like? Where would you like best to live? When…"

Deirdre turned her head to smile at him.

"I've been wondering," she said, "if you thought of me only as a fellow researcher or whether you'd noticed that I'm a person, too. Hmmmmm. There's a restaurant in Manila where they still cut their steaks along the muscle instead of across it, but where they make some unheard-of dishes. That place has some of my favorite foods. And…"

"Next time we're in Manila we'll try it," said Terry. "Now, I know a place…"

The *Esperance* went on. Presently, the moon rose and moonlight glinted on the waves while the stars looked cynically down on the small yacht upon the sea. And two people talked comfortably and absorbedly about things nobody else would have thought very interesting.

When Terry turned in for the night he realized pleasantly that he was very glad he'd let himself be persuaded to join the *Esperance's* company.

Dawn came. Terry was already on deck when the *Esperance* threaded her way into a small harbor. There were palm trees along the shore, and there was a Philippine town with edifices ranging from burnt brick to stucco to mere nipa huts on its outskirts. Two-man fishing boats were making their way out from the shore on which they'd been beached. From somewhere came the staccato, back-firing noise of an old automobile-engine being warmed up for the day's work. It would undoubtedly be the bus for Manila. But it was not thinkable that Terry should take it, now.

The yacht dropped anchor and lay indolently at rest while her crew breakfasted and the morning deck routine was being performed. Then Deirdre appeared in shore-going clothes of extreme femininity. Davis too was dressed otherwise than as usual.

"We're going ashore to the shipyard," he told Terry. "If you'd like to come—"

"I've something to do here," said Terry.

Two of the crew-cuts got a boat overside and headed it for the shore. Terry got out the recorder and the submarine ear and horn. He set up his apparatus for a test. Tony came from belowdecks and watched. Then he came closer.

"If I can help," he said tentatively.

"You can," Terry told him. "But let's listen to what the fish are saying, first."

He dropped over the submarine ear and started the recorder to play what it picked up, but without recording it. Sounds from underwater came out of the speakers. The slappings of tiny harbor-waves against the yacht's planking; the chunking, rhythmic sound of oars from a fishing boat which was rowing after the half-dozen that had gone out earlier; grunting sounds. Those were fish.

Terry listened critically, and Tony with interest. Then Terry brought out the fish-driving paddle. He turned on the tape, now, to have a record of the sound the paddle made.

"Whack this on the water," he suggested, "and we'll hear how it sounds."

Tony went down the ladder and gave the water surface a few resounding whacks. There were tiny, violent swirlings. For thirty or forty feet from the *Esperance's* side there were isolated, minute turmoil's in the water. Three or four fish actually leaped clear of the surface.

"Not bad!" said Tony. "Shall I whack some more?" Terry reeled back a few feet of the tape, which contained the whacking sounds. He re-played them, listening critically as before. Tony had returned to the deck. The whackings, as heard underwater, were not merely impacts. There was a resonance to them. Almost a hum. Rather grimly, Terry substituted this tape-reel with the recording he'd made the night before. He started the instrument and found the exact spot where the object from the depths had fallen back into the sea. He stopped the recorder right there. He hauled up the submarine ear and plugged in the horn to the audio-amplifier, as yet untested, which should multiply the volume of sound from the tape. Then he put the horn overside.

He switched on the recorder again. The tape-reel began to spin. The sound went out underwater from the horn. Underwater it was much louder than when it had been received by the *Esperance's* microphone. Here it was confined by the surface above and the harbor-bottom beneath. It must have been the equivalent of a loud shout in a closed room—only worse.

The fish in the harbor of Barca went mad. All the harbor-surface turned to spray. Creatures of all sizes leaped crazily above the surface, their fins flapping, only to leap again, more frantically still, when they fell back. A totally unsuspected school of very small flying fish flashed upward in such frenzied haste that some tried to climb too steeply and fell back and instantly flung themselves into the air again.

Terry turned off the playing recorder. The disorder at the top of the water ceased immediately. But he heard shrill outcries. Children had been wading at the edge of the shore. They stampeded for solid ground, shrieking. Where their feet and legs had been underwater they felt as if a million pins and needles had pricked them.

Something flapped heavily on the *Esperance's* deck. Tony went to see. It was a three-pound fish which had leaped clear of the water and over the yacht's rail to the deck.

125

Tony threw it back into the water.

"I guess there's not much doubt," he said painfully.

"Of what?" demanded Terry.

"Of what...I had guessed," said Tony.

"And what did you guess?"

Tony hesitated.

"I guess," he said unhappily, "that I'd better not say."

He watched with a startled, uneasy expression on his face as Tony put the apparatus away.

Time passed. Davis and Deirdre had been ashore over an hour. Then Terry saw the small boat leave the shore and approach. It came deftly alongside, the two passengers climbed up to the deck, and all four crew-cuts hauled the boat back inboard and lashed it fast.

"Our dredge isn't ready yet," said Davis. "It looks good, but there'll be a delay of a few days."

Deirdre examined Terry's expression. "Something's happened. What?"

Terry told her. Davis listened. Tony added what he'd seen, including the fish that had leaped high enough out of the water to land on the *Esperance's* deck.

"After the fact," said Davis, "I can see how it could happen. But..." He hesitated for a long time and then said, "This is another case where I've been making guesses and hoping I was wrong. And like the others, proof that my early guess was wrong makes another guess necessary. And I dislike the later guess much more than the first."

He moved restlessly.

"I'm glad you only tried it once, here," he said unhappily. "We're due up at Thrawn Island anyhow. You can work this trick out in the lagoon up there. If there's no reaction to the dredge when we try it, we can try this. But it might be a very violent poke at something we don't quite believe in. I'd rather try a gentle poke first."

He turned away. In minutes Nick was belowdecks starting the yacht's engine, two others of the crew-cuts were hauling up the anchor, and the fourth was at the wheel. Without haste, but with celerity, the *Esperance* headed for the harbor-mouth and the open sea.

They had their midday meal heading north by west. Late in the afternoon Deirdre found occasion to talk to Terry about Thrawn Island.

"It's the China Sea tracking station for satellites," she told him. "Some of the staff are friends of my father's. It's right on the edge of the Luzon Deep, and the island's actually an underwater mountain that just barely protrudes above the surface. There are some hills, a coral reef and a lagoon. It's also terrifically steep, and you can use the fish-driving device as much as you please without startling any Filipino fishermen."

"You've been there before," said Terry.

"Oh, yes! I told you a fish wearing a plastic object was caught in the lagoon there. That was when the station was being built. The men at the tracking station fish in the lagoon for fun, and now they're naturally watching out for more…oddities."

The *Esperance* sailed on. The crew-cuts went about their various chores and talked endlessly, among themselves and with Deirdre, when she joined in. Terry felt useless. He trailed the submarine ear overboard and set the recorder to work as an amplifier only. At low volume it played the sounds of things below. He kept half an ear cocked toward it for the mooing sound he'd picked up at the place where the ocean glittered. He heard it again now, and again found it difficult to imagine any cause for it. The sounds uttered by noisemaking fish are usually produced in their swim-bladders. The purpose of fish cries is as obscure as the reason for some insect stridulations, or the song of many birds. But a long-continued fish noise would involve a swim-bladder of large size. At great depths, if a considerable cavity were filled with gas, under pressures running into tons to the square inch… Terry could not quite believe it.

He did not hear the mooing sound any more, as the yacht went on its way. Other underwater sounds became commonplace, and he tended not to hear them. From the deck around him, though, he heard arguments about wave mechanics, prospects in the World Series, the virtues of Dixieland jazz, ichthyology, Copeland's contribution to modern music, the possibility of life on other planets, and kindred topics. The crew-cuts were taking their summer vacations as able seamen on board the *Esperance*, but they had as many and as voluble opinions as any other undergraduates. They aired them on each other.

The afternoon passed. Night fell, and dinner was a session of learned discussion of different subjects, always vehemently argued. Later Terry took the yacht's wheel, Deirdre sat comfortably nearby, and they discussed matters suitable to their more mature status. They were much less intellectual than the crew-cuts. In a few days they developed an interest in each other, but each of them believed this was just a very pleasant friendship.

Eventually, the moon rose. It was close to midnight when Nick bobbed belowdecks and came up with a report that they'd been picked up by the Thrawn Island radar and were proceeding exactly on course. Half an hour later a tiny light appeared at the edge of the sea. The *Esperance* headed for it, and presently there were breakers to port and starboard, the engine rumbled, down below, and the yacht lifted and fell more violently than ordinary. Then once more she was in glassy smooth water; the air was very heavy with the smell of green vegetation. Certain rectangles of light became visible. They were the windows of the Thrawn Island satellite-tracking installation.

The *Esperance's* sails were lowered and she moved toward the lights on engine power only. There was no movement ashore, though Nick had talked with the island on short-wave.

After a little while the searchlight was put in operation and began to reach out like a pencil of brilliant white light. It darted here and there and found a wharf reaching out from the shore to deep water. The *Esperance* floated toward it, her engine barely

128

turning over. There was still no sign of activity, except for the lighted windows.

The engine stopped, then reversed, and the yacht drifted gently until it contacted the wharf's snubber-pilings. Jug and Tony jumped ashore with lines to fasten the yacht. Still no sign of life.

"Queer," said Davis, staring ashore. "They knew we were coming!"

A moving light suddenly appeared in the sky. A fireball, which is an unusually lurid type of shooting star. It came over the tree-tops and crossed the zenith, leaving a trail of light behind it. It went on and on, seemingly slowing down, which meant that it was descending from a very high altitude. Its brilliance became more and more intense, then it dimmed. At this point the fireball seemed to plunge downward. Then its flame went out and only a faint, dull-red speck in motion could be seen.

It plunged down beyond the trees on the far side of the lagoon. Or so it seemed. Actually, it might have plunged into the sea, miles away. Then there was a faint noise, which was something between a rumble and a hiss. The sound went back across the sky along the path the fireball had followed. It died away.

There was silence. Shooting stars as bright as this one are rare. Most meteors are very small, but they are visible because of the attrition produced by their falling bodies in the atmosphere that sets them on fire. They usually appear at around a seventy-mile height, but frequently they are vaporized before they have descended more than thirty miles. Sometimes they explode in midair and strew the earth with fragments. Sometimes they strike ground, leaving monstrous craters where they have fallen. Most meteors fall in the sea. But a meteor has to be at least down to twenty miles from sea level before its sound can be heard.

Someone came out of a building and moved toward the wharf, an electric lantern bobbing in his hand. Halfway out to the yacht he called, "Davis?"

"Yes," said Davis. "What's happened?"

"Nothing," said the man ashore. "We were watching for that bolide. It was picked up by space radar a couple of hours ago, but then we figured it to land farther on than it did."

It was an educated voice, a scholarly voice.

"Big?" asked Davis as the light drew nearer.

"We've seen them bigger, but not much." The man with the lantern reached the end of the wharf. "Glad to see you. We've got some fish for you, by the way. We caught them in the lagoon. They're waiting for you in the deep-freeze. There's a *Macrourus violaceus*, if we read the books right, and a *Gonostoma polypus*. They match the pictures, anyhow. What do you make of that?"

"You haven't got them!" said Davis incredulously. "You can't have them! I'm no fish specialist, but those are abyssal fish! They can only be caught at a depth of two or more miles!"

"We caught 'em," said the man cheerfully, "on a hook and line, in the lagoon, at night. Come ashore! Everybody'll be glad to see you."

Davis protested, "I won't believe you've got that kind of fish until I see them!"

The man with the lantern stepped down to the yacht's deck.

"All you've got to do is look in the mess hall deep-freeze. The cook's complaining that they take up space. Nobody wants to find out if they're good to eat. Most unwholesome-looking creatures! And how are you, young lady?" he asked Deirdre. "We've missed you. Tony, Nick, Jug…"

Deirdre introduced Terry.

"Ha!" said the man. "They got you enlisted, eh? They were talking about it a month ago. You've solved the problem by now, I daresay. Including how these very queer fish happen to be in our lagoon instead of miles down in the Luzon Deep. When you find time, tell me!"

"I'll try," said Terry reservedly.

The man went down into the after-cabin and Davis followed him. Deirdre said amusedly:

"Dr. Morton's a dear! Don't take him seriously, Terry! He loves to tease. He'll hound you to tell him how deep-sea fish got up here and into a shallow lagoon. Please don't mind!"

"I won't," said Terry. "I'll tell him tomorrow, I think. I believe now I know how it happened, but I want to check it first."

CHAPTER FIVE

When Terry awoke, next morning, the reflections of sunlight on water came in through the porthole of his cabin. He watched the shimmering contortions of the light spots on the wall. His thoughts went instantly back to the subject they'd dwelt on before he went to sleep. The man with the spectacles—Dr. Morton, but his doctorate was in astronomy instead of medicine—had said that Deirdre and her father had discussed enlisting him in the Esperance's company a month ago. Deirdre'd come into the shop of Jimenez y Cía. only four days before. Some of the delay could have been caused by time spent in simple sailing from one place to another, mostly on wholly futile errands. They'd gotten a fish-driving paddle at Alua. That'd take some days of sailing each way. Apparently, they'd been fumbling at some vague idea of trying to find out what would produce the facts they'd noted. 'Very queer fish,' Davis had said of some of the catches La Rubia had made. The abyssal fish mentioned last night would be very queer fish to catch in a lagoon. Yes...

He lay still, surveying other aspects of the situation. Davis had called on an aircraft carrier for electronic items, and the Esperance was in constant touch with somebody by short-wave radio. It might be the same carrier. The Manila police department was on very cordial terms with Davis, and the staff of a satellite tracking installation saved odd specimens of fish for him.

The *Esperance's* enterprise was plainly not a brand-new adventure. It had been carried on for some time. They had had technical aid of the very highest caliber, but they hadn't gotten anywhere yet. It did appear that Terry had added a minor specialty to the arsenal of investigative techniques. Without the data gathered on recorder-tape, their idea of the events of two nights before would be very different. The sea would have seemed very bright, then the glowing area would have been noted to have grown smaller, and something resembling a whale would have been seen leaping high above the water. Then the brightness would have faded out. It would have been mysterious enough, but an entire aspect of the phenomenon would have gone unnoticed. There was still no answer to any of the far-reaching questions Terry had asked himself, but most of them had never been asked before. Sea noises had proved to be closely connected to whatever had to be found out. What was known about them was due to his findings. He'd established a new frame of reference.

And he'd discovered the solution of a minor problem before the problem was even stated. He had only to prove it. Then, of course, there would be other problems arising from it.

He got up, put on swimming trunks, and duck trousers over them. He slipped into a sweat shirt and went upon deck. Deirdre hailed him.

"Good morning! Everybody's over at the tracking station, arguing about the bolide that went over last night. According to the radar, it plunged into the sea, miles and miles away."

"What should it have done?" asked Terry. "I'm not familiar with meteorites. Are they planning to dive for it?"

"Hardly!" Deirdre laughed. "It landed in the Luzon Deep." She waved a hand in an inclusive gesture. "This island's on the brink of it. A bathyscaphe might go down there—in fact, I think it's scheduled; you know, the one I said was coming to

Manila on the oceanographic ship? A bathyscaphe can go that deep, but it's not likely to hunt for meteorites."

"Ah," said Terry judicially. "Then what difference does it make where it hit?"

"It didn't fall the way it should have," said Deirdre. "It was spotted by space radar away out, and they tried to compute its path, but they figured it wrong. Now they're trying to make it come out right by allowing for the effect of the earth's magnetic field on a metal meteorite. They're arguing and waving equations at each other."

"Let them," said Terry. "I have trouble enough with fish. Do you think I could borrow a boat?"

"We've always been able to," said Deirdre. Then she added, "I've kept your breakfast hot. While you eat it I'll get a boat."

She went below, and an instant later was up again.

"I have a feeling," she said, "that something interesting is going to happen. I'll be back."

She swung lightly to the wharf and headed for land. Terry went below, to find his breakfast laid out on the cabin table. He settled down to it, but first pulled a book from the shelves. It was a volume on oceanography, and its pages showed that it had often been referred to. He found the Luzon Deep described. Its area was relatively small, a mere ninety-mile-long chasm in the sea-bed. But it was second only to the Mindanao Deep in its soundings, and a close second at that. Its maximum depth was measured at twenty-seven thousand feet. Over five miles. There was a mention of Thrawn Island as being on the very edge of the Deep. According to the book, the island was the peak of one of the most precipitous and tallest submarine mountains in the world. Three miles from where Thrawn Island lay, there were soundings of twenty-eight thousand feet and upward. This depth extended as a trench…

The staccato roaring of an outboard motor sounded some distance away. It bellowed toward the yacht, swung about, and cut off. Terry gulped down his coffee and went abovedecks, just as Deirdre was fastening the small craft alongside the yacht.

"Taxi?" she asked amiably. "I got the boat. Where to?"

Terry swung down and took the steering grip. He headed the boat away. There was a box for bait, a few fishing lines, and even two highly professional fish-spears on board. Fishing was not necessarily a sedentary pastime here.

"We try the lagoon entrance," he said. "I've an idea. I noticed something last night, when we came in."

"Do you want to brief me?"

"I'd rather not," he admitted.

Deirdre shrugged without resentment. The little craft went sturdily toward the passageway to the open sea. She formed an arrowhead of waves as she moved. She neared the points of land at the ends of the coral formation enclosing the lagoon. Thrawn Island was not an atoll. But the beaches were made of snow-white coral sand. Outside there was clear water for a space and then a reef on which the seas broke.

Terry headed the boat toward the open sea. Almost immediately after, there was nothing but the reef and the sea between the boat and the horizon. He slowed the boat almost to a stop, well within the reef's tumult. She swayed and rolled on the surging water.

"Stay here," he commanded. "I want to swim out and back."

He pulled the sweat shirt over his head. He jumped overboard, leaving Deirdre in charge of the boat.

The world looked strange to him when waves rolled by higher than his head. A few times the sky narrowed to the space between wave-crests. Other times he was lifted upon a wave-peak, and the sky was illimitably high and large, and the breaking seas on the nearby reef merely roared and grumbled to themselves.

He swam out, away from the land. Suddenly his body began to tingle. He stopped and paddled, analyzing the sensation. One side of his body felt as if the most minute of electric currents entered his skin. It was not an unpleasant sensation. Deirdre, in the small boat, was fifty yards behind, watching him. As he swam on, the tingling grew stronger. He dived. The tingling did not vary with depth. He came up, and he was farther out than he'd realized.

He suddenly knew that he'd been incautious. There are currents, which flow in and out of lagoons. A barrier of reef affects them, too. Terry found himself swimming in an outward-bound current, which pushed him out and away from the island.

Within seconds the sensation in his body changed from a mere tingling to torment. For a moment it was just very much stronger and slightly painful, but a moment later it felt as if he swam among flames. It was unbearable. His muscles were not contracted, as if by an electric shock, but he couldn't control their reflexes. He found himself splashing crazily, trying to fight his way out of the anguish, which engulfed him.

He went under. His body had taken complete control over his mind, and he found himself swimming frantically, underwater. He couldn't reach the surface. His body tried to escape the intolerable agony in which it was immersed but couldn't.

He heard a roaring sound, but it meant nothing. The roaring grew louder. Finally, he did break surface for a few seconds, and he gasped horribly, but then he went under. The roaring grew thunderous, and he broke surface again…

Something seized his flailing arm and pulled him up. The arm ceased to experience the horrible sensation of being in boiling oil. His hand recognized a gunwale. He swarmed up the solid object with hands helping him, and found himself in the boat, gasping and shivering, and cringing at the bare memory of the suffering he'd undergone.

Deirdre stared at him, frightened. She swung the boat's bow shoreward. The outboard motor roared, and the boat raced past the gap in the reef and rushed toward the lagoon opening.

"Are you all right? What happened? You were swimming and suddenly…"

He swallowed. His hands quivered. He shook his head and then said unsteadily. "I meant to…check the reason those queer fish stay in the lagoon. I thought that if they belonged in the depths and were somehow carried out of them, they would try to get back. I found out!"

He felt an unreasonable relief when the lagoon entrance was behind the boat. The glassy water was reassuring. The *Esperance* looked like safety itself.

"I think I know how they got here, now," he added. We underestimated what we're trying to understand. I'll be all right in a minute."

It was less than a minute before he shook himself and managed to grin wryly at Deirdre.

"Was there a hum in the water?" asked Deirdre, still staring at him. "I thought I heard it on the bottom of the boat. Was that the trouble?"

"Yes. I wouldn't call it a hum," Terry admitted. "Not any longer. Now I know what a slow fire feels like."

"You frightened me," said Deirdre, "the way you splashed..."

"I heard the humming sound," said Terry, "last night when the yacht came up to the island. We were perhaps a half-mile off-shore. It was very faint, but I had the amplifier turned down low. The hum was at its loudest just before we passed the reef, but nobody else noticed. When Dr. Morton said there were abyssal fish in the lagoon, I knew why they'd be there. I made a guess at what might drive them there. I went to find out if I was right. I found out!"

"The hum?" asked Deirdre again. When he nodded, she said: "What are you going to do now? What do you think makes the hum?"

"I'm trying hard not to guess what makes the hum," Terry told her. "Insufficient data. I need more. I think I'll ask what other odd phenomena have turned up in this neighborhood. Foam-patches on the sea? I can't imagine a connection, but still..."

He swung the little boat alongside the docked *Esperance* and held out his hand to help Deirdre to the dock. His hand was wholly steady again. She accepted the help.

"We'll go to the tracking station?"

"Yes. Everybody seems to be there," said Terry.

They heard a babble of voices coming from the satellite-tracking station. As they approached the buildings, Terry looked around. Off at one side there was the very peculiar aerial system by which tiny artificial moons circling the earth could be detected by their own signals. Minute spheres and cylinders and spiky objects and foolish-looking paddle-wheels, whirling in their man-appointed rounds, sent down signals with powers of mere fractions of a watt. This system of aerials picked up those miniature broadcasts and extracted remarkable amounts of information from them. It was possible to determine the satellites' distance more accurately, by a comparison of phase-changes in their signals, than if steel tape measures were stretched up to make physical contact with them. The accuracy was of the order of inches at hundreds of miles. Floating where the stars were bright and unwinking lights against blackness and the sun was a disk with writhing arms of fire, the small objects sent back information that men had never possessed before and did not wholly know what to do with now that they did. And there were other objects in the heavens, too. There were satellites, which no longer signaled back to earth. Some had their equipment worn out. Some objects were satellites, which had failed to function from the beginning. Some were mysteries.

The bolide of the night before was a mystery. As Terry and Deirdre entered the wide verandah of the recreation building for the station's personnel, they heard Dr. Morton protesting, "But that's out of the question! I agree that we never know any more about what the Russians throw out to space than what we find out for ourselves. That's true! But this wasn't a terrestrial object! If it was a satellite that wasn't launched right, it had to be sent up from Russian territory. It wasn't. That's positive! If we assume it was a satellite that had already made several orbital turns, we must admit it would be an impossible shift in apogee for it to come down at the angle it did!"

Deirdre and Terry sat down as someone else said hotly, "Our observations were wrong. They had to be! The earth's magnetic field couldn't affect the speed of an object *outside* the atmosphere! Our observations say it slowed down. It couldn't!"

Davis lifted a hand in greeting. The argument stopped for a moment. Deirdre was known, but Terry had to be introduced. He was sitting beside a bald young man who explained in a low tone, as the argument resumed. "They're having fun. They argued for days when our radar picked up an empty second stage in orbit. They're still ready to dispute for hours about a supposed retrograde satellite that was spotted last year, was watched for four turns, and then disappeared. Beer?"

"Too early," said Terry. "Thanks just the same."

Davis said earnestly, at the other side of the room, "I'd feel a lot better if that thing last night hadn't splashed where it did."

"The bolide," said a voice humorously, "is a free animal."

The discussion went on. Terry saw Deirdre talking to a middle-aged woman with a splendid sun-tan and a placid expression on her face. Doug and Tony sat watchfully on the side lines, listening. Doug had been offered, and had accepted, a sandwich. He ate it methodically.

Terry had a sudden feeling of unreality. Less than half an hour before he'd been in torment and, but for Deirdre, on his way to death. On the *Esperance* there'd been so much that was absorbing in the way of fish behavior that he'd forgotten some people were interested in other things. Here a dozen people squabbled over the behavior of a meteorite. Nothing could be of less consequence to the outside world. But in the outside world, people argued about baseball, or golf, or politics...

Doug excused himself and slipped outside. Terry joined him there a little later. Doug was smoking a cigarette, looking at the sky and the palms.

"Pretty heavy discussion," said Terry.

"It's over my head," said Doug. "I got lonesome. It made me think of my girl. She likes to talk: like this. That's why…"

He stopped.

"Is there an aqualung outfit on the *Esperance?*" asked Terry.

"Sure! Two or three of them. Mr. Davis had an idea they'd be useful. Used one of them last week to look at the *Esperance's* bottom-planks. Why?"

"I'd like to poke around the bottom of the lagoon a little," said Terry, with unconscious grimness. "Would you help?"

"Sure!" said Doug.

They went back to the *Esperance*. Doug got out two aqualung outfits. They checked the valves and tanks and connections. Doug brought out two spring guns. In half an hour they were in the outboard, headed for what Doug said was the deepest part of the lagoon.

Arrived there, Terry tested the water with his finger and then went overside. Instead of a spring gun, he used one of the fish spears that seemed to be standard equipment for fishing, here. Doug stayed in the boat to watch.

Terry'd guessed that what he looked for would be in the deepest part of the lagoon. He was right. Within half an hour he'd speared five fish of types that had no business being within two thousand fathoms of the surface. He ignored the lagoon's normal inhabitants. He picked on fish of a dark-red color, which is predominant in the depths but not elsewhere. When the fish had extremely small eyes or extremely large ones, he hunted them determinedly, knowing they were deep-sea fish. He caught five, which was a good haul, even considering his previous suspicions.

Doug inspected the catch as the outboard went back to the yacht. Terry replaced his spear under the gunwale.

"They're queer fish," observed Doug. "I wouldn't want to eat them."

"Neither would I," agreed Terry. "But I feel a certain sympathy for them. I think we've shared an experience."

He did. Fish so far from their normal environment would not have migrated unless they'd been forced to. So these fish must have been driven up from the blissful utter blackness of the abyss, which was their habitat. He had a vivid memory of the kind of urging they'd received, because of his recent swim outside the reef opening. That was the experience he believed they shared.

He got his catch onto the *Esperance's* deck and found some sharp knives in the galley, while Doug put the aqualungs away. When Doug came abovedecks again, he looked distastefully at the work Terry had undertaken.

"Do you like to do that sort of thing?" he asked.

"Hardly!" said Terry. "But I want to get it done."

Doug watched for a moment or two.

"I'm pretty keen about poetry. Sometimes I feel I've got to sweat over a poem that I need to get written. It's hard work. There's no real sense to it. But I feel it's got to be done. I guess that's the way you feel now."

"Perhaps," said Terry.

It wouldn't have occurred to him to liken the writing of verses to the dissection of dead deep-sea fish, but Doug had a point. He went away presently, and Terry completed the highly unpleasant task. He had just finished flushing the deck clean when Deirdre came back from the tracking station. He was already at work on the recorder when she stepped onto the deck.

"You didn't stay," said Deirdre. "I was waiting for a chance to tell my father about the hum outside the lagoon, but he was as deep in the meteor argument as any of them. I still haven't told him."

"There's something else to tell him now," Terry remarked. "I went down with an aqualung. Doug was standing by," he added at her gesture of protest, "and speared some fish that don't belong here. I've dissected them. Their swim bladders had been very skillfully punctured, so if they went or were driven into lesser pressure, they'd leak instead of bursting. That's how they survived coming up from the depths. But the main thing is this."

He held out a small plastic object in his hand. It was about an inch in diameter and two in length, and there were inclusions in the clear material. There were plates and threads of metal. They had that look of mysterious purpose that highly-developed technical devices have.

"This was fastened to the fin of a fish that belongs as far down as a fish can go," he said. "I've found out one of its purposes. When it is in the water, it makes a sound more acute than a whistle every time another sound strikes it. Try that on your piano!"

Deirdre stared.

"I'm saying," he repeated, "that it takes in one sound and gives out another. It's…it could be a relay. What is that for? What's it all about? What does it mean? And I ask just those questions because I don't dare ask who and why!"

"What…what will you do?" asked Deirdre absurdly. "I've no idea," Terry told her. "I've got a feeling that the wise thing to do would be to settle down somewhere and buy a shop, and forget all this. If I don't think about it, maybe it'll go away."

"I'll get my father and see what he says."

"Tell him," commanded Terry, "that I want to try out my fish-driving horn. I'd like to have witnesses. If this foolishness has to be reported to somebody, we need evidence of the facts. I want to drive fish and see how many deep-sea ones there are in this lagoon, and how many of them have spy-devices on them."

Deirdre turned away. Then she turned back.

"Spy-dev—"

"I slipped," said Terry. "I shouldn't have said that. Forget it. Just tell your father I have an extremely urgent impulse to drive fish, and would he come and help."

Deirdre looked at him strangely, and went onto the wharf to search for her father.

Terry paced back and forth on the *Esperance's* deck. In a few minutes Davis and the crew-cuts appeared with Deirdre. But they were not alone. Straggling behind them came nearly all the personnel of the tracking station. There would be somebody on official duty, of course. But here was the bespectacled Dr. Morton; the bald young man who'd offered Terry beer; and the installation cook; a typist, and specialists in radar and other abstruse subjects.

Deirdre said, "I told them about the fish-driving business and they want to see. They stopped arguing about last night's bolide to take ringside seats. All right?"

Terry shrugged. He had the recorder already set up. He'd taken a section of the tape made where the sea was bright, at the place where the loudest of the unpleasant humming noise was recorded. He'd made a loop of it so it would play over and over.

He played the much-amplified sound through the underwater horn held in the air. The result was a raucous bellowing noise. He lowered it into the water. The horn touched the surface and went under.

Instantly, the fish of the lagoon seemed to go crazy. The entire surface broke and writhed and splashed. There was an incredible number of fish. Terry turned the horn on one side. In this way, not all the water was filled with the intolerable noise, but only a net-like beam of it raced across the water. Within that line the fish continued to leap frenziedly. The rest of the lagoon suddenly quieted down. In a little while the beam's space, also, grew quiet. But that was because the fish that had been previously caught in it had escaped.

"I'm afraid," said Terry, "that this isn't going to be very entertaining. I'm going to sweep the beam across the lagoon,

142

pushing the fish ahead of it, until I should have them all in one small area."

It was curious that he felt uncomfortable as he set about his task. But he'd experienced the sensation this sound produced. And it was not very pleasant.

He turned the beam around, slightly. Again, there were sudden splashings. They died away. He turned the beam again. It was a nasty, snarling vibration in the water. So far as fish were concerned, it was more like a wall than a net, because not even the tiniest living creature could penetrate it. Not only fish fled before it. Shrimps and crabs and all types of crustaceans jerked and crawled and swam ahead of its motion. Jellyfish writhed when it touched them. Sea cucumbers contorted themselves. Everything that lived in the lagoon and could swim or crawl or writhe moved before the invisible barrier. Presently, the effect of crowding could be seen, and fish began to leap out of water.

"This is a great advance in civilization," said Dr. Morton. "Men invented guns and destroyed the buffalo and the passenger pigeon! You may have made it possible to depopulate the sea!"

Terry did not answer. The morning sun shone brightly, a gentle breeze made ripplings on the lagoon, the palms waved their fronds in languid gestures, and the surf could be heard booming and splashing on the outer reef. And about two dozen people stood on the wharf or on the *Esperance's* deck and watched a spliced section of recorder-tape go through and through a recorder, which was set to make a sound underwater that could not be heard by the people above.

The fish of the lagoon had crowded themselves into a minor embayment of the shore. There were innumerable leapings there.

"There should be plenty of fish collected now," said Terry distastefully. "I certainly can't herd them ashore."

The outboard boat pushed away from the yacht, its motor roaring. It reached the area in which the water seemed to seethe and surge with the motion of densely crowded swimming creatures. The people in the boat examined the surrounding water, then the boat came back at top speed.

"They're there!" called Davis. "And thick enough to walk on! I clearly saw some freaks that must come up from the bottom! We want to collect them!"

"I speared five just now," Terry told him, "and one of them was wearing this."

He held up the plastic object he'd found. There was silence for a moment. Then Dr. Morton said briskly, "We'll want fish spears. We'll take all the boats and go after some more of these piscatory oddities. Who's best with a spear?"

Davis would go. He could use the two fish spears that were standard equipment for the outboard. The staff of the tracking station scattered to launch other boats. Only Terry and Deirdre remained on the *Esperance*. It was necessary for someone to stand by the recorder.

Boats moved away across the water. One stout member of the island's staff trudged along the shore.

"You're driving them," said Deirdre. "You are right."

"I wish I weren't," said Terry.

"Why?"

"You know how these weird fish got here," he said impatiently. "They were driven here. You know how they've been kept here. I experienced that! I told you why they didn't die when they came up from thousands of fathoms! Now, what's the only possible purpose for their being here? Put it more scientifically! What is the consequence of these happenings, so that to some biological entity it would be a favorable happening?" His tone was sardonic, at the end.

"I don't know."

"I hope I don't either," said Terry dourly.

He was in no amiable mood. He'd made too many guesses like those Davis had mentioned. He was beginning to have less and less hope that they were untrue. Each new development made any imaginable cause of these events just so much more appalling to think about.

In an hour, three boats came back from the small bay into which all the fish of the lagoon had been crowded. Terry turned off the underwater horn. A stout man walked slowly along the shore with a heavy burden of known edible fish. He was the island's cook, and he had speared them from the beach. The boats, altogether, had speared and captured not less than sixty specimens of fish normally found only many thousand feet below the ocean's surface. Upon inspection, all of them were found to have deftly punctured swim bladders, punctured with so slender a barb that the opening would close by itself, except when serving for the release of intolerably expanding gas.

Before noon, seven more plastic objects had been found among the deep-sea fish. Three seemed identical to the one Terry had found. Two others were identical to each other but of a different kind, and the last two were of two different types altogether. Only those like the one tested by Terry seemed sensitive to sounds, which they changed into other sounds at a twenty-thousand-cycle frequency, or higher. The rest did nothing that could be detected.

During the afternoon, news came to distract the absorption of the tracking station staff in the lagoon's fish. The short-wave operator came running to the wharf, waving a written message. The deck of the *Esperance* was not a pretty sight, just then, with the dissection that had been taking place on it. Jug was beginning to flush the debris overside.

The short-wave operator arrived. Dr. Morton read the message. He raised his voice.

"Here's a fancy one!" he told the assembled company. "Space-radar's picked up a new object coming in from nowhere. It will probably orbit once before it hits the air and burns. By the line of motion it should pass nearly overhead here. We're alerted to get it under observation and watch it!" He waved the message in a large gesture. "We've got to get ourselves set up! The argument on the path of last night's bolide and why it fell where it did is again in order. We'll see what we can do about computing the fall-point of this!"

He headed for the shore. The staff followed, babbling. Somebody's mathematics would be verified, and with it his views on the possible effects of terrestrial magnetism on objects approaching the earth.

"We ought to get these plastic things to Manila," Davis said slowly. "They need to be compared to others. But I think we'll wait and see this bolide first."

A heated argument started in the tracking station staff. From Dr. Morton downward, almost to the station's cook, the most varied predictions were made. The official computation from Washington, made from the observed course and height and speed, predicted that the bolide would land somewhere in the South Pacific. Dr. Morton predicted a fall in the China Sea, within a certain precisely stated number of miles from Thrawn Island. Other predictions varied.

At exactly fourteen minutes after eight—a time way ahead of the official schedule but exactly as Dr. Morton had predicted—the bolide passed overhead. It was an amazing spectacle. It left a trail of flame behind, across thirty degrees of sky. It went on and on...

Less than ten minutes later the short-wave radio informed the island that the shooting star had been seen to fall in the sea. It had been observed by a plane, which was then circling over the area in which the *Esperance* had encountered the circle of shining sea. The plane was there to see if the phenomenon would occur again. It didn't.

But the plane saw the bolide as it struck the sea, and huge masses of steam and spray arose. The bolide was not white-hot, then, as when it passed over Thrawn Island. It was barely of dull-red brightness. It hit the sea and sank, leaving steam behind.

The water was forty-five hundred fathoms deep at that point.

CHAPTER SIX

Fourteen hours later the *Esperance* made ready to sail from Thrawn Island. Her purpose was to carry the plastic objects to Manila, where they would be turned over to specialized laboratories to be studied. Five such objects had been found before: one in the Thrawn Island lagoon, while the satellite-tracking station was under construction, and four attached to exotic fish brought to market by the commercial fishing boat *La Rubia*. Now there were eight more, of four different kinds. To the laboratories would go Terry's observation that one kind of these objects absorbed sound at audible frequencies and retransmitted it at much higher ones, but only under water. All this was very interesting and very puzzling.

But a serious disturbance had arisen at the tracking station.

Dr. Morton came to the *Esperance* before her departure. He had a problem. He'd predicted to the minute, and almost to the mile, the landing of the bolide of the night before. That was the first accurate prediction of the kind in history. But his forecast stood alone in its precision. Nobody else had even come near being right. Now he was being insistently queried by astronomers the world over. They wanted to know how he'd done it. In particular, they wanted to know how he'd figured that the bolide would lose just so many feet per second velocity, neither more nor less, in a three-quarter orbit around the world. Nobody else had such a figure in his equation for the landing spot. Dr. Morton had. His prediction had been exact. Where did he get that necessary but inexplicable figure?

He beckoned Davis and Terry to go below with him, in the *Esperance's* after cabin. Terry hesitated.

"You may as well hear my troubles," said Morton vexedly. "You're largely responsible for them."

Terry followed uneasily. He didn't see how Dr. Morton could hold them responsible. He had guarded his own guesses about the *Esperance's* discoveries against even the slightest expression. He couldn't let himself believe in their correctness, but he was appalled at the inadequacy of all other explanations of past events.

"In sixteen months," said Morton annoyedly, down below, "we've spotted six bolides coming in to land in the Luzon Deep. That's out of all reason! Of course, it could be a mathematical series of wildly unlikely coincidences, such as probability says may happen sometimes. Up to last night that seemed to be a possible explanation."

Davis nodded. His expression was odd.

"But now," said Morton somehow indignantly, "that's ruled out! It's ruled out by last night's bolide, and yesterday's fishing experiment, and that business of the shining sea, plus those damned plastic gadgets and deep sea fish thriving in shallow water! There's no reasonable explanation for such things, and they're not mere coincidences!"

"I'm afraid," admitted Davis, "that they're not."

"The obvious explanation," said Morton doggedly, "I refuse to name or consider. But nevertheless the question is not whether a theory or an explanation is unlikely or not. The question is whether it's true!"

Davis nodded. Terry had to agree. But the way people are trained in modern times puts a great emphasis on reason, often at the expense of fact. Terry felt the customary civilized reluctance to accept a statistically improbable idea.

"I'm on a spot," fumed Morton. "I calculated that the damned bolide would slow after it went into orbit around the earth. I calculated that it would slow exactly so much. Do you want to know how I figured how much it should slow down? I'll tell you! I calculated exactly how much it would have to slow to be able to fall into the Luzon Deep! It did slow. It did fall there. But how am I going to explain that to Washington?"

Terry suddenly felt a warm sympathy for Morton. It is bad enough to dispute with oneself when something incredible happens. But Dr. Morton had gone out on a limb. He'd been caught psychologically naked telling the truth, and now he was asked to explain it. And he couldn't.

"This thing has got to come to a head!" he said angrily. "Sooner or later they'll find out that I don't calculate where it'll land by its behavior in space but by its landing spot! Davis, you've talked about stirring something up. For Heaven's sake, do it! You may save my reputation! And you…"

"I'll try to think of something," said Davis reservedly.

"I've got to have proof that my suspicions are right or wrong before I'm ruined. I know what you're planning to do. Do it! Is there anything that can be done here to help?"

Davis spread out his hands helplessly. But Terry said, "Yes. Send a boat every so often to listen at the gap in the reef. Put an oar overboard and put your ear to the handle. You should hear the underwater hum, if it's still there. It was there this morning."

Morton looked at him suspiciously. "Why check on it? Should it change?"

"Perhaps," said Terry. "We've speared most of the deep-sea fish in the lagoon. Maybe we've interfered with…the reports from the plastic objects, telling what was happening up here. There may be a reaction. If so, most likely the humming will stop, and after a longer or shorter time begin again. And then, if my guess is right, there'll be more deep-sea creatures in the lagoon."

"Ha," said Morton. "I think you and I have the same kind of delusions! All right. I'll see that that's done. You two do the rest."

He went abovedecks. When Terry got on deck, Dr. Morton's angular figure was already marching along the wharf to the shore.

There was no ceremony of departure. The *Esperance* cast off and her engine started. She moved toward the lagoon entrance under power only, but her sails were hoisted as she floated on, and Jug Bell was trimming the jib when she cleared the opening to the sea.

The humming in the water was still audible to the submarine ear, close to the land. It occurred to Terry to take a bearing on the source of the sound, noting both the compass direction and the vertical angle from the reef. If his vertical-angle reading was accurate, a line from the reef to the source of the sound would touch the bottom at twenty-seven thousand feet down, between four and five miles away.

The *Esperance* sailed on. The humming duly faded away. Terry left the recorder picking up undersea sounds, without recording them. It relayed the underwater sounds to the people on deck. It was in Terry's mind to keep at least half an ear cocked to it, in case the mooing sounds, heard and recorded elsewhere, should come again.

They did not. The *Esperance* went methodically on her way, headed south by east, under sail. A slowly swaying horizon of unbroken sea was all about. There was nothing in the least unusual or mysterious to be seen anywhere.

Presently, Terry found himself in conversation with Deirdre, and the world seemed so blatantly normal that their talk dodged all unusual trends. They talked about their childhoods, about things they had done and places they had seen.

At about four in the afternoon Nick bellowed, *"Thar she blows!"* in a fine attempt at proper whaling ship style, and all the *Esperance's* company joined to watch a spouting far ahead. The yacht changed course a little, and presently reached a pod of sperm whales at the surface. The huge dark bodies moved leisurely through the water. Jug displayed great erudition on the subject and explained in detail how their spouting proved them to be sperm whales. Deirdre pointed out a baby whale close beside a larger one.

They sailed on, leaving the whales behind. The crewcuts, inevitably, argued about them. They canvassed all the information and misinformation they possessed and came up with a heated discussion about whales, how they can swim down to the enormous depths without suffering from the bends on rising again. Then the conversation turned to the food they eat.

Whalers, in the old days, had found snouts of squids and undigested sections of squids' tentacles in the stomachs of harpooned sperm whales. There were reports of sections of tentacles four feet thick, implying a startling total size, all of which proved that the whales had been at the bottom of the ocean, where such gigantic squids can be found. These were the reports of reliable whaling skippers. Certainly the scars made by the tentacular arms of huge squids, indicating battle, have been found on the skin of sperm whales, and there have been reports of battles on the surface between whales and squids of sizes most naturalists would be unwilling to certify. In such cases it was assumed that the squids had been attacked at the bottom of the sea and had followed the whale to the surface when it came up in need of air. Certainly only an enormous squid would be able to sustain a battle with a whale.

Terry listened to the discussion. Everybody had his own opinion.

"You'd never settle the argument, unless you could put a camera and a flash gun on a whale and get an instrument-report from it."

Which was not a new idea, of course. But it was curious that the thought of sending self-reporting instruments down to the bottom of the sea had been suggested by his own suspicion that similar instruments had been sent up from below. Sounding lines had been lowered with thermometers and nets and sampling machines. Core-takers had been dropped to get samplings of abyssal mud. But tethered instrumentation is never more than so useful.

Deirdre said something. Terry realized that she'd repeated it. He'd become absorbed in the possibilities of instrument-reporting from the surface to the depths and back again.

"You're not listening," protested Deirdre. "I'm talking about the bathyscaphe that ought to be in Manila any day now."

"I'm trying to picture myself going down in a bathyscaphe," said Terry hastily. "I don't think I'd like it."

A bathyscaphe is a metal sphere with walls and windows of enormous thickness, hung from a metal balloon filled with gasoline for flotation. It is lowered to appalling depths with the help of heavy ballast, and is equipped with electric motors for independent motion. It carries powerful electric reflectors, which allow as much as thirty or forty feet of visibility. It rises to the surface again when its ballast is dumped. There are only three such undersea exploring devices in the whole world.

"I'm not at all sure you wouldn't like it," said Deirdre.

Terry scowled at his own thoughts. There are opinions a man holds firmly without ever being aware of them, unless they are challenged, and if that happens, he is deeply suspicious of the challenge because it suggests that his opinion needs to be re-examined. Terry had been gathering scraps of information here, and unquestionable items there, resisting a conclusion all the while.

It seemed fantastic to think that the plastic objects carried by deep-sea fish out of their natural environment were actually man-made instruments—telemetering apparatus closely comparable to the devices used to transmit information from outer space. It was wildly imaginative to suppose that they transmitted information from the water surface to the depths of the ocean; that fish had been driven up from the abyss in order to report what went on at the surface. Report to whom? It was the most fantastic of fantasies to think that there was curiosity, in the Luzon Deep, about the manners and customs of the inhabitants of the surface waters and of those areas not covered by the sea.

But Terry stopped short. There were limits to the ideas he would allow his brain to think about.

Deirdre walked away, and he assured himself he never thought of anything so ridiculous as the conclusions he had just reached. Presently, dinner was served, and Terry painstakingly acted like a perfectly rational person. After dinner Davis, as usual, settled himself down to enjoy a program of symphonic music from San Francisco, many thousands of miles away. And Deirdre vanished from sight again.

Later on Terry found himself alone on the *Esperance's* deck, except for Nick at the wheel—a mere dark figure seen only by the light of the binnacle lamp. There was a diffused, faint glow coming from the after-cabin hatch. Up forward, one of the crew-cuts plucked a guitar, and Terry could imagine Doug dourly trying to read poetry despite the noise. The sails were black against the sky. The deck was darker than the sea.

Terry's guesses haunted him. He assured himself that he did not entertain them even for an instant. They were absurd! A part of his mind argued speciously that if they were absurd there was no reason not to test them. If he was afraid to try, it would imply that at least part of him believed them.

He picked up one of the plastic objects, and moved the recorder close to the lee rail. It still transmitted faithfully, at minimum volume, the washing of the waves as heard from beneath, and occasional small sounds from living creatures, generally far away in the sea. Heeled over as the *Esperance* was, his hand could reach down into the rushing waters overside.

He came to a resolution. He felt foolish, but by now he was determined to try an experiment. Tiny light-blue sparks flashed where the water raced past the yacht's planking. When he dipped his hand, water piled up against his wrist and a streak of brightness trailed away behind.

He tapped the plastic object against the hull. One tap, two taps, three taps, four taps. Then five, six, seven, eight. He went back to one. One tap, two, and three and four. Five and six and seven and eight.

The recorder gave out the tappings the underwater microphone had picked up. It seemed to Terry that the loudspeaker struggled to emit the shrillest imaginable sounds in strict synchrony with the tappings.

Then Deirdre's voice came quietly, very near.

"I don't think," she said evenly, "that that's a fair thing to do."

He'd been bent over the rail in an awkward position.

He straightened up, guiltily. "I know it's nonsense, but I was...ashamed to admit..."

"To admit," Deirdre concluded for him, "that by tapping numbers with a plastic spy-device, you hoped to say to whom it might concern that we've found a communicator, and we know what it is, and we're trying to get in touch with the intelligent creatures who made it."

To hear his own self-denied guesses spoken aloud was appalling. Terry instantly disbelieved them entirely.

"It's ridiculous, of course," he protested. "It's childish..."

"But it could be true," said Deirdre. "And, if true, it could be dangerous. Suppose whatever put those plastic gadgets on the fish doesn't want to be communicated with? Suppose it feels that it should defend the secret of its existence by killing those who suspect it? I wasn't spying on you," she added. "I heard the tappings down below."

Then she was gone. He saw the interruption in the light from the after-cabin hatch as she went below.

He was suddenly filled with horror at the idea that if his guesses did prove to be right, he might have endangered Deirdre. And then he ceased to feel foolish. He felt like a criminal instead.

For a long, long time he listened with desperate intensity to the recorder, lest he hear some reply to his signals.

But no answer came. The sounds from undersea remained utterly commonplace.

When morning arrived he was in a state of desperate gloom. At breakfast Deirdre acted as if she considered the incident closed. And, such being the nature of men, Terry felt worse than before.

He was not wholly at ease again, even when that afternoon the *Esperance* sailed in past Cavite and Corregidor and into Manila Bay. A new ship was at anchor in the harbor. It was a stubby, stocky ship, which Davis regarded with interest.

"That's the *Pelorus,*" he told Terry as the yacht passed within a mile, on the way to her former anchorage. "She's the hydrographic ship with the bathyscaphe on board. We'll visit her. I'll get Nick to call her on short-wave."

He went forward, where Nick was making ready to drop the anchor. Davis took over the chore, and Nick went below.

"Are you going ashore?" asked Deirdre.

Terry shrugged. "I've no reason to."

She looked relieved. "Then you'll stay with the *Esperance* until—things are settled one way or another? I mean, you're really enlisted?"

"Until there are no more ways left for me to blunder," said Terry distastefully. "I'm about through the list, though."

"Not at all!" protested Deirdre. "Tapping numbers was really a very good idea. I was horrible! I scolded because you'd kept it a secret from me. I'd have been proud if I'd thought of it first!"

Nick came back and spoke to Davis. Davis came aft.

"The *Pelorus* will send a boat as soon as we've anchored," he told them. "They've heard something and want to see the plastic objects."

"I'd like the long end of a bet that they don't believe in them, or us," Terry said abruptly. "They're established authorities on the ocean bottom. They know a lot. They probably know so much they can't really believe there's anything more to know than what they're busy finding out now."

Davis shook his head. He was confident. The *Esperance* anchored, almost exactly where she'd been when Terry first came on board. Within half an hour a boat arrived from the *Pelorus*. Terry repeated his refusal to go along. Deirdre went along with her father.

They came back a little over an hour later. At first Davis was almost speechless with fury. Then he told Terry, choking on his rage, "According to them, the plastic objects are a hoax. The hum is a school of fish. We aren't trained observers. At Thrawn Island they're astronomers and they simply don't know anything about biology. And we should realize that it's starkly impossible for intelligence to develop where the oxygen supply is limited. It's unthinkable that abyssal fish should have their swim bladders punctured so they won't explode from release of pressure when they come to the surface. Those in the lagoon aren't abyssal fish, just unfamiliar species!"

"Well?" Terry asked.

"Oh, they're going to make a bathyscaphe dive!" said Davis as angrily as before. "As a matter of courtesy to somebody— not us. They'll make it where we found fish packed in a circle. That happens to be the deepest part of the Luzon Deep, in any case. They don't object to our sending our dredge down first. They will be politely interested if it comes back up."

"I," announced Deirdre, "I am so mad I could spit!"

"There's no use in our staying here," said Davis, seething. "Our dredge should be ready. We'll go up to Barca and tow it to the point we want to send it down."

He ordered Nick to get ready to lift anchor.

"One question," Terry said finally. "Did you mention the bolides?"

"No!" snapped Davis. "Would I want them to think I was crazy?"

He stamped away.

The *Esperance* put to sea again. She sailed north along the coast. At dinner everybody was quiet. It was the only meal, since Terry's joining, that had not been enlivened by an elaborate argument on some subject or other. Davis was still in an abominable mood. He knew it, and held himself to silence.

Later, Terry and Deirdre talked together. They refrained tacitly from speaking of marine biology or any reasons for tapping plastic objects against the *Esperance's* hull. They discussed only trivia, but somehow Terry found any subject absorbing, when he was with Deirdre.

After a while she went below, and he stayed abovedecks, smoking. The moon had not yet risen when he turned in.

They sailed into the small harbor of Barca at ten in the morning. By twelve, local boatmen had towed out an ungainly object some thirty-two feet long. They tethered it to bitts at the *Esperance's* stern. By one o'clock they had loaded on her deck a large, folded sack of sailcloth and half a dozen specially-cast concrete blocks with eyed iron rods cemented in them. At half-past one Deirdre, who had gone ashore in one of the yacht's own boats, came back with innumerable supplies she'd bought. At two o'clock the *Esperance* went out to sea again.

The towed object was a construction around a central wooden spar with an iron tube at its top end and half a dozen lesser spars linked loosely to its bottom. A mass of fishnet was fastened to the smaller spars and heavy ropes were holding the spars and the net in place during its tow. There was a hook for attaching the main spar to the concrete sinkers.

"It opens like an umbrella," explained Deirdre. "We'll hoist it upright barely out of the water, and fasten on the weights. The canvas bag fits on that iron pipe. When you let it go, it sinks like an umbrella that's tightly closed, but when it touches bottom the weights spread it out and an explosive charge automatically goes off in that iron tube. It's special explosive. The gas it makes inflates the canvas bag, which can't burn underwater, and that floats the whole thing back up with the ribs of the umbrella stretched out and spreading the net between them. It should catch anything it encounters as it rises. As the pressure lowers, the excess gas can escape through a relief-valve. This dredge is experimental. If it works, it can be modified to do lots of things."

"Such as poking at things we don't believe in," said Terry drily. "That explosion ought to stir up anything in its neighborhood. It'll be much more disturbing and audible than a few light taps against the *Esperance's* hull!"

Deirdre grinned ruefully and did not answer.

The bulky tow slowed the yacht. She did not reach the position of the fish-filled circle until after nightfall, and it was necessary to have plenty of light by which to locate the inflated bag when it came to the surface, so nothing could be tried until the following morning. A short while before daybreak, lights appeared at the horizon. Red and green sidelights and white central lights. It was a steamer. It came closer and closer. Presently, it turned and headed upwind and went dead slow, barely keeping steerage. It was the *Pelorus*.

Dawn arrived in a golden radiance which thrust aside the night. The *Pelorus* shone brightly in the first rays of the sun. A large object was hoisted out of her hold. Its shape was that of a gravid goldfish, with a smaller sphere hanging beneath it. It went overside, slowly, and there it floated, rolling wildly on the waves. For a very long time nothing seemed to happen. Then the water-level of the float sank a little. It was being filled with gasoline, which is lighter than water and practically incompressible.

On the *Esperance*, the tow had been pulled alongside and the yacht's powerful winch hauled it upright. The yacht heeled over from the weight. The crew-cuts fastened the canvas sack in place, and Davis loaded the explosive charge into the iron tube. The crew-cuts cleared the nets. This preliminary operation seemed promising, and it was quite likely that the dredge would operate as it was designed to do.

The *Pelorus* whistled impatiently. Nick abandoned his job and went below to the short-wave set. He returned shortly after.

"The *Pelorus* says she'll be ready to send the bathyscaphe down for a test dive in two hours," he reported. "She says she will object if our gadget is floating free at the time, on the chance that it might interfere with the bathyscaphe. She asks if you can send our dredge down right away and get it over with."

"Tell them yes," said Davis. "In five minutes."

He compressed his lips. The *Esperance's* device, though clumsy, was fundamentally simple. Five minutes later the top of the central spar was level with the water. "Cut away," said Davis.

Doug slashed the single rope holding the dredge. It sank immediately.

The recorder gave off the sound of waves. Occasionally, very occasionally, a chirping or a grunt could be heard. Twenty minutes. Thirty.

There was a "crump!" from the loudspeaker, which reported underwater events. The sound seemed to come from very far below. Even a small amount of explosive makes a very considerable concussion when it goes off so far down, and the shock travels in all directions instead of merely upward. The recorder picked up that concussion as a deep-bass sound.

The sun shone. The wind increased. Waves marched in serried ranks from here to there.

A long, long time later the inflated canvas bag came up and was floating on top of the waves. The *Pelorus* whistled. Nick went below. A few minutes later he came up again to report.

"The *Pelorus* says not to cast our dredge adrift. They're sending the bathyscaphe down unmanned, to test all apparatus before a manned dive. They don't want any debris in the sea."

"Tell them we send them a kiss," snapped Davis, "and they needn't worry!"

The *Esperance* approached the floating bag. Jug swung out on the lifting boom and hooked it. The winch hauled it out of the water. The concrete weights were gone. What the nets had captured was not pretty to see. A dead fish with foliated appendages had come up from far below, to judge by what its unpunctured swim bladder had done to it in uncontrolled expansion. Davis said curtly it was *Linophrine arborifer*, belonging two thousand fathoms below. An angry-looking creature, similarly dead, was *Opisthoproctus grimaldi*. It belonged deeper than the other. There were other specimens. A *genostoma* of a species the books didn't picture; a *Myctophum*; and various other creatures, mostly as grotesque as their scientific names. All were abyssal fish. They had died while rising from a pressure of several tons per square inch to surface-pressure only.

"It worked," said Davis curtly. "I almost wish it hadn't. Let it down into the water again. We'll jettison it when the *Pelorus* gives us permission."

Time passed. More time. Still more. The bathyscaphe was now in the water, practically awash. Only a small conning tower showed above the waves. Men swarmed around it.

There came a query from the *Pelorus*. The *Esperance* gave assurance that the deep-sea dredge had returned to the surface and would be kept there.

The bathysphere was allowed to sink.

The recorder on the yacht began to pick up deep-toned mooing sounds from the depths.

Presently, the mooing sounds ceased.

Two hours later, waves broke over an object completely awash on the ocean. The *Pelorus* steamed cautiously toward it. Boats went down from her sides and surrounded the float.

After a long time the *Pelorus* got alongside and men quickly fastened the huge buoy to the ship. Then the down-wind sea changed its appearance. A reek of gasoline reached the *Esperance*.

"Something happened," said Davis dourly. "They're dumping the gasoline—not even pumping it aboard. Let's get out of the stink."

The *Esperance* beat to windward. The *Pelorus* began to lift something large and ungainly out of the water. The *Esperance* went downwind to take a look at it.

The yacht went past no more than fifty yards away, just as the bathyscaphe left the water and swung clear.

The bathyscaphe's conning-tower was gone. It had been torn away by brute force. The three-inch-thick steel globe... Half of it was gone. The rest was crushed. The sphere, which had been designed to resist a crushing pressure of ten tons per square inch, had been ripped in half! It had been bitten through. Bitten!

There was no comment by anybody on the *Esperance*.

Half a mile from the oceanographic ship, Davis said in a peculiarly flat voice, "Cut away the dredge. We won't try to use it again."

Someone slashed the inflated canvas bag. It collapsed. Somebody cut away a rope. The free dredge sank, slowly. It would never come up again.

The *Esperance* changed course. She headed north by west. There was still no conversation at all. The yacht seemed to tiptoe away from the scene of the bathyscaphe's destruction.

A long time later, Deirdre said tentatively, "Have you been making guesses, Terry?"

"Guesses, yes," he admitted.

"Such as?"

"Your father denied that the dredge was designed to stir up whatever gathered the fish together and then carried them down to the bottom of the sea. I was right there with him in the denial, but that's what we intended, just the same. We said we didn't believe there was anything there, so it couldn't do any harm to poke it. We poked, all right! Our dredge, and then the bathyscaphe…"

'But what…"

"And a bolide fell right there a couple of nights ago," said Terry irrelevantly. "I wonder what the entity on the ocean-bottom thought of the bolide. Hm." He paused. "I wonder, too, what the bolide thought of what it found down there. Is that too crazy for a sane man to think, Deirdre?"

She shook her head.

"Why is my father working on this business?" she asked. "And why are the boys helping, and why do radar stations tell us what they find out, and why did the Philippine Government ask the *Pelorus* to make a bathyscaphe dive at just that spot?"

Terry blinked at her.

"Too crazy for official notice, eh?" he said, "but too dangerous not to check up on! Is it absolutely certain that the bolides are bolides?"

"No."

"Thanks," said Terry. He pursed his lips as if to whistle. "I've been thinking of this thing as a puzzle. But it isn't. I'm very much afraid it's a threat!" He paused. "Y-y-es. I've just made a new guess. It adds everything together. I do hope its wrong, Deirdre! I've got cold chills running up and down my spine!"

CHAPTER SEVEN

As the *Esperance* sailed northward, she looked almost unreal. From a distance she might have been an artist's picture of an imaginary yacht heeled over in the wind, sailing splendidly over a non-existent ocean. The sky was a speckless blue, the sun was high.

But she was real enough, and the China Sea around her was genuine, and what had taken place where the *Pelorus* lay now hull-down, stowing a ruined bathyscaphe in her hold, had unquestionably taken place.

Something monstrous and terrible was hidden in the dark abyss below the yacht. The ferocity of its attack on the bathyscaphe was daunting. And ferocity has always, somehow, a suggestion of madness about it. But the humming sound in the sea was not the product of madness. It was a technical achievement. And plastic objects with metal inclusions...

Davis joined Deirdre and Terry. Before Davis could speak she said, "I can't imagine any guess that will add everything together, Terry."

Davis made a jerky gesture.

"Today's business is beyond all reason," he said unhappily, "and if there ever was an understatement, that's it! If there can be any conceivable motive for the plastic objects, which the *Pelorus* dismisses as hoaxes, the motive is to use them to find out something about surface conditions; that is, for surface conditions to be reported back. And that's not easy to imagine.

But try to think of something easier! And yet, such mindless ferocity as attacked the bathyscaphe…that wouldn't be curious about the surface!"

"No-o-o-o," agreed Terry. "It wouldn't. But we'd set off a bomb down below to stir things up. A couple of hours later the bathyscaphe went down. A stupid and merely ferocious thing of the depths wouldn't associate a bomb that exploded with a bathyscaphe that came down two hours later. It took intelligence to make the association of two falling objects with danger."

Deirdre beamed suddenly.

"Of course! That's it! Go on!"

"Curiosity implies intelligence," said Terry carefully, "and intelligence is a substitute for teeth or claws. We don't assume that the fish that carry the plastic gadgets made them. Why assume that whatever attacked the bathyscaphe did it of its own accord? We believe that something else makes the deep-sea fish come up into the Thrawn Island lagoon, don't we? Or do we?"

"We pretend we don't," said Deirdre.

Davis nodded reluctantly.

"Yes, we pretend we don't," he agreed. "But if intelligence is involved, I find myself getting frightened! We humans are always terrified of strange types of intelligence, anyhow. If it's intelligence that isn't human…"

Nick came up from below.

"Thrawn Island calling," he reported. "They say the hum at the lagoon opening stopped for some forty-odd hours and then started again. They ask if we're coming. I said we were on the way. They're standing by. Anything we should tell them?"

"We'll get there some time after sunset," said Davis. "And maybe you should tell them about the *Pelorus* and the bathyscaphe."

Nick grinned briefly. "I did. And the guy on Thrawn Island said 'Hooray' and then explained that he said that because he couldn't think of anything that fitted the idea of something biting holes in three-inch steel." He added, "I can't think of a proper comment, either."

"We'll get to Thrawn Island after sunset," repeated Davis. "Then we'll see what we find in the lagoon—if anything."

Nick started back toward the bow. He stopped.

"Oh, yes! It wasn't a scientific guy talking, just the short-wave operator. The science staff is all busy. He said they heard an hour ago that another possible bolide's been spotted by a space-radar back in the US. It was picked up farther out than one's ever been spotted before. Five thousand miles high."

Davis nodded without comment. Nick went forward and disappeared below.

A school of porpoises appeared astern. They caught up with the *Esperance*. They went rocketing past, leaping exuberantly for no reason whatever. They cut across the yacht's bow and zestfully played around her two or three times, then went on, toward a faraway horizon. They managed somehow to give the impression of creatures who have done something they consider important.

"It's said," said Terry, "that porpoises have brains as good as men's. I wish I could get one or two to talk! They might answer everything! I'm getting obsessed by this infernal business!"

"I've been at it for months," said Davis. "In the past week, though, with you on board, I have found out more things I don't understand than I believed existed!"

He walked away. Deirdre smiled at Terry.

"My father paid you a tribute," she said. "I think we've been wasting time, you and I. We do a lot of talking to each other, but we haven't been applying our massive brains to matters of real importance."

"Such as what?" asked Terry dourly.

"Foam," said Deirdre. "Big masses of foam seen to be floating on the sea. Always over the Luzon Deep. Photographed by a plane less than a month ago. Reported by fishermen much more often than you'd suspect. At least once a ship sailed into a foam-patch and dropped out of sight, exactly as if there were a hole in the sea there. Let's talk about that."

They settled down on the after-cabin roof and began a discussion on the foam-patches, for which there was no hint of an explanation. Then Deirdre mentioned that when she was a little girl she'd always been fascinated by the sight of her father shaving. The foam—the lather—entranced her. And somehow that led to something else, and that to something else still. A full hour later they were talking enjoyably about matters of no conceivable relationship to large patches of foam seen floating on the ocean's surface where the water was forty-five hundred fathoms deep.

Davis came to a halt beside them.

"Morton's just been talking to me from Thrawn Island," he said abruptly. "He's very much upset. It's about that prospective bolide that was spotted from Palomar. It's been night there for two hours."

Terry waited.

"Morton," said Davis, "would like us to try to photograph it when it comes in, back where the *Pelorus* was this morning."

Terry stared. Shooting stars are not rare. On an average summer night anybody can see at least three in an hour's watch of any one quarter of the sky. Bolides are a rare kind of shooting star. Still, many people have seen one or two in their lifetime. But nobody plans ahead of time to observe a bolide, and still less does anybody ever plan in advance to watch a meteorite arrive on the earth's surface, whether on land or sea. It is simply not thinkable.

"We'll go back and try," said Davis. He seemed embarrassed. "Morton says there's no sense to it at all, and that if we do get photographs they'll be considered fakes. He's really wrought up. But he asked if I thought I could get a plane out from Manila to watch it fall—if it comes. I'm going to try that too." He added, more embarrassed still, "Of course nobody'd pay attention if I explained why the plane should go there. I'll have to say that I'm just looking for something else peculiar to happen at that spot. The *Pelorus* must have already reported that one peculiar thing has happened."

Terry opened his mouth, and closed it again. Davis went away.

"You had an idea," said Deirdre accusingly. "What?"

"I was thinking of Horta," said Terry. "Police Captain Horta. A very honest man with no scientific knowledge at all. Nobody with a scientific education would pay any attention, but I could get him to tell a few others who know as little as he does, and if the damned thing does turn up, there'll be proof it was foretold. If it doesn't arrive—" Terry shrugged, "I've no scientific reputation to lose."

"Wonderful!" said Deirdre warmly. "But you wouldn't have proposed it but for me! I'll put things in motion!"

She vanished. Within minutes the *Esperance* came about in a wide semicircle and headed in the direction from which she had just come. Deirdre stayed out of sight for a long while. When she came up it was to tell Terry that Nick was calling on the short-wave set. He'd raised the flattop in Manila Bay. The flattop had raised the shore. Telephone calls were being made to here and there and everywhere to get Horta to a short-wave station to take a call from Terry.

It was near sunset when the complicated call was ready and Horta's voice came into a pair of headphones Terry was wearing in the *Esperance's* radio room.

"I need," said Terry slowly, "to have a number of people in Manila know now of something that's going to happen out at sea tonight. They'll be needed to testify that they knew of the prediction before the event. Can you arrange it?"

"Par supuesto," said Horta's voice cheerfully. "Are we not *amigos?* What is the prediction and who should know?"

"The prediction," said Terry doggedly, anticipating disbelief and protest, "is that at twelve minutes after nine o'clock tonight a large meteorite will fall into the sea where—hmm—where *La Rubia* catches her fish. No, you'd better not locate it that way. I'll give you the position."

Davis, standing by, wrote the position in latitude and longitude and handed it to him. He read it into the transmitter.

"Have you got it?" he demanded. "Is it written down?"

"Ah, yes," said Horta tranquilly. "I will see that they make a memorandum of the matter. Shall I tell three or four persons, or more? I have news for you also. Jimenez…"

"Look here!" said Terry sharply. "I want this thing to be past all doubt! Everybody who's ever been worried about *La Rubia* should know about this! There should be no possible doubt about it! But there should be disbelief, so people who don't believe will try to verify that it didn't happen, so they can crow over the people who thought it would, or might."

"Ah!" said Horta. "You wish you stick out the neck! It is serious! Now tell me again!"

"At twelve minutes after nine tonight," said Terry doggedly, "A shooting star will fall into the sea at…" He named the latitude and longitude Davis had given him. "That is where *La Rubia* catches her fish."

"A shooting star will fall there?" protested Horta. "But who knows where they fall?"

"You do," said Terry. "This one, anyhow. Now, will you see that a number of people know about it?"

"It is cr-azy!" objected Horta. Then he said, "I will do it."

The short-wave call ended, with Horta too much disturbed to refer again to Jimenez.

By sunset Doug had gotten out the gun-cameras. Doug held an impromptu class on deck, showing the other crew-cuts exactly how to aim the cameras and expose the films, and what button to press to change film automatically between shots. He was unhappy because he did not know how bright the object to be photographed would be, for his lens-settings. He was even more unhappy because the bolide might travel at practically any angular velocity, so he didn't know how to set the shutters. But the focus would be infinity, and if he used the fastest possible film, he could stop most motion with a hundredth second exposure.

Instead of reaching Thrawn Island shortly after sunset, then, the *Esperance* was back above the place where the dredge had been dropped and the bathyscaphe wrecked. The *Pelorus* was gone. The people on board that ship must have been very upset. The bathyscaphe had cost more money than is usually allotted to most scientific researchers, and now it was smashed. How would they justify themselves? They could hardly blame the *Esperance*.

The yacht sailed in a closed pattern over this area of the Luzon Deep. Deirdre served dinner on deck. Stars shone down almost instantly after a sunset of unusual magnificence, even for the China Sea. Tony brought his guitar aft, and a contagious feeling of exhilaration spread about the *Esperance* and an improvised party took place on deck. Maybe the mood for festivity arose from the realization that at least nine-tenths of the world's population would have graded them as lunatics, had it known their project for the evening.

It would have been unjust, of course. Terry reflected that it had not been their idea to make an appointment with a shooting star. They were doing it out of some sort of professional courtesy, "from one set of crackpots to another," Terry phrased it in his own mind. It was a wild attempt to secure proof of the starkly impossible. So there was chatter, singing, and some dancing. The high spot was perhaps the time when Jug bashfully serenaded the rigging and the stars above it with howling melodies he'd learned in college.

Eventually, Nick went down to the short-wave set. Doug passed out the gun-cameras again, after checking each one. Nick popped his head out of the hatch.

"Dr. Morton's been calling like crazy," he reported. "The bolide's made four orbital turns, coming in all the while. It ought to touch the atmosphere next time around. ETO is nine-twelve-seventeen-seconds. I told him we're all set."

His head disappeared.

"Don't forget!" Doug said anxiously. "The cameras will feel like shotguns but don't lead your target! And don't forget to press the film-changer!"

Terry lifted his gun-camera experimentally. It did feel like a shotgun. And then, suddenly, he disbelieved everything: the purpose of the *Esperance's* original investigation; the phenomena that had been observed; the guesses that had been made. It was pure insanity! He felt a quick impatience with himself for becoming entangled in anything so ridiculous.

Deirdre leaned toward him and whispered forlornly, "Terry! It's dreadful! I've just had an attack of common sense! What are we doing here? We're crazy!"

He put his hand consolingly over hers. The act was unpremeditated and the sensation was startling. He found that they were staring at each other intently in the starlight.

"I think…" said Terry, unsteadily, "that it's very sensible to be crazy. We've got to…talk this over."

Deirdre smiled at him shakily.

"Y-yes, we will."

Then Davis pointed out positions for the camera operators. The bolide's course should be three hundred fifty degrees, not quite on a north-south line. It might land short of, or beyond, the *Esperance*. Or it might pass many miles to the east or west. Dr. Morton needed as many pictures of it against recognizable stars as could possibly be secured.

Suddenly, there was a faint, dull rumbling in the heavens. It grew louder. Presently, cruising lights appeared in the sky. They maintained a fixed relationship to each other. They looked like moving stars, flying in formation from star-cluster to star-cluster.

Nick popped abovedecks again.

"The planes just called us," he reported. "They've just had a Loran position-check and they're on the mark. They've got orders to observe any unusual phenomena occurring around nine-twelve P. M., Manila time. Using civilian terminology, it sounds like they're saying the Philippine Government asked them to come out and take a look."

"It's five after nine now," said Davis.

The *Esperance* headed into the wind. Her bow rose and fell. Waves washed past, and roarings trundled about under the stars overhead, and very tiny lights moved in a compact group across the firmament.

Time passed.

At twenty-two seconds after nine-twelve—which is to say at twenty-one hours, twelve minutes, twenty-two seconds—a light appeared in the sky from the north. It grew steadily brighter. It suddenly flared very brightly indeed, then dimmed, and continued to rise above the horizon. Seconds later it flared again, very briefly.

Terry found himself aiming the gun-camera. He pulled trigger and changed film and pulled trigger and changed film.

The bright light ceased to climb. It grew steadily brighter and brighter, and then it flared for the third time—Terry's mind asked skeptically, 'Breaking rockets?' —and the light was so intense that the cracks in the yacht's deck-planking could be seen. Then the extra brilliance vanished, and suddenly the moving light was no longer white, but reddish.

Terry aimed again and fired the gun-camera.

The light passed almost directly overhead. Terry had the impression that he felt its heat upon his skin.

It plunged into the sea two miles beyond the *Esperance*. The shock-wave caused by the impact tapped on the yacht's side-planking a few seconds later. Starlight shone upon a plume of steam.

Then there was nothing but the noise of the circling planes above. Then a sound, as of thunder. It disappeared northward. It was the sound of the bolide's passage, arriving after the object itself had dived into the sea.

The people on the *Esperance* were dumfounded. Nick went below and came up again a few minutes later.

"The planes were calling," he reported. "They say they noted the unusual phenomenon. They ask if they should stay around for something else."

"I think," said Davis caustically, "that that's all that's scheduled just now. Tell them so."

The *Esperance* went on steadily again, a trifle west of north. Davis was below, talking via radio to Dr. Morton at the satellite tracking base.

Terry and Deirdre went to look for a place where they could talk over something privately. It was of enormous importance to them, but it was not connected with fish or meteorites or plastic objects or anything at all but the two of them. And to them the yacht seemed crowded with people, even though there was nobody else abovedecks but one of the crew-cuts at the wheel.

When the *Esperance* entered the lagoon the next morning, though, their private talk had evidently come to a satisfactory conclusion. Deirdre smiled at Terry without any reason whatever, and he looked at once smug and embarrassed and uneasy, as if he possessed a new status to which he was still unaccustomed.

The recorder, trailing a submarine ear overboard, had duly reported the presence of the hum in the water, just outside the lagoon. It had not been operating for forty hours or thereabouts. During that time the fish inside could go out of the lagoon, if they chose. And other fish could come in. Terry said suddenly, as the yacht went under power toward the tracking station wharf, "Suppose there was a cone of noise just outside the lagoon, and the flanks of the submarine mountain under us were included in the cone? And suppose the cone grew smaller, like the other one. What would happen?"

Deirdre shook her head, smiling at him.

"The fish," said Terry, "could escape into the lagoon."

"Probably," agreed Deirdre.

"And if fish could be driven downward along a certain path," said Terry, "the way we saw it happen, why, fish could be driven up in a certain path, too."

"Obviously," said Deirdre.

"So if something wanted to replace the fish in the lagoon, or to add to their number, why, it would puncture their swim bladders far, far down, and then drive them up to the surface and into the lagoon, and then keep the noise going to keep them inside."

"Is this a new idea?" asked Deirdre.

"N-n-o," admitted Terry. "I've had it for some time."

"So," said Deirdre, "have I."

The *Esperance's* engine stopped, and she floated to gentle contact with the wharf. Members of the tracking station staff made the yacht fast. With others, Dr. Morton came on board. His expression was the picture of unrelieved gloom.

"I'm in a nice spot!" he told Davis. "I predicted a second bolide correctly! I had to use a different retardation factor to make the math come out right. Now I'm asked to explain that! How can I tell them I knew where it would fall, and only had to compute when?"

"Come below and look at the pictures we got," said Davis.

They disappeared down the after-cabin hatch. Terry knew about the pictures. Doug had developed them with sweating care, developing each negative separately and adjusting the development-time to the varying exposures of the bright object.

There was a total of twenty reasonably good pictures of the bolide, from its first appearance to its plunge into the ocean, two miles from the *Esperance*. Doug had enlarged some of them. There were distinct star-patterns in most. In nearly all, though, the object was more or less blurred by its own motion. In those taken when it flared most brightly, the blurriness was especially marked. There was only one picture of professional, if accidental, quality, and it was the least convincing of all. It showed the fore-part of a conical shape traveling point-first.

Nobody would conceivably believe that it was a meteorite. It looked artificial.

Terry and Deirdre, as it happened, stayed on deck. The people of the tracking station made a babbling uproar. It appeared that the most important event in history, as history was viewed on Thrawn Island, had taken place the night before. It was revealed—Terry had not suspected his own success—that in asking Horta to see that there was foreknowledge of a meteoric fall, Terry had arranged for the matter to be taken immediately to high Philippine Government officials. The American flattop, at their request, had sent planes to the place of the fall, with orders, which were enigmatic, only until the descending object appeared. Then every man in every plane knew that he'd been sent there to see it.

So there could be no question but that Dr. Morton had predicted it. That meant that he knew more about meteoric objects than anybody else in the world. What he had to say was of vast importance, and Thrawn Island shared in his achievement. But it was a strictly professional triumph. The news would not break in the newspapers. No ordinary reader would believe in it. And nobody anywhere would believe in Morton's knowledge of the place of the fall before he began to calculate.

Terry observed that the people of Thrawn Island were definitely no longer interested in fish. They'd kept their eyes open for oddities because a deep-sea fish with a plastic object attached had been caught in the lagoon a long while before. They'd been intensely interested when Terry herded all the lagoon fish into one small inner bay, and they speared sixty fish that had no business being at the surface. They'd found eight more plastic objects. Such things had been interesting, if not important. But now the head of the Thrawn Island staff had computed the place and time of arrival of a meteoric mass from space! And he did it when that mass was five thousand miles out! From a professional standpoint, this was stupendous! They tried to make Terry see how important it was.

Davis and Morton came up from below. They headed for the shore. The crew-cuts trailed off to the land with most of the visitors. Only Deirdre and Terry remained on the yacht, with a mere short-wave operator from the island.

"We're going to have a fancy lunch, with champagne and speeches," the operator said hopefully. "You'll come?"

"Naturally!" said Terry. "But first we're going swimming. We haven't had a chance to be overboard since the last time we were here."

"We'll be back in time for lunch," Deirdre assured the operator, "but swimming here is so wonderful! We've been talking about it for days!"

She went below to change. The operator shrugged. After a further attempt to interest Terry in the celebration of an astronomical first, he went ashore. Terry went with him to get the outboard motorboat he and Deirdre had used before. He was already wearing swimming trunks.

A little later the small boat putt-putted away from the *Esperance* upon the glassy-rippled waters of the lagoon.

There was a very great tranquility everywhere. The booming roar of the surf came from unseen rollers on the reef outside. Seabirds squawked. Palms along the edge of the lagoon waved their fronds very, very gently.

"How far will you go before we swim?" asked Deirdre. "All the lagoon's perfect. One place is as good as another."

He cut off the motor.

"Hmmm. There's a deep place yonder," he observed. "That's where I went with the aqualung and speared the freak fish. Stay away from it."

She jumped over in a clean dive. He joined her in the water. She came up, blowing bubbles.

"All right, Terry. What are your troubles?"

"That bolide bothers me," he told her. "It had a specific destination! It was meant to hit the water over the Luzon Deep!"

174

She dived again. This time Terry followed her. The underwater world was beautifully bright, with ripplings making everything seem to shimmer because of the changing light. When they came up again Deirdre said, "Funny!"

"It had a purpose!" insisted Terry. "There were others before it, and they had a purpose too! That's not funny!"

"I didn't mean that," said Deirdre. "I meant...just now, under the water... What's that?"

There was a swirling at the surface, some tens of yards away. It was not the curling eddy made by a fish about to break surface. It was too big a disturbance for that. It looked as if something stirred, barely submerged, but something very large. Terry, staring, thought of a porpoise cavorting just below the ripples. Or perhaps a shark. But sharks and porpoises are too small to have made this eddying. It reappeared.

"Get in the boat!" snapped Terry. "Quick!"

While she climbed in he let himself sink, his eyes open. There was a clouding of the water underneath, where the surface-disturbance had been. It was mud from the bottom, which had been stirred up. He could see nothing clearly through it, though nearby and around him he could easily see the colorings of coral and fan sponges, and he could see small fish darting here and there.

He broke surface. Deirdre bent anxiously over the gunwale. "What is it?"

"I don't know," he said curtly. "But give me a fish spear."

"You won't..."

"I just want to have something in my hand," he told her impatiently, "while I look."

He took the spear she handed him, and sank once more. Again something moved in the deeper part of the lagoon. It was a fretful motion, as if a creature or creatures tried to burrow away from the light shining through the water. Whatever moved, a thick cloud of debris from the bottom floated all the way up to the surface.

Terry came up for air.

"There's something queer there," he said shortly. "I don't know what."

He went under and swam cautiously nearer to the disturbance. He was within a few feet of the curling cloud of obscurity when something like a gigantic worm came out of it. Or maybe it was like an elephant's trunk, only no elephant ever had a trunk so huge. It was a dull and glistening writhing object. Its end was rounded. The tip of the worm-like thing must have been a foot in diameter, and it came out of the mud cloud for four feet, then six, then, fifteen feet. It thickened only slightly in that length. It groped blindly in the brightness.

Terry swam back quickly, and the object reared up and made a groping sweep through the clear water. Some peculiar white disks suddenly appeared on the underside of the long tentacle. They looked like sucker-disks, able to grip anything at all. The monstrous tentacle fumbled for Terry, as if guided by the pressure-waves his movements generated.

Terry froze. Deirdre moved in the boat almost directly overhead. Something clanked in the boat and he heard it. The boat was probably rocking, making the pressure-waves that a creature from the abyss would depend upon for guidance where eyes would not serve at all.

The thick, bulging tentacle reached toward the sound at the surface, now ignoring Terry, though he was nearer. He was still. The white sucker-disks on it's under side had several rings of a horny, tooth-like substance at their rims. The smallest were about four inches wide. The fumbling object felt blindly in the water. Deirdre stirred again in the boat. The visible portion of the groping monstrosity was already longer than the boat. The whole creature would be enormous! If this groping arm rested upon the gunwale of the boat, it could easily swamp it.

It groped for the boat, coming horribly out of a cloud of mud. It reached out. In another instant it would touch...

Terry plunged his fish spear into the worm. It jerked violently. There were enormous thrashings. Other similar white-disked arms thrust into view, fumbling somehow angrily for the creature—Terry—which had dared to attack it.

He darted for the surface. Something unspeakably horrible touched him, but it was the smooth and not the suckered side of the groping worm. Terry's head was now above water. He grasped the gunwale to pull himself in, in a fever of haste. But the thing that had touched him before came back. It grazed his leg, for just a second. Where it touched, his flesh burned like fire.

"Start...motor!" gasped Terry. "Get away!"

Something touched the stern-board of the boat. Deirdre pulled the starter of the motor.

"Get in!" she said tensely. "Quickly!"

She saw him, straining every muscle by pure, agonized instinct against the irresistible force of whatever clung to his skin. The horrible tentacle stretched, and part of its length took a new grip. It crawled upon him... Deirdre saw the look on his face.

She snatched up the second spear and stabbed past him, into the crawling beast. There was a most violent jerking. She stabbed again. She panted. She gasped. She stabbed and stabbed, sobbing with fear and horror. And Terry tumbled in over the gunwale, released. As soon as he fell onto the floor-boards he painfully dragged himself toward the motor at the stern. Something bumped the boat underneath. Terry pulled the starter and the motor suddenly roared. But the boat didn't start immediately, and it jerked once more. The whirling propeller-blades had touched one of the groping tentacles and cut it. Tumult arose.

The boat surged into motion and Terry, with clenched teeth, sent it into a crazy, skidding turn to avoid a surface swirl, and then another frantic swerve when something showed momentarily above the surface. The boat zigzagged along. A grisly, writhing object rose above the water, flailing, a fish-spear sticking in it. The small, skimming boat dodged and twisted at its topmost speed... It suddenly straightened out and almost flew across the water toward the land.

CHAPTER EIGHT

Echoes of the outboard's roaring motor came back from the trunks of palm trees that lined the lagoon's shore as the tiny boat raced across the water. Deirdre was ashen-white. She turned her eyes from the water, and they fell on the round raw places on Terry's leg where the sucker-disks had bruised it horribly. She shuddered. She still had the sensation of being pursued by the monster. Back where Deirdre's spear had finally liberated Terry, startled and convulsive motions continued, followed by a final gigantic splash. Terry drove the boat on at top speed.

The monster sank again in the spot where the lagoon was deepest. It had come from depths where there was no light; from an abyss where blackness was absolute. Now, having lost its victim, it returned peevishly to such darkness as it could secure.

Terry said curtly, as the small boat raced for the *Esperance* and the wharf, "That creature was driven up from the Luzon Deep into the lagoon to replace the gadget-carrying fish we speared!"

Deirdre stammered a little.

"Your l-leg... You're bleeding..."

"I'm pretty well skinned in a couple of places," he said shortly. "That's all."

"Could it be poisonous?"

"Poison," said Terry, "is a weapon for the weak. This thing's not weak! I'm all right. And I'm lucky!"

"I'd have jumped over with my spear, if..."

"Idiot!" said Terry gently. "Never think of such a thing! Never! Never!"

"I wouldn't want to l-live—"

A new reverberating quality came into the echoes from the shore. The pilings of the wharf were nearby, now. They multiplied the sounds they returned. The *Esperance* loomed up. Terry cut off the motor, the little boat drifted to contact, and Deirdre scrambled to the yacht's deck, and then took the bow line and fastened it. This was absurdly commonplace. It was exactly what would have been done on the return from any usual ride.

"Go tell the others what we found," said Terry. "I'm going to see if there's more than one of those things around."

"Not…"

"No," he assured her. "I'm only going to use the fish-driving horn."

Deirdre looked at him in distress.

"Be careful! Please!" She kissed him suddenly, scrambled to the wharf, and set off at a run toward the shore. Terry stared hungrily after her. They'd come to a highly personal decision the night before on the *Esperance*, but it still seemed unbelievable to him that Deirdre felt about him the way he felt about her.

He went forward to set up the fish-driving combination. One part of him thought vividly of Deirdre. The other faced the consequences that might follow if the bolides were not bolides, and if the plastic gadgets and the nasty-sounding underwater hums were products of an intelligence which could make bolides change their velocity in space; which made them fall in the Luzon Deep in the China Sea and nowhere else.

He set up the recorder with its loop of fish-driving hum. He put the horn overboard, carefully oriented to spread its sound through all the enclosed shallow water of the lagoon. He turned the extra amplifier to maximum output, to increase the effectiveness of the noise, and turned on the apparatus.

The glassy look of the lagoon-water vanished immediately. Fish leaped crazily everywhere, from half-inch midgets to lean-flanked predators a yard and more in length. There was no square foot in all the shallows where a creature didn't struggle to escape the sensation of pins and needles all over its body. And these pins and needles pricked deep.

Flying-fish soared crazily, and they were the most fortunate because so long as they flew, the tormenting water-sound did not reach them. But many of them landed on the beach, and even among the palms.

In the spot where blind and snakelike arms had tried to destroy Terry and Deirdre, the lashing and swirling was of a different kind. Something there used enormous strength to offer battle to a noise. The water was whipped to froth. Twice Terry saw those rope-like arms rise above the water and flail it.

This particular sort of tumult, however, appeared only in one spot. So there was only one such creature in the lagoon.

When Davis and the others came down from the tracking station, Terry turned off the horn. He was applying soothing ointment to the raw flesh of his leg.

"There's a monstrous creature out there," he said evenly when a white-faced Davis demanded information. "Heaven knows how big it is, but it's something like a huge squid. It may be the kind that sperm whales feed on, down in the depths."

Others from the tracking station arrived, panting.

"Oh! I'm tired of being conservative!" added Terry fiercely. "I'm going to say what all of us think! There's something intelligent down at the bottom of the sea, five miles down!"

He glared challengingly around him.

"Who doesn't believe that?" he demanded. "Well, the reporting gadgets don't report any more. We killed the fish that carried them. So that whatever-it-is down on the sea-bed has very cleverly sent up something we ignorant savages wouldn't dare to meddle with! We would be terrified. But we'll show *it* what men are like!"

Dr. Morton said gently, "Perhaps we should notify the *Pelorus*. The biologists on board there..."

"No!" said Terry grimly. "I have a private quarrel with this monster. It might have killed Deirdre! And Davis already tried to tell those biologists something! Tell them about this, and they'll want proofs they wouldn't look at anyhow. We'll handle this ourselves! It's too important for them!"

"Much too important," said Deirdre firmly. "The shooting stars aren't shooting stars and there's something down in the depths just like Terry says. He's right that we can't consider sharing our world with—beings that come down from the sky, even if they only want our oceans and don't care about the land. He says that we wouldn't get along with creatures that know more than we do, and we would especially resent any space ships coming uninvited to start colonies on our world while we're not advanced enough to stop them! If that's what they're doing, they have to be fought from the very first instant to the very last moment there's one of them hiding in our seas! Terry's right!"

"I haven't heard him say any of those things, young lady," said Morton drily, "but they're true. And I don't like the idea of a sea monster being in the lagoon anyhow. Especially one that tries to kill people. Still, fighting it…"

"There are a couple of bazookas on the *Esperance*," said Terry sharply. He looked at Davis. "If you're willing to risk the yacht, we can drive the beast aground, or at least to shallow water, with the submarine horn. Then the bazookas should be able to destroy it. Will you take the risk?"

"Of course you'll use the *Esperance*," said Davis. "Of course!"

"Then I'll want," said Terry, unconsciously taking command, "somebody at the engine and somebody at the wheel. I'll run the horn. But, frankly, if that monster lays one sucker-arm on the *Esperance*, it may be goodbye. Any volunteers?"

In minutes the *Esperance*, her engine rumbling, pulled away from the dock. She had on board all her original company except Deirdre—firmly left ashore by her father and Terry—and in addition she carried Dr. Morton and the most enthusiastic amateur photographer of the tracking station staff. He was shaky but resolute, and was hanging about with an imposing array of cameras, for both still and motion pictures. The

Esperance's sails were furled and she went into battle under bare poles. Davis was busy manufacturing improvised hand grenades for himself and Morton.

The sun was nearly overhead. Terry asked Morton questions about the lagoon. They finally chose a minor inlet as the place to which the creature must be driven, if possible. There it could be immobilized by the intolerable sound from the recorder. There it could be destroyed.

"I wonder," said Morton wryly, "if I can present a dead giant squid as part of the explanation for my computed orbits for the last two bolides!"

The *Esperance* moved steadily toward the place where Terry had nearly been killed.

The enterprise was risky. The *Esperance* was sixty-five feet long. The creature it was to attack was much larger, and if one of its kind had crushed the bathyscaphe, it had sufficient strength and ferocity to make a battle cruiser a much more suitable antagonist. But the true folly of the effort was its purpose.

It all started when a fishing boat—*La Rubia*—went to sea and caught remarkable quantities of fish, of which four specimens had had plastic artifacts fastened to them. Then Terry began checking on certain noises he heard in the sea, which provoked an incomprehensible crowding of millions of fish into a small area, from which they swam down to depths where they could not survive. Now the killing of this squid was supposed to cast a light on the mystery of the nine bolides, which had fallen into a particular part of the ocean.

Terry had the undersea horn turned vertically so that it would transmit a blade of sound wherever he aimed it, instead of spreading all through the lagoon. He turned it on.

The water before the *Esperance* suddenly speckled and splashed from the maddened leaps of fish of every possible size. He turned it off. He aimed it where the ripples showed the presence of something huge beneath the surface. He turned it on again.

There were convulsive writhings. A long tentacle emerged briefly and then splashed under again. The writings continued. Terry adjusted his aim. Crazy leapings of smaller creatures showed the line of the sound-beam, as tracer-bullets show the paths of bullets from a machine gun. He cut off the sound for an instant and turned it on again at full volume, pointed where the monster must be. There was explosive tumult underwater. Huge arms flailed above the surface. But once again the creature fled.

The *Esperance* followed slowly, now. The monster had reacted to the stinging sound-beam as if cowed. But it was a deep-sea creature. It did not know how to move when squeezed into a shallow water, which hampered its movements. It seemed frightened to discover itself trapped between the lagoon-bottom and the surface. And it was dazzled by the brightness to which it had been driven. Left unattacked, even for an instant, it tried to burrow away from the light, and again it made a dense cloud of mud from the bottom. Then it became quiet, as if hiding.

Grimly, Terry lanced it with the painful noise. The water frothed. Monstrous tentacles appeared and disappeared, and once part of the creature's body itself emerged. It was cornered into a minor inlet, and there the water grew more shallow and the monster did not want to go to where its motions would be even more confined.

It seemed to flow into the deepest part of the miniature bay. It was as if it felt certain of a haven there. When the tormenting noise-beam struck again, the abyssal monster flung itself about crazily. A terrible, frustrated rage filled it. Its arms fumbled here and there, above water and below. It hauled itself upright so that a part of its torpedo-shaped body broke through the surface. The monster was mad with fury. It plunged toward the *Esperance*, not swimming now, but crawling with all its eight legs in water too shallow to submerge it. Its effort was desperate. It lifted everything from the water, and splashed everything down again, all the while crawling toward its enemy.

Terry saw Nick and Jug steady the aim of their bazookas. Davis ran toward the bow with hand grenades. The huge squid came crawling, and with every foot of advance the pain-noise grew more unendurable. Suddenly the creature uttered a mooing cry and retreated. The cry was like the mooing noise Terry had picked up from the depths.

It went aground. It struggled to climb ashore, to do anything to escape its tormentors. It foamed and splashed...

Despairing, it turned to face its tormentors. Its body reared almost entirely out of the water, now. It sagged flabbily. It reeled as its arms strained. Its eyes rose above the surface, blinded by the light. They were huge eyes. Squids alone, among the invertebrates, have eyes like those of land beasts. They flamed demoniac hatred. A beak appeared, not unlike a parrot's, but capable of rending steel plates. The beak opened and closed with clicking sounds that were singularly horrifying. It snapped at the yacht, which was beyond reach. One of the tentacles wrenched violently at something. It gave. The arm rose above the water. A thorny mass of branched coral flew through the air and splashed close beside the *Esperance*.

"Shoot!" said Terry, somehow sickened. "Dammit, shoot!"

Nick and Tony aimed closely. The bazookas made their peculiar, inadequate sounds. The bazooka-shells, like small rocket-missiles, sped through the short distance. They struck. Their shaped charges detonated, again with inadequate loudness. They did not explode in a fashion to tear the creature to bits. Instead, they sent lancing flames a thousand times more deadly than bullets into the squid's flesh.

It fought insanely. It uttered shrill cries. Its arms tore at its own wounds, at the water, at the lagoon-bed as if it would rend and shatter all the universe in its rage.

The bazookas fired again and again.

It was the eighth missile from the bazooka, which ended the battle. Then the enormous body went limp. Its horny beak ceased to try to crush all creation. But the long, thick, sucker-disked arms thrashed aimlessly for a long time. Even when they ceased to throw themselves about, they quivered and rippled for a considerable period more. And when it seemed that all life had left the gigantic beast, and the men from the satellite - tracking station stepped on the monstrous body, it suddenly jerked once more, in a last attempt to murder.

The squid's body, without the tentacles, was thirty-five feet long. The largest squid, the Atlantic variety, captured before had a mantle no longer than twenty feet. That relatively familiar creature, *Architeuthis princeps*, came to a maximum total length of fifty-two feet. Counting the two longest arms of this one, it reached eighty. It could not possibly swim in water less than six yards deep. It did not belong in a coral lagoon, but it was there.

It was close to sunset when the last tremors of the great mass of flesh were stilled. Terry was in no mood for eating, afterward. He skipped the evening meal altogether, and paced up and down the veranda of the dining hall, at the satellite-tracking station. Inside, there was a clatter of dishes and a humming of voices. Outside, there was a soft, warm, starlit night. The surf boomed on the reef outside the lagoon.

Deirdre came out and walked quickly into Terry's arms. She kissed him and then drew back.

"Darling!" she said softly. Her voice changed. "How is your leg? Does it still hurt?"

"It's nothing to worry about," said Terry. "I'm worried about something else. Two things, in fact."

"Name one!" said Deirdre, smiling.

"I'd like to get married soon," said Terry ruefully.

"To whom?" she asked, jokingly.

"But I have to have a business or an income first. I think, though, that with a little hard work I can start up my *especialidades electrónicas y físicas* again, and if you don't mind skimping a little…"

"I'll adore it," said Deirdre enthusiastically. "What else would I want? What's the other thing you worry about?"

"That monster," said Terry with some grimness. "Pouf!" said Deirdre. "You've killed it!"

"I don't mean that one," said Terry more grimly. "I mean the one that sent it. I wish I knew what it is and what it intends to do!"

"You've already found out more than anybody else even dared to guess!" she protested.

"But not enough. We've stirred it up. It sent small fish in the lagoon here and elsewhere to report back to it. We can't guess what the fish reported, but we know some of it was about human beings. Whatever is down at the bottom of the sea must be interested in men. Remember? It made a patch of foam that swallowed up one ship and all its crew. It's interested in men, all right!"

"True, but…"

"We dropped the dredge, which implied that we were interested in it. The bathyscaphe indicated more interest on our part. To discourage that interest—or perhaps in self-defense—it wrecked the bathyscaphe."

"It, Terry?" asked Deirdre. "Or *ellos*, they?"

"They," he corrected himself coldly. "We killed the fish that were reporting men's doings from here. That was insolence on our part. So the hum at the lagoon entrance went off and, after two nights, started again—and then this huge squid was found in the lagoon. It should have been able to defend itself against us. It was sent up here because it was capable of defending itself! But we've killed it just the same. So now what will come up out of the depths? And what will it do?"

Deirdre said firmly, "You'll be ready for it when it comes!"

"Maybe," said Terry. "Your father once mentioned an instrument he'd like to have to take a relief map of the ocean bottom. Changed around a little, it might be something we need very badly indeed. The horn we've got is good, but not good enough. I'll talk to the electronics men here."

There was a noise of scraping chairs, inside the dining hall. People came out, talking cheerfully. There was much to talk about on Thrawn Island today. The killing of a giant squid had been preceded by a specific guess that linked it to meteoric falls in the Luzon Deep. Logically, the excitement had grown.

Terry found his electronics specialists, and explained to them the type of apparatus he was interested in. He asked if it was included in the island's technical stores. He wanted to assemble something capable of emitting underwater noises of special quality and unprecedented power. There is not much power involved in sound through the air. A cornet player manages with much effort to convert four-tenths of a watt of power into music. A public-address system for a large area may give out fifteen watts of noise. Terry described a device, which could use a small amount of power, serving as a sonar or a depth-finding unit, and then, with the throw of a switch, turn kilowatts into vibrations underneath the sea. If powerful and shrill enough, such vibrations could be lethal.

A technical argument ensued. Terry's demands were toned down to fit the equipment at hand. Then three men went with him to the island's workshop. They took off their coats and set to work.

Three hours later someone noticed an unknown vessel making its way into the lagoon. She was stubby and small, and had short thick masts with heavy booms tilted up at steep angles. Her Diesel engines boomed hollowly, louder than the surf. As she entered the lagoon, a searchlight winked on and flicked here and there. It finally found the wharf where the *Esperance* was moored.

Men of the tracking station staff went down to the wharf to meet the small row boat that was now coming ashore.

A short, stout, irate fishing boat skipper waved his arms and shouted angrily. What had *los americanos* done to keep *La Rubia* from catching fish? Why had they changed the arrangement by which the starving wives and children of *La Rubia*'s crew were fed? He would protest to the Philippine Government! He would expose the villain of *los americanos* to the world! He demanded that now, instantly, the original state of affairs be restored!

A fish leaped out of the water nearby. Where it leaped, and where it fell back, bright specks of luminosity appeared. Even the ripples of the splashes glowed faintly as they spread outward. The skipper of *La Rubia* stared. And now the people of the island realized that the look of the water was not altogether commonplace. Little bluish flames under the surface showed that many fish darted there. There were more fish than usual in the lagoon. Many more. The lagoon had suddenly become a fine place to catch fish. Some care would be needed, of course. There were doubtless coral heads in plenty. But still...

The skipper of *La Rubia* abruptly returned to his fury and his protests. *La Rubia* had gone to the place where she always found fish. Always! There was a humming in the water there, and fish were to be found in quantity. But yesterday the American ship had been there, and also this very yacht! *La Rubia* stayed out of sight lest the *americanos* learn her fishing secrets. But it was useless. When the two American ships were gone, there was no longer a humming in the sea and no more fish for the crew of *La Rubia* to capture for their hungry wives and children. And therefore he, Capitan Saavedra, demanded that the *americanos* restore the previous state of affairs.

Davis would have intervened, but the chubby skipper erupted into wilder and more theatrical accusations still.

Let them not deny what they had done! Fish were always to be found where there was a humming in the sea that *las orejas de ellos* heard and reported to him. But that humming was not in its former place. It was here! At the entrance of the lagoon! The fish were here, also! *Los americanos* had moved the fish so the crewmen of *La Rubia* could not feed their wives and children. *Los americanos* wished to take all the fish for themselves! But fish were the property of all men, especially fishermen with starving wives and children. So he, Capitan Saavedra, would fish in this lagoon, and he defied anyone to stop him.

"Certainly," said Terry. *"Seguramente!"* He added in Spanish: "We'll lend you a short-wave contact with Manila to make any complaints you please. I'm sure all the other fishing boats will be glad to hear where you've been catching fish, and where you've found the fish have moved to! Calm yourself, Capitan, and help yourself to the fish of the lagoon, and any time you want to call Manila we'll arrange it!"

He moved away. He went back to the electronics shop, while Morton and Davis and the others talked encouragingly to Capitan Saavedra. Presently they suggested that he accept their hospitality, and the Capitan and his oarsmen went up to the dining hall, where they were served dinner, and a more friendly mood developed. In time the Capitan said happily that he would wait till sunrise to lower his nets, because he didn't want to risk losing them on the coral heads. A few drinks later the Capitan boasted about his own system of fishing, as practiced by *La Rubia*. The starving condition of his crew's wives and children ceased to be mentioned.

In the presence of so accomplished a liar, nobody of the tracking station staff mentioned a giant squid hauled partly, but only partly, out of the water. They suspected that he would not believe it. They were sure that he would top their real feat by an imaginary one. So the four crew-cuts listened politely, and fed him more drinks, and learned much.

In the workshop the most unlikely device Terry'd described took form. In effect, it was an underwater horn, which was much more powerful than it looked. Submerged, and with power from a group of amplifiers in parallel, it would create a tremendous volume of underwater noise. That sound would run through a tube shaped like a gun-barrel. It would travel in a straight line, spreading only a little.

The same projection tube could also send out the tentative beep-beep-beep of sonar gear, or the peculiar noise a depth-finder makes. So the instrument could search out a distance or find a target, and then fling at it a beam of humming torment equal to bullets from a machine gun.

It would have taken Terry, alone, a long time to build. But he had three assistants, two of whom were very competent. By dawn, they had it ready to be mounted upon the *Esperance*. It was placed hanging from the bow, mounted on gimbals, so that it could point in any direction. It was firmly fixed to the yacht's planking.

There was plenty of activity on *La Rubia*, too, at daybreak. That squat and capable fishing boat prepared to harvest the fish in the lagoon. She got her nets over. She essayed to haul them. Some got caught on the coral heads rising from the lagoon's bottom toward the surface. Capitan Saavedra swore, and untangled them. He tried again. Again coral heads balked the enterprise. The nets tore.

A helicopter came rattling into view from the south. It grew in size and loudness, and presently hovered over the tracking station. Then it made a wide, deliberate circuit of the lagoon. At the inlet where the squid lay almost entirely in the water— but fastened by ropes lest it drift away—above that spot, the helicopter hovered for a long time. It must have been taking photographs. Presently, it lowered one man by a line to the ground. Obviously, the man could not endure any delay in getting at so desirable a biological specimen. Then the helicopter went droning and rattling to the tracking station, and landed with an air of weariness.

La Rubia continued to try to catch fish. They were here in plenty. But the coral heads were everywhere. Nets tore. Ropes parted. Capitan Saavedra waved his arms and swore.

The *Esperance* rumbled forth and circled away from the wharf, and headed out toward the entrance of the lagoon. The singular contrivance built during the night was in place at her bow. She passed *La Rubia*, on whose deck men frantically mended nets.

The *Esperance* passed between the small capes and the first of the ocean swells raised her bow and rocked her. She proceeded beyond the reef. The bottom of the sea dropped out of sight. Terry switched on the submarine ear and listened. The humming sound was to be expected here.

It had stopped. It was present yesterday, and even during the night, when *La Rubia* came into the lagoon. But now the sea

190

CREATURES OF THE ABYSS

held no sound other than the multitudinous random noises of fish and the washing, roaring, booming of the surf.

Deirdre was aboard, of course. She watched Terry's face. He turned to the new instrument, and then dropped his hand.

"I think," he said carefully to Davis, "that I'd like to make a sort of sweep out to sea. It's just possible we'll find the hum farther out."

Deirdre said quickly, "I think I know what you're up to. You want to survey a large area of the ocean while something comes up. Then you can direct that "something" to the lagoon mouth by using your sound device, so the…whatever-it-is has to take refuge in the lagoon. Since we've killed the squid…"

"That's it," said Terry. "Something like that happened when we speared the fish. The squid took their place. Now we've killed the squid. Just possibly…"

They found the humming sound in the water four miles offshore. They traced it through part of a circle. If something were being driven upward, it could not pass through that wall of humming sound.

"That proves your point," Davis said. "Now what?"

Without realizing it, he'd yielded direction of the enterprise to Terry, who had unconsciously assumed it.

"Let's go back to the island," said Terry thoughtfully. "I've got a crazy idea—really crazy! I want to be where we can duck into shallow water when we try the new projector."

The *Esperance* swung about and headed back toward the island. The sea and the distant island looked comfortingly normal and beautiful in the sunshine. Under so blue a sky it did not seem reasonable to worry about anything. Events or schemes at the bottom of the sea seemed certainly the last things to be likely to matter to anyone.

Terry had the *Esperance* almost between the reefs before he tried the new contrivance. If it worked, it should be possible to make a relief map of the ocean bottom with every height and depth on the seabed plotted with precision.

He started to operate the new instrument. First he traced the steep descent from the flanks of the submarine mountain whose tip was Thrawn Island. He traced them down to the abyss which was the Luzon Deep. Then he began to trace the ocean bottom at its extreme depth, on what should have been submarine plains at the foot of the submerged mountain. The instrument began to give extraordinary readings. The bottom, in a certain spot, read forty-five hundred fathoms down. But suddenly there was a reading of twenty-five hundred. There was a huge obstruction, twelve thousand feet above the bottom of the sea, more than twenty thousand feet below the surface. The instrument scanned the area. Something else was found eighteen hundred fathoms up. These were objects of enormous size, floating, or perhaps swimming in the blackness. They were not whales. Whales are air-breathers. They cannot stay too long in deep waters, motionless between the top and the bottom of the sea.

The instrument picked up more and more such objects. Some were twenty-five hundred fathoms from the bottom, and two thousand from the surface. Some were twenty-two hundred up, and twenty-three hundred down. There were eighteen hundred-fathom readings, and twenty-one, and twenty-four, and nineteen. The readings were of objects bigger than whales. They rose very slowly, and appeared to rest, then rose some more, and rested…

Blank faces turned to Terry. He licked his lips and looked for Deirdre. Then he said evenly, "We go into the lagoon. And if we come out again—if!—we leave Deirdre ashore, unless these readings have been cleared up. There are chances I'm not willing to take."

The *Esperance* headed in. It was not possible for the new instrument to tell what the large objects were. They could be monstrous living creatures, perhaps squids, and one could only guess that their errand was to deal with the surface-creatures—men—who speared fish and giant squids and set off explosions in the Luzon Deep.

CREATURES OF THE ABYSS

Or the rising objects could be, say, bolides that had dived into the Deep from outer space and were now coming to the surface to make sure that the native creatures of earth did not again disturb the depths taken over by beings from another planet.

CHAPTER NINE

The sun rose high in the sky as the *Esperance* returned to the wharf. Davis went ashore and held lengthy conversations with Manila by short-wave radio. The biologists essayed to investigate the squid. *La Rubia* still attempted to catch fish. All efforts seemed to tend toward frustration.

When Terry walked over to see his victim at close range, he found the biologists balked by the mere huge size of the squid. There were literally tens of tons of flesh to be handled. Squid have no backbone, but a modified internal shell is important to biologists for study. The biologists wanted it. The gills needed to be examined, and their position under the mantle noted, and their filaments counted. The nervous system of the huge creature must have its oddities. But the actual preservation of the squid was out of the question. The mere handling of so large an object was an engineering problem.

Terry consulted the frenziedly swearing Capitan Saavedra, who was ready to weep with sheer rage as he contemplated torn nets, and fish he could not capture. Squids were an article of commerce. Terry took the Capitan to view this one. His crew would help the biologists get at the scientifically important items, and for reward they would have the rest of the giant— more than they could load upon *La Rubia*. This would make their voyage profitable, and the Capitan would have the opportunity to tell the most stupendous story of his capture and killing of the giant. With the evidence he'd have, people might believe him.

Presently, the crewmen of *La Rubia* clambered over the monster, huge knives at work under the direction of the men from Manila. There was bitter dispute with the tracking station cook, who objected to the use of his refrigeration space to freeze biological material before it was sent to Manila by helicopter.

In mid-afternoon the *Esperance* left the lagoon again. The sonar-depth-finder probed the depths delicately. The objects in mid-sea, it appeared, had been rising steadily. Their previous position had averaged twenty-five hundred fathoms deep. They were now less than two thousand fathoms down, and there were many of them. Unfortunately, the *Esperance* was not a steady enough platform for the instrument. But a fairly accurate calculation was made, and if the unidentified objects continued their ascent at their present rate, they would surface not long after sunrise. Then what?

Increasingly urgent queries came by short-wave, asking for Dr. Morton's explanation of how he had computed the landing place and time of the latest bolide. His accuracy was not disputed. But astronomers and physicists wanted to be able to do it themselves. How had he done it?

Terry came upon him sitting gloomily before a cup of coffee in the tracking station. Davis was there too.

"I wish I hadn't done it," Morton confided. "It's one of those things that shouldn't happen. It's bad enough to have a giant squid to account for. They tell me it's a new species, by the way. Never found or even described before. One of the *Pelorus* men tells me it's an immature specimen, too. It's not full-grown! What will a grown-up one be like?"

"I have a hunch we'll find out when those submerged giants reach the surface," said Davis unhappily.

Terry said, "The one we killed couldn't get out of the water. I wonder if the adult forms can walk over the land!"

Davis stared. "Should we send Deirdre to safety on the *Esperance?*"

"Safety?" asked Terry. "On a boat? When a mass of bubbles from undersea could provoke such a turmoil in the water that no ship could stay afloat? That's how one ship disappeared. It might be the *Esperance's* turn next. Who knows?" Then he added, "There's no limit to the size of a swimming creature!"

A bald-headed member of the tracking station staff walked in. He carried an object of clear plastic. It was a foot and a half long, about six inches in diameter. There was an infinite complexity of metallic parts enclosed in the plastic.

"I caught one of the fishermen making off with this," he said in a flat voice. "It was fastened to one of the squid's shorter arms. The fishermen didn't want to give it up. The skipper claimed it as treasure-trove."

He put it down on the table. Davis, Terry and Morton looked at it. Then Morton shrugged his shoulders, almost up to his ears.

"The intelligent being that made it," said Davis, "apparently came down from the sky in a bolide. That's easier to believe than that a submarine civilization of earthly origin lives down in the depths. But why would anybody prefer the bottom of the sea to—anywhere else on earth? Where would such a creature come from?"

Deirdre walked in and stood by the table, watching Terry's face. The bald-headed man said, "I could believe some pretty strange things, but you can't make me believe that a creature can develop intelligence without plenty of oxygen. There's not much free oxygen at the bottom of the sea."

"But there's something intelligent down there," said Davis doggedly. "If it has to have free oxygen, you've only raised the question of where it gets it. Maybe it brings it."

Deirdre shook her head. "Foam," she said.

The four men stared at her. Then Terry said sharply, "That's it! On the *Esperance* there's a picture of a huge mass of foam on the sea. A ship dropped right out of sight right into it. Deirdre found the answer! Something down below needs free oxygen.

In quantity. Why not get it from the water? What to do with the hydrogen that is left? Let it loose! It'll come to the surface, make a foam-patch…"

Dr. Morton said with a sort of mirthless geniality, "I add a stroke of pure genius! Davis just asked what would be the origin of a creature, which preferred the depths of the sea to any other place on earth. What's to be found down there that's missing everywhere else? Cold? No. Moisture? No. Just two things! Darkness and pressure! At the bottom of the Luzon Deep the pressure is over seven tons to the square inch. There's no light—I repeat, none—below three hundred fathoms. Down at the sea-bottom it's black, black, black! Now, where in the universe could there be creatures capable of riding down here in a bolide, and in need of an environment like that?"

Terry shook his head. He remembered seeing a book on the solar planets, in the after-cabin of the *Esperance*. He hadn't read it. The others on the yacht must have.

"How about Jupiter?" asked Deirdre. "The gravity's four times the earth's, and the atmosphere is thousands of miles thick. The pressure at the surface should be tons to the square inch."

Morton nodded. With the same false geniality he added, "And there'll be no light. Sunlight will never get through that muggy thick atmosphere! So we consider ourselves to be rational beings and guess that the bolides come from Jupiter! But I must admit that the last bolide was headed inward toward the sun, and from the general direction of Jupiter. So-o-o-o, do we warn the world that creatures from Jupiter are descending in space ships and are settling down under water, at a depth of forty-five hundred fathoms? Like hell we do!"

He got up and walked abruptly away.

"I…" said the bald-headed man, shaking his head incredulously, "will put this gadget away and go back to carve some more squid."

"I'll talk to Manila," said Davis drearily. "Something is coming up from below. There shouldn't be any ships allowed to come this way until we find out what's happening."

Deirdre smiled at Terry, now that they were alone.

"Have you anything very important to do just now?"

He shook his head.

"If the things that are coming up are—space ships, we can't fight them. If they're anything else, they can't very well fight us. If we wanted to attack something at the bottom of the sea we'd have to fumble at the job. We wouldn't know where to begin. So maybe, if a submarine power wants to attack at the surface of the sea, it may find it difficult, too."

He frowned. Deirdre said, "Let's go look at the sea and think things over!"

She very formally took his arm and they walked out. Presently, they stood on the white coral beach on the outer shore, and talked. Terry's mind came back, now and then, to how inadequate his previous guesses about the impending menace had been. It seemed now that the menace must be much worse than he had imagined. But there were many things he wanted to say to Deirdre.

As they talked, they were disturbed. The helicopter, which had left before noon loaded down with biological material for Manila, was approaching again. It landed by the tracking station. Then they were alone again.

When night fell, they were astonished at how quickly time had passed. They went back to the station. The helicopter was on the ground. The biologists had stopped their work, exhausted but very excited by their discovery of a new species of squid, of which an immature specimen measured eighty feet. It had offered extremely interesting phylogenic material for the Cephalopoda in general. The photographs they'd taken were invaluable, from a scientific viewpoint.

The crew of *La Rubia* had returned to their boat.

The *Esperance* had been out beyond the reef once more. The unidentified objects were still rising. They had risen to less than a thousand fathoms from the surface, well before sundown. At this same rate of rise, they should reach the surface some time after midnight. What would happen after that?

"What will happen depends," said Terry, "on how accurate their information about us is. It depends on their instruments, really. I suspect their ideas about us are weird. I find I haven't any ideas about them."

At dinner, Davis said worriedly, "I talked to Manila. The mine layer that was in the Bay left harbor yesterday. The flattop picked it up by radio and they're both going to come on here tomorrow. I had to talk about the foam. They weren't impressed. The squid does impress them, but the foam—no. I hate," he said indignantly, "to try to convince people of things I couldn't possibly be convinced of myself!"

They talked leisurely. Somebody mentioned *La Rubia*. It had been more or less expected that her skipper would turn up for drinks and conversation again. But he hadn't. The conversation turned to the plastic objects. They might or might not pick up sounds. It was not likely they'd respond to light. Certainly, complete images would be meaningless to creatures that had evolved in blackness and without a sense of sight. They might respond to pressure-waves, such as are known to be picked up by fish when something struggles in the water, even though man-made instruments have not yet detected them. They might furnish data of a sensory kind that is meaningless to humans, as pictures would be to Jovians. *If* there were such things...

"Why argue only for Jupiter?" asked Deirdre. "Venus is supposed to be mostly ocean. There could be abyssal life there."

The crew-cuts joined in the argument, but tentatively, because there were many experts present.

Midnight came. The open sea outside the reef showed nothing unusual. The waves glittered palely at their tips. There were little flashings in the water where an occasional surface fish darted. The stars shone. The moon was not yet risen.

Two o'clock came. The *Esperance* people were divided. Terry and Davis were too apprehensive to sleep. Deirdre'd gone confidently to the yacht to turn in. The crew-cuts slept peacefully, too. Davis said uneasily, "I've got a feeling that the…objects are at the surface, or very close to it, but that they simply aren't showing themselves. I think they're lying in ambush. The squid that was killed must have had trouble getting into the lagoon. They probably won't try to get the big ones in. They'll wait…"

Terry shook his head.

"We killed that little one—save the mark!—and its death was probably reported in some fashion. So maybe they'll use the big ones on the surface as bait for another kind of weapon. Foam, for example. We know how a ship simply dropped out of sight, as if into a hole."

"I know!" said Davis drearily. "I told the flattop about that. But I don't think they really believe it."

At two-thirty Davis and Terry went down to the yacht. They stood on the deck. They kept watch by mere instinct. There was no activity anywhere. Faint noises were coming from *La Rubia*. Maybe her crew was repacking the hastily loaded masses of squid-flesh. The last-quarter moon rose at long last, and shone upon the glassy-rippled water of the lagoon. Star-images danced beside its reflection.

A little after three, quite abruptly, the Diesels of *La Rubia* rumbled and boomed. The dark silhouette of the ship headed across the lagoon toward its opening. Terry swore.

"She lifted her anchor without making a noise," he said angrily. "Her skipper wants to get to Manila with his catch before it spoils! Damnation! I told him not to leave without warning. Anything could be waiting outside!"

He raced for the shore and the outboard motorboat. Davis shouted down the forecastle and pelted after him. Terry had the outboard in the water by the time Davis arrived. He jumped in and pulled the starter. The motor caught.

The outboard went rushing across the water. Its wake was a brilliant bluish luminescence.

The booming of the Diesels grew louder. Capitan Saavedra thought he had put over a fast one on *los americanos*, who had moved the fish from where he regularly captured them in vast quantities and gathered them in a lagoon where his nets tore. They had given him most of a monster squid, true, but they had reserved certain parts for themselves. They were undoubtedly the most valuable parts. So when labor officially ceased at sundown, *La Rubia*'s skipper only pretended to accept the idea. In the last hour his crew had quietly completed loading *La Rubia* with squid. They'd been carefully silent. They'd lifted anchor without noise. Now *La Rubia* headed for the lagoon entrance, heavy in the water but with precise information about what coral heads needed to be dodged. She had on board a cargo history had no parallel for. Her skipper expected to be rewarded with fame, as well as cash.

When the outboard motor rushed toward *La Rubia*, Capitan Saavedra zestfully gave his engines full throttle. When the racketing, roaring motorboat arrived beside his ship, and Terry shouted to him to stop, he chuckled and drove on. In fact, he left *La Rubia*'s pilot-house to wave cheerfully at the two men. They frantically ran close and shouted to him above the rat-tat-tatting of their own motor and the rumble of his Diesels.

La Rubia reached the lagoon entrance with the smaller boat close at her side, and Terry still shouting.

But Capitan Saavedre did not believe. Maybe he did not understand. Certainly he did not obey. Ocean swells lifted and tossed the motorboat. It became necessary to slow down, for safety. But *La Rubia* went grandly on, into the open sea.

"We can't force him to stop," said Davis in a despairing voice. "He won't. I only hope we're wrong, and he gets through!"

The outboard stayed where it was, and swells tossed it haphazardly. *La Rubia* switched on her navigation lights. She drove zestfully to the southward. She sailed on, dwindling in size, as the drone of her Diesels diminished in volume.

Looking back, Terry saw the *Esperance* approaching from the lagoon, dark figures on her deck. Terry shouted, cries answered him, and the *Esperance* came to a stop as the motorboat drew alongside.

Terry and Davis scrambled to her deck while one of the crew-cuts led the smaller boat astern and tethered it.

"We're safe enough here," Terry said bitterly, "and since you've come, we can stay and watch if anything happens. If only she keeps on going…"

But *La Rubia* did not. Her lights showed that she had changed course. She changed course again. Her masthead light began to waver from side to side. She wallowed in such a way that it was clear she was neither on course nor in motion any longer.

Nobody gave orders, but the *Esperance's* engine roared. The action from this point on became an automatic and quick response to an emergency.

The schooner-yacht plunged ahead at top speed. Terry switched on the recorder and the ultra-powerful sound projector. Davis bent over the searchlight. Two of the crew-cuts readied the bazookas.

Suddenly, a flare went off on *La Rubia's* deck. Her stubby masts and spars became startlingly bright. Screams came across the waves, even above the growling of the surf and above the noise of the *Esperance's* engine.

The flare shot through the air. It arched in a high parabola, bright in the sky, and fell into the sea. Another flare was ignited.

The *Esperance's* searchlight flicked on. A long pencil of light reached across the waves as she raced on. More screamings were heard. Another flare burned. It arched overside. The *Esperance* plunged on, shouldering aside the heavier waves of open water.

A half-mile. A quarter-mile. *La Rubia* wallowed crazily, and more shrieks came from her deck. Then the fishing boat seemed to swing. Beyond her, a conical, glistening and utterly horrifying monster emerged, a mere few yards from her rail. Enormous eyes glittered in the searchlight rays. A monstrous tentacle with a row of innumerable sucker-disks reached over the stem of *La Rubia.*

Another flare swept from the fishing boat's deck in the direction of the giant squid. It fell upon wetted, shining flesh. The monster jerked, and *La Rubia* was shaken from stem to stem. Hurriedly, Terry pressed the power-feed button, and the sound projector was on. Its effect was instantaneous. The monster began to writhe convulsively. It was gigantic. It was twice, three times the size of the squid captured in the lagoon. Terry heard his own voice cry out, "Bazookas! Use 'em! Use 'em!"

Flaring rocket missiles sped toward the giant. Davis flung one of the hand grenades he'd manufactured. The yacht plunged on toward the clutched, half-sunk fishing boat. The hand grenade exploded against the monster's flesh. Simultaneously, the bazooka-missiles hit their target and flung living, incandescent flame deep into the creature's body. Those flames would melt steel. They bored deeply into the squid, and they were infinitely more damaging than bullets.

The creature leaped from the water, as chunks of its flesh exploded. It was a mountainous horror raised from the sea. As it leaped, it had squirted the inky substance, which is the squid's ultimate weapon of defense. But, unlike small squid, this beast of the depths squirted phosphorescent ink.

The beast splashed back into the sea, and the wave of its descent swept over the deck of *La Rubia.* The fishing boat nearly capsized. But the monster had not escaped the anguish of its wounds. It fought the injured spots as though an enemy still gnawed there. It was a struggling madness in the sea.

The *Esperance* swung to approach the half-sunken trawler, and Terry kept the searchlight on the turmoil. The beast knew panic. It was wounded, and the abyss is not a place where the weak or wounded can long survive. Its fellows would be coming…

They did. Something enormous moved swiftly under the sea toward the wounded monster. It could be seen by the phosphorescence its motion created, as it approached the surface. There was a jar, a jolt. Some part of it actually touched the *Esperance's* keel. The huge monster moved ahead, but a trailing tentacle flicked up to what it had touched a moment before.

The ugly tentacle trailed over the yacht's rail. The rail shattered. The forecastle hatch was wiped out. The bowsprit became mere debris, which dangled foolishly from the standing rigging.

The *Esperance* bucked wildly at this fleeting contact.

Nick fired a bazooka-shell, but it missed. Holding fast, Davis flung a grenade. It detonated uselessly. It was then that Deirdre screamed.

Terry froze for an instant. There had simply been no time for him to think that Deirdre might be aboard. It was inexcusable, but nothing could be done now.

Tony had been knocked overside by the shock of the contact with the giant, and was swimming desperately trying to follow the yacht and climb back on board. Terry flashed the searchlight about. He found Tony, splashing. The *Esperance* swung in her own length while Terry kept the searchlight beam focused. More shrieks came from *La Rubia*. Davis threw a rope and Tony caught it. They hauled him aboard, and the *Esperance* turned again to pluck away the trawler's crewmen.

There were unbelievable splashings off to port. Terry flung the lightbeam in that direction. It fell upon unimaginable conflict. The monster that had passed under the yacht now battled the wounded squid. They fought on the surface, horribly. A maze of intertwining tentacles glistened in the light, and their revolting bodies appeared now and again as the battered creature fought to protect itself, and the other to devour. Other enormous squids came hurrying to the scene.

They flung themselves into the gruesome fight, tearing at the dying monster and at each other. There were still others on the way...

The sea resounded with desperate mooing sounds.

The *Esperance* bumped against *La Rubia*. Frantic, hysterically frightened men clambered up from the deck of the sinking trawler to the yacht. As soon as they were aboard they implored their rescuers to head for land, immediately.

"Get 'em all off!" bellowed Terry, in command by simple virtue of having clear ideas of what had to be done. "Get 'em all off!"

The stout skipper of *La Rubia* jumped over the yacht's rail. Without orders, the yacht's engine bellowed. The *Esperance* turned toward the shore, which now seemed very far away.

Something splashed to starboard. The sea glowed all around it. Terry poured the pain-sound exactly in that direction. The monster went into convulsions. The yacht swerved away to keep its distance. She raced on, past the spot where the giant flailed its tentacles insanely about. It mooed.

The *Esperance* raced at full speed toward the island.

About a mile ahead, the surf roared and foamed on the coral reef almost awash.

Back at the scene of the battle of monsters, there was a sudden break in the conflict. One of the wounded giants broke free. It may have been the one the *Esperance* had first attacked; perhaps it was another, which might have been partly devoured while still fighting.

In any case, one of them broke loose and fled, with the hellish pack after it. It is the instinct of squids, if injured, to try to find some submarine cavern in which to hide. The monster dived, and the others pursued it. There was no opening in the reef barrier—not underwater. But there was an opening on the surface. The crippled beast had to find a refuge, or be torn to bits. It may have been guided by instinct, or perhaps the current flowing into or out of the lagoon furnished the clue. In any case, the fleeing creature darted crazily into the channel used by the *Esperance* for passage. For a little way, it proceeded underwater. Then it grounded itself. Hopelessly.

And the pursuing pack arrived.

The sight from the *Esperance's* deck was straight out of the worst possible nightmare. Glistening serpentine tentacles writhed and flailed the seas. They tore the swells to froth. The pursuers had flung themselves savagely upon the helpless one. The gap in the reef was closed by the battling giants. They slavered. They gripped. They tore. They rent each other…

Terry saw a tentacle as thick as a barrel, which had been haggled half through and dangled futilely as its stump still tried to fight.

And more giants came. Terry shouted, and the *Esperance* turned. He could see large patches of phosphorescence under the surface. And suddenly, he noticed that a few of them had swerved toward the *Esperance*. As they approached the sound-horn stung them. They went into convulsive struggling, as the sound played upon them, and they passed the *Esperance* by.

Davis found Terry beside the sound-weapon's controls, watching the sea with desperate intensity.

"Listen," said Davis fiercely, "we're out at sea and we can't get back into the lagoon! We'd better get away from here!"

"Across deep water?" demanded Terry. "That dangerous foam can come up from deep water, but maybe not from shallow water. We've got to stay close to the reef until the flattop comes and bombs these creatures if it will ever come!"

Davis made a helpless gesture. Terry said crisply, "Get the 'copter to hang over the reef and report on the fighting there. Tell it to report to the flattop. They may not believe us, but they may send a plane anyway. And if the ships come, they'll have to believe about the foam! Tell them to listen for it underwater. They've got sonar gear."

Davis stumbled away. Presently, the dark figure of Nick lowered himself through what had been the forecastle hatch. Davis followed him.

Deirdre came over to Terry.

"Terry..."

"I'm going to beat in the heads," said Terry, "of those idiots who came after your father and me without throwing you on the wharf first!"

"They'd have wasted precious time," said Deirdre calmly. "I wouldn't have let them. Do you think I want to be ashore when you..."

There was the faintest of palings of the horizon to the east. Terry said grimly, "I'm going to try to find a passage through the surf, to get you ashore. I'm keeping the *Esperance* in shallow water—inside the hundred-fathom line—but I don't trust it. Certainly I don't trust a ship to make you safer!"

"It's going to be daybreak soon," she protested. "Then..."

"Then we won't be able to see what goes on underwater," he told her. "Those...creatures down below are smart!"

There was a racketing, rumbling roar from the island. A light rose above the tree-tops. Presently a parachute-flare lit up. Then there was another, as if the men in the helicopter did not believe what they saw the first time.

"Terry," said Deirdre shakily, "I'm...glad we found each other, no matter what happens..."

Davis came up from below.

"The flattop's only a few miles away. They're now proceeding at top speed. The mine layer's following. They'll be here by sunrise."

Far away to the east, some brightness entered into the paling of the sky. A drab, colorless light spread over the sea. The ocean was a dark, slate blue. Swells flattened abruptly about a quarter-mile away. Terry aimed the sound-weapon and pressed the button. Something gigantic started up, and the top of a huge squid's mantle pierced the surface. The giant leaped convulsively, high above the water, save for trailing tentacles. It was larger than a whale. It fell back into the sea with a loud splash, and moved away quickly.

Color came into the sky. The sun's upper rim appeared. Flecks of gold spread upon the sea.

Far, far away at the horizon a dark speck appeared. As the sun climbed up over the edge of the world, the speck turned golden. There was a mist of smoke above it. A plane took off from the ship. Another plane followed.

Fighter planes flashed toward the island. One of them zoomed sharply, like a bird astonished at something it has seen below. It whirled and came back over that spot. There was the rasping whine of a machine gun. Something like a giant snake reared up and fell back again. And now more planes appeared.

Sunrise was suddenly complete. Terry stared out over the sea. And he could not believe his eyes, accustomed as he was to the highly unlikely, now. Giant squids were afloat at the surface. He saw one here, and another there, and another, and another... They were emerging by tens, by scores.

"They've been sent up," said Terry very grimly, "by an entity that didn't evolve on the earth. They're...domesticated, in a way. They're watchdogs for whatever arrives in bolides that fall in the Luzon Deep. They are the reason for the shining circle of sea from which thousands of tons of living fish were drawn down into the abyss. The creatures—the...*ellos* who listen to what fish and fishermen say—they keep these things as domestic animals. And they have to feed them. Those mooings were the...cries of these things waiting to be fed. Try to imagine that, Deirdre! In the blackness of the pit, in the abyss at the bottom of the sea..."

A tentacle broke surface. Terry swung the sound-beam. A mantle reared above the waves. A bazooka shell hit it. Something huge and stupid and monstrous fought the impalpable thing that hurt it...

Davis approached.

"These," he said absurdly, "aren't the creatures that made the plastic objects. Maybe we ought to try to open communication with their masters. Why should we fight? If we prove we can defend ourselves..."

"I suspect," said Terry, "that all intelligent beings think the same way, intelligently. If we landed on another planet, on some part of that planet that the natives didn't use but we could, it wouldn't be sensible for those natives to welcome us! Trade with us, perhaps. But let us settle down, no!"

There was a bomb explosion out at sea. A plane had dropped a hundred-pound bomb on a monster at the surface. The flattop was now distinct. Golden, almost horizontal sunlight struck upon it. Off to the west a plane dived steeply, something dropped from it, and the plane leveled off. A three-hundred-foot fountain erupted from the surface. Then there came absolute proof that intelligence lay behind all this. It was not human intelligence, to be sure. Men are tool-using creatures nowadays. They imagine robots for fighting, and nowadays they make them, but many centuries ago men ceased to try to use animals as combatants in war.

The creatures under the sea had not. They'd send up giant squids to do battle with men, as men once sent elephants against the Macedonian army. It was naive. But the generals, the tacticians, the strategists of the Deep did not remain wedded to the one weapon. Already, they saw that beasts could be fought by men. So their instruments of battle changed. Doubtless, orders were given, and five miles under the sea something, - something men could not have duplicated—began the transformation of seawater into gas, in quantities past imagining. Tiny, tiny bubbles were produced by some un-guessable engine, and rose toward the surface, in a steady stream. At the bottom they were under a pressure of tons to the square inch. But the pressure lessened as they rose, and as they rose they swelled. A bubble, which was pinhead-size at the sea-bed, grew to be the size of a basketball a half-mile up, and would have been the size of a house a mile up, except that then it separated into smaller ones. They rose and rose and expanded and separated. Five miles up from their origin, at little more than atmospheric pressure, they made a rising column of insubstantiality. At the surface they became foam. But under the foam there was more foam, and under that still more. A ship sailing from normal ocean water into such airy stuff would drop like a stone into the miles-long cone of semi-nothingness. Nothing solid could float there. Nothing substantial could rest its weight upon such rushing thistledown.

And the first of the bubble-weapons appeared at the surface in the form of a patch of foam. Its source—and hence the place of its appearance—could be moved. It could be shifted under any ship, though there would be a time-interval, always, before the foam at the surface was exactly above the gas-generating engine below. It could be moved to anticipate the movements of a ship. But there was always that time-lag.

The *Esperance* headed back toward the heap of monsters at the break in the reef. Other giant squids emerged and joined the pack. A plane came over and bombed it. The *Esperance* turned away. The mine layer from Manila appeared at the horizon. The flattop made a sudden violent turn, and more foam appeared upon the water. It curled and writhed and piled up to be ten—twenty—thirty yards in height.

The flattop fired a shell into it. There was a gigantic flash and flame, and for an instant there was no foam, but only peculiarly pock-marked ocean surface, instantly covered by more foam which piled up as before.

"Gas," said Terry grimly. "Hydrogen. You guessed right, Deirdre!"

Now the flattop shot off plane after plane, as if they were projectiles. They swung in the air and flew low to drop bombs in the now wobbling, moving, sweeping patch of white stuff. It was a huge discoloration of the ocean surface. It was almost in diameter as the flattop's length. Now the carrier dodged it warily.

There were dull concussions everywhere. Giant squids writhed in death-agonies. White foam-patches appeared here and there—but somehow haphazardly—as if fumbling for the ships. One patch swept close to *La Rubia*, and that small derelict seemed to tremble. And then the fishing boat touched the very edge of the white stuff, and was engulfed in it. She vanished instantly, as if she had fallen into a hole in the sea. When the foam-patch passed on, the sea was empty.

The effect of the foam, actually, was that of a gigantic, slavering, blind gullet straining to devour. It moved erratically over the surface. Terry called to Deirdre, "Have Nick tell the flattop that the foam only comes up from deep water. If they can get inside the hundred-fathom curve they're safe! Maybe even five hundred. Maybe more. But the foam only comes up from deep water!"

The mine layer came on from the horizon at topmost speed. Apparently, they had received warning from the carrier, because the ship suddenly began to zigzag. The carrier itself adopted the unpredictable change-of-course system, which had been originally designed to frustrate submarines lying in wait. Both ships adopted it just in time. A ravening area of foam appeared directly before the mine-layer's bow just as she turned aside. The mine layer dumped a mine. Terry saw it go overboard. But it would have five miles to sink before it hit bottom.

Terry called Davis and jerkily explained that the mines would have to be armed when they went overboard—set so that they would explode when they hit bottom. He explained that depth-bombs might be useful against squids, but if they went off at a fixed depth they would be harmless against the enemy, which deployed the squids.

The carrier, in the middle of a ninety-degree zigzag turn, found her bow projecting into a foam-patch. The bow sank deep. The carrier's propellers were out of the water as her bow pointed downward. Had the foam stayed still for two seconds, the carrier would have slid into the column of gigantic ascending bubbles and plunged to destruction. But the foam swerved sidewise.

The carrier escaped, and was infinitely cautious after that. She made short, swift, unpredictable dashes this way and that... Her anti-aircraft guns rumbled and rattled at things upon the surface. Presently, her depth-finder discovered an underwater extension of the island's mountain-foundation, and the ship took refuge where the water was less than a hundred fathoms deep. There she lay, shooting off planes and retrieving them, her guns flashing at whatever targets appeared.

Twice, as it happened, snaky, monstrous arms flung themselves up and heaved at the flattop as if the giant squids hoped to overturn even an aircraft carrier by their weight. But those arms were blasted to nothingness. The only damage they did was that a twenty-foot section of tentacle—writhing independently on the flight-deck—broke the landing-gear of a returning plane, which collided with it.

The mine layer ploughed across the sea. From time to time she heaved something overboard. Nothing seemed to happen. But each mine was, nevertheless, so adjusted that it could explode any time it touched something underwater. They did not allow the usual time so that the mine layer could get away. The mine layer had ample time, because the mines had to go slowly spinning down five long miles to the bottom of the Luzon Deep.

Twenty mines went down before the first one detonated. The concussion was felt on the *Esperance*, twenty-seven thousand feet up and in shallow water. Then another, and another, and another. The mine layer continued to sow her destructive seed. Far behind her, a monstrous spouting of gas and spume rose up hundreds of feet. There was another concussion, and another…

The *Esperance* quivered, and Terry said grimly to Deirdre, "We set off five pounds of explosive down the Deep, and the bathyscaphe returned all smashed. What will the creature do now? I wish we could get some mines down to the bottom there!"

Davis came up, beaming—but shaking.

"The carrier's sending some planes down to drop eggs at the spot where the fish were dragged down!" he said zestfully.

Gigantic, terrifying masses of gas leaped skyward where the gases released by the exploding mines finally reached the surface. The mine layer zigzagged, and dropped a mine. She zigzagged again, and dropped another. Presently, she took refuge beside the carrier. The *Esperance* drove over and came to a stop between the two armed vessels. Someone shouted down by megaphone from the carrier's deck, "What happened to you? What hit your bowsprit?"

Terry shouted back, "You shot those beasts. We've been wrestling with 'em!"

An enormous eruption of gas... Then the underwater ear began to emit an unprecedented sound. It was a rushing sound, but it was only vaguely like the noise of whatever had come up from the depths last Tuesday night. This was powerful beyond imagining.

"Something's coming up!" roared Terry. "Better alert for a real fight now!"

Deirdre said with a little gasp, "The real creatures are coming up! Terry! The...things that come in the bolides..."

He said savagely, "They've been shaken up badly by the concussions underwater. They resented five pounds of explosive! There's been four hundred pounds in every mine! If they try to fight after what they've taken down below..."

The rushing sound from underwater was a loud, throbbing hum, which had no relationship with the humming sound that drove fish. Two spoutings of gas from mine-explosions shot up. There were more concussions in the water.

Then something broke surface. It was huge, and looked like a rocket. It leaped. No, it dashed upward, toward the sky. It flashed skyward, accelerating as it rose. Something else broke the surface and headed for the heavens. This one was globular.

There were dull concussions coming from far underwater, and more rockets broke surface and shot skyward.

Anti-aircraft guns were fired. Shell-bursts came close, but not close enough. Not less than twenty enormous rockets leaped out of the water and shot up toward the sky. Some observers claimed there were more than thirty. Down to southward, where the bathyscaphe had been crushed, the planes that were dropping mines reported that four other objects broke loose from the ocean and fled for empty space at speeds too great to be estimated.

Terry looked suddenly astonished.

"But...of course!" he told Deirdre. "When you need high pressure, of course you've got a weakness. You can't take concussions! Anything underwater is completely vulnerable to bombs! Whatever was down there has found out that the natives—we aborigines—have a weapon they can't face. Primitive stuff. Explosives! Chemical explosives! And creatures that can travel between planets and undoubtedly have atomic power and—who knows what else—can't fight back if we drop submarine mines on them!"

A last object broke surface and hurtled skyward. Behind it, deep, deep down, there was a titanic explosion.

"Ah!" said Terry. "That was a time-bomb! They've gone home for good!"

* * * *

A task force of a private yacht, a fishing boat, a satellite-tracking station, an airplane carrier and a mine layer had driven off an invasion of earth. But the public could not be told that the earth had been invaded. The people who had been involved in this secret adventure had to be satisfied with the realization that they had saved mankind.

After a jubilant dinner Terry and Deirdre sat in the veranda.

Davis came out. He blinked at the night.

"Deirdre? Terry?"

"Here," said Terry.

Davis joined them. They had drawn apart a little.

"Good news by short-wave," said Davis. "Those rockets were picked up by radar. They divided into two groups. One headed sunward. The other headed for deep space. My guess is

Venus for one group and Jupiter for the other. They couldn't have come from Mars. But they've gone home. Both groups."

Terry paused, and then said wryly, "Two races! Some of the bolides were bullet-shaped and some were globular. That figures. But two races capable of space travel and both in our own solar system!"

Davis grimaced. "We've been talking about it. Our guess is that the Venus race developed in deep water, and therefore at high pressure. And anything that developed on the solid surface of Jupiter would also be accustomed to extremely high pressure."

Terry nodded. He was not exactly absorbed in what Davis had to say. But he said suddenly, "I make a guess. They didn't want to start a colony here. The sea-bottom here is too cold to be comfortable for the beings from Venus, and far too hot to suit those from Jupiter. But both needed terrific pressure. In order to keep contact with each other, in order to do business, they could have set up a trading post here. To meet and trade. Neither one could take over the earth. When you think of it, we couldn't take over Venus or Jupiter! Maybe that's the answer!"

"Eh?" said Davis.

"We won't have to fight as planets," said Terry, "when we have space-ships like they do. We couldn't gain anything by fighting. All we can gain by is trade. They'll be pleased. It must have been horribly inconvenient to have to set up a trading post here on earth. There were always the natives, you know. Lately, they've noticed that we've been getting restless. We have been. I imagine that now they'll wait for us to make spaceships and start up interplanetary trade."

Davis said, "Very true. There's going to be the devil of a mess, though. Morton will still have to explain the accuracy of his prediction about the bolides' landings. I suspect he'll be censured for assuming anything as unlikely as the truth has turned out to be."

Terry did not answer. Deirdre was saying something, and he did not hear at all.

"There are still loose ends," added Davis. "For instance, how do you suppose they controlled those squids down below? What did they use for eyesight? How the devil would Jovians and Venusians agree on a meeting place in our oceans?"

Terry answered what Deirdre'd said. She smiled at him. They'd forgotten that Davis was there.

THE END

If you've enjoyed this book, you will not want to miss these terrific titles…

ARMCHAIR SCI-FI, FANTASY, & HORROR DOUBLE NOVELS, $12.95 each

D-1   **THE GALAXY RAIDERS** by William P. McGivern
SPACE STATION #1 by Frank Belknap Long

D-2   **THE PROGRAMMED PEOPLE** by Jack Sharkey
SLAVES OF THE CRYSTAL BRAIN by William Carter Sawtelle

D-3   **YOU'RE ALL ALONE** by Fritz Leiber
THE LIQUID MAN by Bernard C. Gilford

D-4   **CITADEL OF THE STAR LORDS** by Edmund Hamilton
VOYAGE TO ETERNITY by Milton Lesser

D-5   **IRON MEN OF VENUS** by Don Wilcox
THE MAN WITH ABSOLUTE MOTION by Noel Loomis

D-6   **WHO SOWS THE WIND…** by Rog Phillips
THE PUZZLE PLANET by Robert A. W. Lowndes

D-7   **PLANET OF DREAD** by Murray Leinster
TWICE UPON A TIME by Charles L. Fontenay

D-8   **THE TERROR OUT OF SPACE** by Dwight V. Swain
QUEST OF THE GOLDEN APE by Ivar Jorgensen and Adam Chase

D-9   **SECRET OF MARRACOTT DEEP** by Henry Slesar
PAWN OF THE BLACK FLEET by Mark Clifton.

D-10   **BEYOND THE RINGS OF SATURN** by Robert Moore Williams
A MAN OBSESSED by Alan E. Nourse

ARMCHAIR SCIENCE FICTION CLASSICS, $12.95 each

C-1   **THE GREEN MAN**
by Harold M. Sherman

C-2   **A TRACE OF MEMORY**
By Keith Laumer

ARMCHAIR MASTERS OF SCIENCE FICTION SERIES, $16.95 each

M-1   **MASTERS OF SCIENCE FICTION, Vol. One**
Bryce Walton—"Dark of the Moon" and other tales

M-2   **MASTERS OF SCIENCE FICTION, Vol. Two**
Jerome Bixby: "One Way Street" and other tales

Made in United States
North Haven, CT
22 July 2022